WHO WAS CORMAC MAC ART—
BEFORE HE BECAME THE FAMOUS REAVER,
BANE OF SORCERERS,
AND CHAMPION OF EIRRIN?

—and then Cormac mac Art was oblivious of the proffered meat, and the voices of these his companions, for he was no longer with them . . .

He stood in a fine shining chariot drawn by two horses with the spirit of spring breezes. Mourning was on him for his driver just slain, and he hurled again his spear of victory into the ranks of the gathered enemy, and its gleaming bronze point drove through a man so that he died. And then another leaped forward, and tore free that much-blooded spear, the *gau-buaid*, and hurled it even as Cormac whipped up his fine team of horses—

No! Not Cormac; no son of Art was he, but him born Setalta and later called the hound of the smith, Chulan—Cuchulain he was. And he, Cormac who was Cuchulain, cried out, for life and time were closing on him, and in his anguished mind he heard anew the druid's words of his youth:

"If any young man should be taking up arms this day, his name will be greater than any other name in Eirrin."

He looked down then, he who was not yet Cormac for centuries were in the way of it, and he felt the cold that came . . .

ROBERT E. HOWARD'S
OTHER GREAT HERO
CORMAC MAC ART
· THE ·
MISTS OF DOOM

ANDREW J. OFFUTT

ACE FANTASY BOOKS
NEW YORK

to
Jodie of the Erin-born
until further notice

THE MISTS OF DOOM

An Ace Fantasy Book / published by arrangement with the Estate of
Robert E. Howard and Andrew J. Offutt and Glenn Lord

PRINTING HISTORY
Ace edition / November 1980
Second printing / January 1984

ISBN: 0-441-53504-6

Ace Fantasy Books are published by The Berkley Publishing Group,
200 Madison Avenue, New York, New York 10016.
PRINTED IN THE UNITED STATES OF AMERICA

CONTENTS

Introduction:
With Gratitude

Though this novel appears as the fourth in the series, it is technically the first in that cycle of the Irish hero of the late fifth century, Cormac mac Art. Herein is chronicled all the information we have concerning Cormac's early life, his youth, the death of his father and the orphaned youth's employment in Leinster as warrior—and the events that led up to Cormac's long series of adventures away from his beloved homeland; the reaver or pirate Robert E. Howard wrote of in *Tigers of the Sea*.

If you are discovering Cormac for the first time, this is the beginning and the best place to begin the cycle. If you've been with us through *Tigers of the Sea* and Offutt's *The Sword of the Gael, The Undying Wizard,* and *Sign of the Moonbow,* you will surely welcome this look into Cormac's origins—including his first meeting with Samaire of Leinster.

Accounts of the later events of Cormac's adventurous life were found and authenticated with relative ease. The stories had been passed down orally in the Irish tradition and more than one writer of the fifth through tenth centuries had written of his exploits: as commander of a crew of piratic reavers and the subsequent years as reaver with Wulfhere the Dane; of his adventures in

Britain and Denmark and the little kingdom of Galicia; among the Tuatha de Danann within the Emerald Isle; of his crossing of life-paths with Arthur of Britain and with Hengist, among the first of those from oversea to carve out sword-lands in Britain to become England, of the matter of the sigil-ring of Egypt; of his perilous struggles with such sorcerers as Thulsa Doom, Tarmur Roag, Lucanor of Antioch, and others.

Some of these adventures have appeared in the books previously mentioned; others are to follow as Offutt and Ace Books continue to present the cycle for the modern reader.

More difficult to unearth were the facts of his youth, before he became the famous reaver, bane of sorcerers, and Champion of Eirrin. The task of tracking down and assembling these accounts fell to my friend Geo. W. Proctor.

Like Howard who first discovered and began chronicling the Cormac cycle, Proctor is a Texan and a lover of high adventure, particularly heroic fantasy. His own tales of weapon-men and images are included in my anthologies of new heroic fantasy, *Swords Against Darkness,* and he is working on his own novels.

It was Geo. Proctor who tirelessly tracked down, along vermiculate paths leading into and through numerous sources, *Macghnimhartha na Cormaic:* The Youthful Deeds of Cormac. From a crumbling monastery near Cashel came the scraps of laboriously recopied—in Latin!—manuscript, *Partha na Lagen,* and realized that this "partha (mac Othna) of Laigin or Leinster" was indeed Cormac, written of as his cloak-name or alias. From the musty library of an aged scholar—now deceased—living near Dublin that was Dubh-linn (and formerly

Baile Atha Cliath or Ath-Cliath), came into Proctor's hands the nigh-unreadable *Longes mac Airt:* the *Exile of Art's Son.* In the Leinsterish archives is proudly recorded *Tain Bo an-Ard Riogh:* The Cattle-Raid of the High-king or the Driving off of the High-king's Kine.

Laboriously Proctor checked and cross-checked, questioned and collected, compiled and discarded, and somehow pieced together the story of a heinous plot by High-king and priest . . . and the story of young Cormac. His work does shame on scholars and historians (whom in truth I have caught out in errors, in my own researches—while doubtless making errors of my own).

Geo. and I were already in contact, and I am the chronicler and supposed expert. To me he sent his account—and two copies of his pages and pages of notes. Pleading gross ignorance of Gaelic, I asked him to compile it all into a sort of narrative, in outline form. (We agreed to leave out The Matter of the Queen's Chamber, and the Story of the Twelve Picts, as being surely fanciful, apocryphal additions by later enthusiasts.)

Proctor complied, and once I had rewritten his outline I obtained his approval of that version. It was also patiently explained to me that "Ceann" is *not* "Sean" but simply *Ken* and that the "family name" of the Leinsterish royal house, *Ceannselaigh,* would be pronounced simply KEN-sley. He also confirmed the name "Conan": it is very old Irish, as are Crom and indeed the word *amra,* which means eulogy. Howard did like his Celts—I mean, Kelts.

The volume, then, is my narrative based on an outline by Geo. W. Proctor of Tay-has, and we are all indebted to him.

Andrew J. Offutt—Kentucky, U.S.A.

Though the rain had ceased just before sundown,
the clouds remained. The setting Eye of Behl rayed
its gold and crimson across a sky of greys and deep
slate. The spectacular effect lasted only a few
minutes ere the sun was gone and the sky became a
wash of slate and indigo and the absolute black of
onyx. Night ruled. The imposing buildings standing
aloofly apart atop the hill called Tara were become
but shadows, some limned darkly against the sky,
others spectrally pale.

Fog and mist were permanent inhabitants of this
land, which they and the forests had owned long
before the coming of the Fir Bholgs, and then the
Tuatha de Danann, and finally the Celts. It crawled
the ground now, so that the peasantish houses
huddled so closely all about the base of the hill
were as if aswim in the cold fog. Some indeed were
invisible beneath their dripping roofs of wattle and
sod. No women or children were abroad, and few
men. Even so close past sunset, many were already

abed, for wakeful life and the work of the day began with Behl's eastward appearance each morn, when pearl and nacre displaced the dark of night and were followed by rich gold. Thus came daily the manifestation of the god of the Celts, whether they abode here in this land, or over in Gallic or Frankish lands. For not yet had the new god, him of the Jews and then of Rome on which the sun had set, usurped the ancient power of Bel, or, depending upon where he was worshiped, Baal, or Beal, or Ba'al or Behl.

This night, strangely, the fog rose up the hill among the houses of the nobles and even among the rath structures of the *righ-danna,* the many who in this way or that claimed kinship to the *Ard-righ,* the High-king. Aye, on this haunted night the fog eddied and crept even about that most noble lord's own abode, the *rig-thig.*

Through it, his feet and robed legs vanishing into the ever-moving gray, walked a man who neither strode nor strolled. Hooded he was, rendered bodiless by the robe and faceless by the night. Almost silently, picking his way with a long holly staff, he moved toward his goal.

A peasant, in leggings and leathern stockings, a patched brown cloak and flapped cap of hareskin, touched his forehead when his path downward crossed that of the robed man ascending; the former was late wending homeward from the house of his lord who had spoken not complimentarily to him of the peasant's care for his granary, for it was unpatched and the cats were hard-worked and fat from the catching of invading mice.

"Lord Druid," the peasant said by way of greeting, and no more, and kept walking.

Nor did the druid in the hooded robe, the deep

11

green of the forest, speak or otherwise acknowledge the respectful greeting. He but climbed on, a bottle-green phantom in the night of darkness and fog-damp and dripping eaves. His staff of holly made tiny sucking noises when he drew it up with each pace.

"Some of those in the service of Crom and Behl," the peasant muttered, but not so loudly as to be heard by aught of ears other than his own, "count themselves too high among mere men . . . *other* mere men," he added, for all of his sea-bounded land were proud and few acknowledged themselves lowly—when they were not within lordly earshot.

He wended on to his little house of stout wood and roof of wattle and thatch with its dangling, dripping tie-stones, and when his wife Faencha did chiding on him for his tardiness, he was sharp with her. In a morose silence he ate his porkish supper and drank ale that was little more than barley-water whilst she overbusied her good self with her embroidery.

The man in the druidic robe meanwhile approached the wall that had been raised about the splendid house of the High-king; of oak was the wall, and over half a foot in thickness.

There he came upon two men in bronze-decorated helmets and close-pulled cloaks of scarlet wool. Their bare, fog-wet hands were fisted about the hafts of long spears, each banded twice with bronze. Nor said they aught, but only stared. The newcomer's flowing sleeve whispered with the extending of his arm. They gazed on his fist, and at the signet there, and they nodded. The gate was opened respectfully for the faceless man, who passed through without the speaking of a word.

"Good it is to see a druid abroad and wearing a

ring of the High-king himself, Cairthide," one of the sentries muttered, whilst they closed the gate, "and his wife and so many others believers in the New God."

"Good it is to be knowing a druid's about at all, on such a night as this!" Cairthide said. His sigh emerged tremulously for he shivered. "A good night for hearth and ale—and locked door!"

His companion coughed and sniffed.

Through the grounds of the High-king strode the hooded man who seemed to have no legs. Outbuildings for storage and creaming and smithing and the housing of animals had been scattered randomly, so that it was no straight course he took. The fog was both thinner and lower to the wet wet earth as he approached the rising rig-thig, as though the high son of Laegaire was immune, respected even by the powers of earth and water and the sky that had come down this night to blanket the earth.

At the very walls of the High-king's manse, the walker in the fog was again challenged by two men. Helmeted they were, and mailed, armed with swords and bucklers with brazen decor, and long spears and each man draped in a cloak of dark red woollen. These stalwarts took note of the newcomer's long walking-staff, that might have been a cudgel but for his druid's robe.

The robe-swathed man said no word, but again showed them his fist on which flashed a ring of gold and enamel and carbuncle.

"Enter then, Lord Druid," one sentry said, opening the great door.

"And come ye in from such a surly night, Lord Druid," the other said, with a smile, though he did not forget the respectful inclining of his head in its shining round helm.

Robes of dark green rustled like fallen leaves; leather heels fell softly; the holly stick tapped once and then was lifted clear of the floor. Otherwise in silence, the visitor passed them by. From the wall he took a candle, which he waved a bit that it might flare the better while he paced through the dark defense-hall. On his way to the chamber he sought in that high house he saw only a woman abroad. She was not the wife of the High-king, and made a little obeisance as the cowled robe passed. It gave no sign of acknowledgement.

A tawny-haired man in clean green leggings and blue smock of wool sat before the door the visitor approached. The door seemed to crawl with carven knotwork and fantastickal animals, lit and as if animated by the torch burning in a cresset of bronze to either side.

"The lord High-king is receiving no visitors, Druid."

Once again the cowled man displayed his ring, and in silence. The other gazed upon it, blinking.

For the first time, a voice emerged from the hood. In the middle range it was, and a bit strained as though its owner had need to cough. The voice betrayed too a certain shortness of breath, for Tara Hill was no brief or easy climb.

"It is disrespectful ye be, boy, and not minded to hide it. That will come as ye gain in wisdom. Be ye follower of Iosa Chriost?"

"Aye, Lord Druid," the green-legged man said quietly, and belligerence was absent from his voice and manner. More, he had risen and taken a step aside. He stared at the darkness between the edges of the cowl, but the light of three glims showed him only the tip of a nose. The visitor did have a face, then. 14

"Well—open it!"

With apologetic face and attitude, the tawny-haired man rapped twice, paused while he counted mentally to twice ten as his most noble lord had decreed, and opened the door. It swung inward. The young man turned back just in time to wrap his fingers automatically about the candle the visitor had thrust at him.

With a whisper of his robes, the walker in the fog passed into a room alight with no less than four candles; servingmaids would certainly be at the collecting of that wax, later! He paused as if to make certain the door closed securely behind himself; it did. He was in a broad room of red yew, speckled with copper rivets and with floor-to-ceiling hangings on two walls, warmly dark and richly woven and broidered with scrollwork and fanciful animals and twining flowers.

In a carven chair behind a table set near the dancing hearth-fire a man sat, and he lifted his russet-haired head to gaze upon his visitor. High was this man's forehead, for his hair was thinning atop even as at the temple grey usurped the rusty red, and had departed to the breadth of two fingers beyond the hairline of his youth. Jowly his face, though he was paunchy, not fat. Fog-grey eyes fixed their stare on the intruder upon his guarded, fire-warmed solitude, the seated man alone in the loosegirt robe of silver-trimmed darkest blue, collared with beaver. On his chest a broad neck-torc seemed to have grown, become a carcanet studded with jewels and traced with a design of honeysuckle vine picked out in red gold. The over-grown *muin-torch* depended even onto his pectorals. His ten fingers bore five rings, and one of gold and coral center-set with a large carbuncle; was the mate of the ring on the guest's finger.

The latter threw back his cowl with both hands, staff under his arm; the man by the fire smiled. His deep blue robe was split at each elbow and edged there with beaver fur; from those slashes emerged his arms in sleeves of white.

"A fine disguise, Milchu. Come, warm yourself. Indech!"

The seated man called out the last word, whereupon his visitor instantly restored his hood. Behind the door opened; the seated man looked past his guest.

"Mulled ale—no, mulled wine, Indech. And knock first!"

"At once, lord King."

The door closed solidly. The robed man called Milchu moved to the fire.

"It's no talking we'll do till the wine's after being brought, Milchu," the king said. "Add a few oak knots if ye're of a mind to. But it's not for patience I'm known. Ye bring much information?"

"Much information, High—" Milchu broke off in a cough— "king of Eirrin."

"Bodes it ill or else for Lugaid mac Laegair?"

Clearing his throat repeatedly, Milchu tossed several chunky oaktree knots onto the fire. "When the wine comes, Lugaid mac Laegair." His voice was strained; he coughed again.

"No night for being abroad, robed or no," High-king Lugaid said.

And they were silent, the High-king fretting restlessly with the handle of a tall mug on the table before him. Moulded as a fanciful beast was that long thin handle, though the bear thus represented was necessarily long and thin of body, and its ears rose unnaturally long and pointed. The bronze

16

tankard was inlaid about the base with two rows of rectangles in green and red enamel; superbly carven coral formed a knotwork design betwixt the rows of rectangles. Lugaid's ringed fingers seemed to wrestle with the bronze bear.

Come the knock they awaited; High-king Lugaid son of High-king Laegair loudly called "Enter" rather than wait those thirty or so heartbeats he had mandated as wait between knock and entry.

Immediately Indech of the green leggings hurried a sizable pottery jug and two mugs over to the table. He bowed, set them down, looked his question. Receiving an equally silent reply by gesture, he poured both mugs full of dark golden liquid from which rose tendrils of steam. Indech glanced at the fire, seeing that it was blazing up all yellow and snapping. He looked again at his lord. Lugaid waved a hand. With another bow—and a glance at Mulchu, who stood by the fire with his back to the room—Indech departed the chamber with its rush-strewn floor and cold-absorbing hangings over the fine red wood of the yew-tree.

The door closed on him. Milchu turned from the fire. Again with both hands he shot back the druidic cowl. He commenced loosing the laces at the robe's throat; they ran down to a point approximately horizontal with his nipples.

Then did he bare a pectoral pendant that was strange indeed, on the chest of a man in the robe of a druid of the Celts.

The Egyptians of centuries agone had formed the device of the male triad and the woman's parts; a loop atop two straight bars, one set perpendicular to the center of the other so that they formed three. Thus the male and female united, a symbol of the creation of life, and Life everlasting

17

of the faith of Set and Horus and Osiris. After them the Romans used a similar design, formed of timbers, for the execution of criminals. *Ankh,* those of Egypt called it; the Sign of Life. *Crux,* those of the more latterly "world" conquerors termed it; the sign of Death. On it they had slain one Yeshua—Iesu in their tongue, changed in Eirrin to Iosa—for sedition and the stirring up of the common folk against the priests . . . and, far more seriously, against the togaed representatives of Rome's might. Along with the fish, the sign was adopted by the Friends, later called Saints by some and Christians by others.

Though they claimed that this cross, like the open one of old Egypt, represented and promised life everlasting, there were many and many who pointed out that the female was closed against life and further that the sign signified pain and slow death, and a dead god.

Though he had curbed it in himself now, Lugaid had been known to refer to Iosa Chriost who was Iesus Christus as the Dead God, and the thought crossed his mind now as he gazed upon that which hung on Milchu's chest.

No druid wore the cross of Iosa Chriost.

Chapter One:
The Plotters

The cross jumped and gleamed on the chest of the High-king's visitor when the man coughed. Watching this priest of Jesus come out of the disguising robe, High-king Lugaid reflected that it must sore have irked Milchu to wear the robe of the Old Faith over his execution symbol. Iosa was the enemy of all other gods; Christianity and its "Saints" were the enemy of all other beliefs; the druids of the Old Faith and the priests of the New were hardly friends!

Lugaid grinned sourly. Toying with the mug of mulled wine, he reflected on how the former shepherd-slave had returned here to Eirrin—from Rome—preaching the New Faith. He attacked the old ways and beliefs directly, that Padraigh or Patriche, claiming that while as all knew the druids could with their powers bring on darkness, only Jesus the Christus brought light. And he had thrown down the great statue of Crom Cruach and its attending statuary on the Plain of Slecht. Nor had that ancient god of Eirrin, no nor Behl either,

19

done aught to avenge the sacrilege.

Those there were who began to say that Padraigh's god was God. His faith spread throughout the land of mighty warriors. Somehow the sons of Eirrin took the dictates of peacefulness more seriously than the people of the continent; their Saints slew Saints and all the in the name of Jesus whom they called Christus as though it were his name. Soon, Lugaid mused without pleasure, Padraigh had converted many. Aye, even including the wife of High-king Laegair, for he put guilt on her, and on his chief advisor as well, so that Laegair was no enemy of the Saints. Well Lugaid remembered the changes in his mother, and the change in the relationship between her and his royal father.

Yet even that had not been enough for the Saints. They wanted all.

They want *all*, Lugaid the king thought, and his hand clutched the tighter at his tankard.

Still, the Ard-righ of Eirrin was no enemy of the Old Faith either, so that druids remained welcome throughout most of the land. That proved not sufficiently satisfactory to the dark-robed priests who came to Eirrin after Padraigh. That stern man with his great pointed staff preached that which had aided the toppling of the Empire of Rome and now survived it in quest of an empire of its own.

No, Lugaid mac Laegair mused, gazing on the equally stern-faced opportunist Milchu, *the Saints will settle for naught less than ownership of Eirrin—and the world. And this fanatical follower of that dead son of a wright of the Jews . . .*

Lugaid saw Milchu for what he was, for all his ascetic face and pretensions. In the tradition of Padraigh himself was this man, and yet steps beyond

20

him, for the priests had power now in Eirrin, and they were far from averse to using it.

This weasel-face seeks only personal power and influence, Lugaid mused, *and all in the name of his religion. It's more willing this man is even than I or my uncle to set aside his moral convictions and the gentle teachings of his god, for after all there is always their Confession to Him . . . and surely to Milchu mac Roigh the achievement of the goal ever justifies the means used in its attainment! Indeed, when once man on the ridge of the earth feels that the warm breath of his god is upon him, it's little there is he cannot justify in his mind!*

A fitting servant for Lugaid mac Laegair then, Lugaid mac Laegair thought. Once the priest had served his purposes, the man with the ever-set lips and stern brow would easily be handled, one way or the other! *For surely I,* Lugaid Ard-righ thought, *am the superior of any at crafty plotting, though I be plotted against on all sides by so many, at all times.*

He was sure, in point of fact, that Milchu the priest plotted independent of him. For who did not? Were it not for the High-king's supremely powerful uncle Muirchetach mac Erca—*and my own genius*—Lugaid would surely have been wrested from this highest of abodes years agone. Of this he was convinced.

"Ye passed safely and with ease," he said aloud, "for surely none would expect to find a priest of Rome abroad, alurk in the oak-green robe of a druid!"

The priest tossed aside the robe—to the floor, and with the movement his pectoral cross of silver flashed, for fire and candles lit the room well if fitfully. Nor did he show amusement.

21

"It's no priest of Rome I am, son of L—" he began and broke off to cough. "Son of Laegair, but a priest of Iosa Chriost our Saviour—a priest of *Eirrin,* as ye be her High-king!"

With a slow blink of both grey eyes amid the disappearance of his smile, Eirrin's High-king nodded.

"The ways of God are strange," Milchu said. "I but use the tools he places before me, lord King." And he spurned that latest tool, the druidic robe, with his well-shod foot.

"Aye. It's not the psalms of your god ye were to bring me, though, but information. Sit, Milchu. And speak."

Milchu sat, sipped, leaned forward to fix the king with a gaze from the bright round eyes of a fanatic.

"Information, aye. From Connacht."

"Ah, Connacht, Connacht. Long did it supply our land with its High-kings . . . until *I,* grandson of Niall Noiqiallach, united with the other ui-Neill and even those of Leinster, and overthrew Connacht's power and strangle-hold on this hill! Dead is my predecessor Ailill Molt; dead is Connachtish power." He too leaned forward, his hand only toying unconsciously with the design of his mug's handle. "And doubtless Connachtish nobles plot, and plot! Eh, Milchu? Eh, eh?"

"Aye, High-king. There are those in Connacht who plot."

"Ah. Against the High-king of all Eirrin!"

"Aye, High-king. Even against yourself."

"Ah."

A glow that came not from the fire entered into Lugaid's grey eyes, for so he had surmised, and with Lugaid who dwelt ever in the shadow of his mighty uncle Mac Erca and the misty fogs of his own suspicions, to surmise in the matter of plotting

22

was to believe. And in truth gladness was on him for Milchu's confirming his suspicion-become-belief, For had the priest said otherwise, then Lugaid Laegair's son must suspect him. Which would be to disbelieve him.

And one, Lugaid thought, *must believe one's spies . . . so long as one has them watched and checked now and again.*

"Aye," Milchu said again. "And plots are laid up in Ulster, too, lord King, and Munster, and even in Leinster—"

"Aye, aye, and in Meath and even here on Tara Hill!" The king's eyes fair glittered. "But what of Connacht, *priest?*"

"—and we who are united in Christ and who are everywhere, king son of a king, are your eyes and ears and, with some small increase in numbers, your protection."

Milchu spoiled his own dramatic effect then, for whilst he sought to fix the king with a meaningful gaze of steel, that feather the fog seemed to have put into his throat tickled again, so that he coughed.

Power, Lugaid thought. *Increase in numbers, is it? That means increase in* power! *I hear ye, priest. I hear even the words ye speak not.*

"Milchu."

"Lord King?"

"Connacht."

"Let me tell the High-king not of those who plot, but of a perhaps worse danger in Coiced Connachta of the west."

And Lugaid listened with attentiveness and narrowed eyes grey and impenetrable as fog, and forgot the tankard of ale and the mug of good mulled wine.

"It is of a youth only recently turned fourteen I'd
23

be speaking, lord King."

"*Fourteen!* A *boy!* Milchu—"

Milchu but raised a pale, pale hand a little, fingers up, palm to the king. The king stared, silencing himself. And waiting.

"And is ten and four not the age of manhood, lord King?—and most especially when the youthful man in question is rising six feet in height, with an athlete's muscle on him, and druid-taught craftiness in him, and a consummate weaponish skill, a natural talent? And when he all alone but a single moon's passage agone did battle with no less than four *Cruithne* on the rocky shores of westernmost Connacht, and sustained him but a scratch, and left four Pictish corpses to rot in sun and tide?"

Staring bright-eyes, his knuckles nigh white on his tankard's zoomorphic handle, Lugaid gestured impatiently with his other hand, for the spy had paused as if to tease.

"This is fact, Milchu?"

"This—" Milchu broke off coughing, and coughed, nor did he bring up aught of phlegm or curses. Blinking, he sipped, drank, wiped at the corner of his eye with a long thin index finger.

"This is fact, son of Laegair. He cut them down all four as trees are felled in the wood."

"It sounds like legend."

"Ah! Doesn't it! It is what Connachtmen are saying of this youth . . . his name Cormac, son of Art son of Comal."

"Art!"

"Aye."

"Gods of Eirrin, what a name! Legend itself: Cormac mac Art! How *dare* one so named as Art give his son the name of that great High-king of long ago!"

24

"He does, my lord King, and with calculation. For the lord Art of Connacht has naught of the fool about him, and knew what the sound of that name he gave his son would be, in the ears and minds of all men of Eirrin . . . your Eirrin, mac Laegair."

"My Eirrin," Lugaid said, tasting the words and looking ready to smack his lips over them.

"Now this lad has done deeds to call attention to himself so that his name is heard throughout Connacht. And too, to him is applied another name, now. For it's yourself has said it, lord King; his deed sounds like one of legend. For not only did he perform this deed with spear and sword and buckler, and him alone, but when afterward others came upon him he stood against a great standing stone on the shore, with the four death-hacked *Cruithne* at his feet."

"Four," Lugaid muttered.

"Winded he was, and splashed with Pictish gore, and he leaned panting against the great rock rising up from the sand. To those who first came onto the strand, it appeared the lad was *bound* there, that he was dead there, standing . . . as," Milchu said on, emphasizing each several word now, "was Eirrin's greatest hero at his death—"

"Cuchulain of Muirthemne!" Lugaid's voice was an explosive whisper. He pronounced the name of the Irish Akilles or Odysseos/Ulysses; his land's greatest folk-hero whose deeds were known to every lad. And the colour of the High-king came and went as quickly as the aspen by the stream.

"Even Cuchulain," Milchu said.

Then Lugaid cocked his head and came nigh to smiling. "So was it at the death of Cuchulain, Chulan's hound—and was Art's son of Connact dead, then?"

25

"Far from it, lord King. Merely dazed and exhausted was the youth and his long-used arms atremble, whilst all victorious he supported himself against a stone taller than he and four times as broad."

Lugaid's eyes were ugly and his lips tight. "I much prefer a dead legend to a live hero, Milchu—especially with his parentage and that name."

"Aye," Milchu said, and he was silent then, seeing that the High-king pondered.

Known well to Lugaid was Art of Connacht. Well-birthed the man was, a descendant of the family of High-kings so many of whom had come from Connact that it had been called the Cradle of Kings and even Tara of the West. Aye, Lugaid knew of Art mac Comail. A brave and fearless fighter in the service of Connacht's king the man was. For many a year he had done mayhem among the ever-restless *Cruithne,* or Picts, on Connacht's shores.

Art, too, was of the descendants of Niall.

Seventy years dead was Niall, great High-king who had sallied forth into Alba and Britain and even into Gaul over the water. Sons he had in plenty, Fiacaid and Laegair, Conal Crimthanni of the Britonish mother, and Mani, and Conal Gulban and Eoghan and Cairbri and Enna . . . only thirteen years dead was Conal of Tir Connail. And these were the ui-Neill, the descendants of Niall, and so was Art, Comal's son of Connact. Yet he was king not in Tara nor in Connacht.

Without real power the man was, and watched even by his own king for what and who he was. Lugaid knew he was popular and a hero, commander of a rath he protected well . . . a coastal command far from the capital at Cruachan.

I like not the man's arrogance in naming his son Cormac, for that greatest of High-kings whose father was Art Aenfher, Art the Lonely. Too easily, he mused, staring at Milchu while hardly seeing him, *do legends and popular fervors grow. And in Connacht. . . . !*

"And so . . . now even the son of Art of the Connachtish ui-Neill, and him bearing so auspicious and magnetic a name, is a hero . . . "

"Aye, lord King."

"And him but fourteen."

"Aye, lord King."

"With many years ahead of him."

"Lord King, yourself has said it."

Aye, and a threat to the highest crown, Lugaid did not say, *a threat to me!*

"Now . . . Milchu . . . this is fact . . ."

"Lord King, the information comes from one in my service, and him of Connacht, close to Lord Art."

"You will tell me his name."

Milchu bowed to that and made answer at once, for it was no question but a command.

"Eoin mac Gulbain, High-king."

"Gulban! Ah."

"Even so, my lord King. The Lord Gulban's son Eoin is a weapon-man among those who serve the lord Art. A brave man and a loyal warrior, Eoin . . . though he wears another name, keeping his own under a cloak of deception. For he has with Art a blood-feud—"

"Ahhh." And this time Lugaid did not smile, for possibilities of counteractions took shape in his mind nigh as swiftly as plots.

"Aye, lord King," Milchu said with a nod. He

27

knew he need not explain the significance to this ever-mistrustful man, this calculating plotter on Eirrin's highest throne. "Aye. Nor would Eoin mac Gulbain wish good on Art, for he feels that Art was responsible for the ruination of his father and the sinking of his family."

Now Lugaid straightened. Now he took note of his mug, with beaming eye. He drank off a draught of wine.

"What said ye, Milchu, of God's placing tools before us . . ."

Milchu smiled, very thinly, as if with reluctance to allow such interference with his ascetic mien.

"Even so," he said. "And it is of interest that Eoin is baptised as one of us, one of the Saints."

Lugaid was grinning. Shoulders hunched, he leaned forward on his table. "And will do as bids a priest of his faith?"

"It's only a priest of Connacht has stayed him from having his feud-vengeance on Art, lord King. Nor does he refrain with much willingness on him. This has he said of his lord, Art: 'If he did fifty good deeds on me, surely this would be my thanks, I would not give him peace, and him in distress, but every great want I could put on him.' "

"A fine worthy young son of Eirrin! And does he have a brain within him, as well?"

"He stays his hand, lord King."

"Umm. But unwillingly."

"Even so, lord King."

"Ho." Lugaid drank. "Ha. And were a priest to speak otherwise, counsel the opposite course, perhaps point out that Art is a great enemy of Iosa Chriost—"

"In truth, lord King, he is no friend—"

"Surely then would be this fine young man's

holy duty to avenge his poor father!"

"Surely, my lord. Were he to be so convinced." And as if he'd forgot and only just thought of it, Milchu coughed again.

"A bad cough," the High-king commented.

"The . . . night air . . . the fog," Milchu said weakly, bent forward so that his chin was nearly on the table.

He did not move from that strange posture, for the other man's eyes were upon him. The two gazed steadily at each other. Nor did either misunderstand the other. The fire crackled and played games of light and shadow with their faces, though not with their eyes.

So, the Ard-righ of Eirrin thought, *so simple it appears, and now we are come down to it. Will it be so simple, Milchu's agreement to gain? Methinks not. He waits now . . . for he wants something. And that something, whatever it may be, lies here in these hands, for I am High-king in Eirrin!*

"Shall I ask, Priest?"

"My lord?"

"Seek ye not to play at games with me, Milchu, who has played so many for so long, and who wears Eirrin's highest crown!"

"My lord High-king. I—"

"Nor will I bargain as with some merchant over pigs or embroidery-work! Ye know well my meaning. What is it ye'd be having, Milchu, Priest, to . . . counsel with Eoin as to his honour and his duty?"

"My *lord*!"

Lugaid said nothing. Again his fingers were tracing out the shape and the inlays of his tankard's handle. He waited.

At last Milchu leaned back, though he did not relax. "Great honour would accrue to my lord God,"

29

he said reflectively, "and to my lord High-king and thus to Eirrin, were it Lugaid Laegair's son who approved my buiding a fine church in the town of Ath Cliath, with myself as Bishop once it's done, to do glory to both God and the High-king who pleases Him."

For a time Lugaid remained as if frozen. Then he too sat back. He bethought him. Well he knew that men said his crown rested shakily on his thinning russet locks . . . that he was a man who like a child abroad alone at night saw *demain* shapes in every shadow . . .

Such men of course were fools. The demons of treachery, Lugaid was convinced, *did* lurk in all places. The cleverer he, who with such hidden eyes as those of Milchu could pierce the shadows and draw away the dark veils from those who made plots against him. Fail to discover them and surely he'd not be toppled, for there was his uncle Mac Erca with the weaponish host But . . . if Muirchetach mac Erca decided that a High-king who had to be protected, nephew or no, were not worthy of remaining enthroned?

Besides, Lugaid was sure that it was Mac Erca's plan to make the High-kingship more than it was, not only the highest seat in Eirrin, but actually king over the other kings of the Emerald Isle. And were a western ui-Neill to be no longer available to defend that land against Picts . . . or . . . *others,* and his heroic son to be nipped whilst still abudding like a rose never to be seen, an acorn fed as mast to the pigs rather than allowed to grow into a great strong oak . . .

Aye.

Not shaky my crown; neither is my seat on Eirrin's highest chair. Solid both, and to be made the more so for my sons to follow. That is, if I prepare the way for those to follow me . . . preserve crown and throne and thus serve Eirrin best; for how could I do elsewise, the High-king? . . . by removing any who offer the slightest threat to crown, or throne, or honour, and future . . . suzerainty!

Art mocks me by naming his son Cormac!

Cormac mac Art challenges me by bearing the name, by his feat, by suffering himself to be called Cuchulain . . .

Art and his weaponish son threaten Eirrin!

"It seems to me that Art and his weaponish son, Cormac and Cuchulain all combined, are threats."

Milchu had but waited for him to speak it aloud. "It is why I'm after coming direct to yourself, High-king."

"The best time to meet such threats is before they become manifest and thus even more dangerous . . . and harder to remove."

"The thinking of a King of Kings, lord King," Milchu said, and was careful to let his eyes remain flat and bland, lest they bespeak his true opinion of this . . . this fearful puppet of Mac Erca!

"Methinks the god of Rome—and of Eirrin— should be honoured with a fine chapel in Baile Atha Cliath . . . would ye be taking such a commission, Priest?"

"My lord King does honour on me!"

"Assuredly."

"And should I wend my way eastward to Ath Cliath by a westward route, by way of . . . Connacht, lord King?"

The High-king's eyes were hooded, but he leaned forward to end the game with plain words and royally extended forefinger.

31

"Eoin mac Gulbain were better and covered surely with honour an he avenged his father's loss of honour . . . on the man who replaced that father—and on the son!"

"Milchu nodded. His eyes were agleam. He rose.

"Soon, lord High-king of Eirrin, there shall have been but one Cormac mac Art in Eirrin, and him that great king dead these two hundred years! As for the other . . . none shall remember him, after his death at age fourteen!"

Chapter Two:
The Bear

A grassy branch popped loudly in the fire and one of the five men gathered about it shot out a foot to wipe the good-sized spark into the ground. He continued rubbing that foot along the ground; little value a well-made buskin of good cowhide if he burned a hole in its sole. Still, one had to be mindful of the sparks. This forest—*Sciath Connaict,* the Shield of Connacht—had stood here in southern Connacht far longer than any man had lived, and fire in a forest was a terrible thing.

Huddled in furs to ward off the breeze-brought chill of early March, the five men stared at the fire. Eyes of blue and of grey gazed at the great haunch and leg of fresh-slain elk that sizzled on the makeshift spit they'd constructed of good green wood gathered from close round about. Bubbling fat became grease that dripped down to spat and sizzle and pop amid the flames. The aroma that rose thick on the air was enough to make stomachs rumble, and stomachs did.

Beneath their furs two of the five wore mail,

linked in five circles of chain again and again in the manner of Eirrin. Two others wore the far less dear—and more swiftly made—armour coats of boiled leather. Bosses of bronze winked dully. One of these men of weapons, his helm beside him and his dark hair falling loose and sweat-matted nigh to his shoulders within his robe's hood of hare's fur, had bossed his leatherncoat with two great blunted cones of iron. Like huge shining blue nipples, they stood forth an inch from either side of his chest. Another of the five had doffed his plain round helm, too, and was combing tangled wheaten locks with his fingers.

The five stared at the meat, waiting. They swallowed repeatedly.

"Best ye get that pot back on your head, Roich, and forget the beauty of your hair." It was the reddish-bearded man in chainmail who spoke. "This air does a sweaty crown no good, none at all."

"Damned thing's heavy," Roich muttered, but he picked up his helmet.

"That's because ye've a neck like a chicken, Roich," the man beside him said, he in the thick heavy cloak of grey wolf and hare combined.

Roich pushed him angrily and the speaker chuckled, rocking on his buttocks.

"To gain Midhir's advice is one thing, Bran, but to have my ears wounded with that raven's voice of yours is more than a man can bear."

Bran and Midhir chuckled.

The fifth among them wore an enveloping cloak of brown woollen, to which had been sewn a collar of badger. Around his hair a narrow leathern binding, a sort of head-torc or *niamh-lhamn;* on his chest a sun-symbol on a woven silver chain. He it was who spoke now:

"It's with weapon-men of Art mac Comail I set forth as druid companion, and with children about a campfire I find myself. Och, only the youngest among us keeps his peace as a man."

"Once again Edar the Druid speaks sense and truth," the mailed, reddish-bearded man called Midhir said.

The four of them looked at him the druid had singled out; a lad he was, his face showing only the adolescent intimation of a beard to come. It would be black. Black the hair falling below his pot-like helm; nor was his skin fair like Bran's and Midhir's. Yet his eyes were grey-blue, the colour even in the light of the dancing fire of good sword-steel. Was he wore the other coat of chainmail, over a shirt of soft doeskin and leggings of the same. His gaze moved swiftly from one to the other of his companions, returned to the elk's leg over the fire. Praised for his mannish silence, he nevertheless spoke now.

"Midhir . . ." he said, in a voice not quite through its change to that of manhood, for he had recently reached that age at which boys were called men whether they were ready or not, and were so called until old age began to set in—usually at about forty, and usually not of long duration thereafter.

"Aye," Midhir said, looking also at the meat.

Bucking up the knees of his crossed legs, he pressed with his heels. Chain rustled then as he thrust himself easily to his feet without touching the ground with his hands, for all the weight of his muscular self and his chaincoat and helm. His right hand pushed away his furs; his left went in to his hip and came forth with a long dagger.

Behind him, a horse whickered. Another stamped. Midhir paused to glance at the four animals, staked out for the grazing just without the fire's light.

Nearby rested the two carts they had drawn hence from Cruachan. The carts were empty.

Roich twisted half around. "Heard they something I did not?"

"It's but happiness on them to have delivered the annual tribute to our king and have naught to pull but empty carts," Bran said. "And less than a day from home."

"We've been still and so have they," Midhir said. "Morelike they were startled by my getting up to test this meat." And he leaned in toward the haunch and leg of juicy elk.

It was then the thundersome roar exploded from the darkness of the woods. The noise seemed to shake the very twigs of the trees with their fledgeling buds. With wild calls, startled birds vacated their nests. One of the horses, the red-brown, reared and tugged at his leg-tether.

All five men were on their feet in an instant and staring into the darkness.

Mighty crashing noises, slavering snarls, and another roar announced the coming of . . . something. The men's long spears stood from one of the carts like huge needles from a good wife's cushion, and Roich and Bran lurched into movement toward them as if shoved. Driven they were, indeed, by the weapon-man's training that became as instinct.

Was Bran who first snatched his spear, and at that instant the great bear came charging into the little encampment.

Like a jealous guardian of the forest privacy he was, angered at the intrusion of men into his wood, and bent on doing death on them all. Up on his two hind legs he was so that he towered over all; a shaggy brown beast rising eight feet in height. A fleeing ring ouzel hurtled across the little clearing on blurring wings, and a sizable shrew, fearing the bear more than the evidence of its nose, rushed in among the men, headed directly for the fire. It swerved sharply, skidded, and was a brown streak that vanished into the forest again.

Bran could not cast or make a running stab; the bear was already too close, and coming. The weapon-man swung his spear to get it in line with the beast even as he backed a pace. One paw the size of Bran's head snapped the spear, bringing a grunt of pain from him as the haft slammed into his hip. The spear broke, for all its being good season-ed ash.

And then the bear caught Roich, who screamed out in a voice not a man's.

Ere Midhir could abandon dagger and draw sword, the furs flew in a rustle from the lad at his side, and clumbed to the earth. Surely it was worse than unwise for that tall, beautifully constructed youth to do what he did then, all in an instant; he drew both sword and foot-long knife at the same time as he rushed to Roich's aid.

That writhing weapon-man had managed to strike the bear in the nose with no more than his knuckly fist, yet with an angry and pained roar the beast hurled him aside. His gaze lit instantly on that which moved: the rushing youth. A huge shaggy arm leaped out to grasp him. The beast emitted such a fierce growling that it might have been heard through all Connacht, and he moved on the youth as if he had a mind not to stop and tear him up at all, but to swallow him at the one mouthful.

The mailed young man reacted in the manner of a seasoned warrior. So deeply did he chop into the furry arm that the bear's instant yanking back of his limb tore the sword from it's weilder's grasp. The

36

brute had shrieked—but attacked in bleeding rage, rather than fled. The other arm swept forth, and then the wounded one as well. The sword dropped free of riven flesh while the animal seized the source of its pain.

Instantly the young man was being crushed against the great beast, which sought his face or neck with its terrible jaws. Was well for the Connachtish youth he had not removed his coat of linked steel chain, else the awful claws would have ribboned his back and torn him to the bone.

Only just was the youth able to wedge an arm beneath the brute's chin, and his body quivered with strain while he held the yellow-white teeth scant inches from his face. At the same time, his legs braced and the calves knotting within deerskin leggings, the youth plunged his dagger again and again into his ferocious antagonist.

The immediate effect was precious little, though the bear issued more screams of rage that blasted the human's eardrums and fanned his face with the charnel-house breath of the beast; this omnivorous creature must have come recently from its winter's nap and found meat almost at once. Now it sought more. Its prey was incredibly strongly held, squeezed in his carapace of steel links—and in imminent danger now of being crushed even as a steel-backed beetle. His entire body quivered in the strain of muscular tension. Surely his life was measured in seconds.

Straining to keep massively powerful jaws and great teeth from his face, he desperately re-directed the aim of his dagger—and plunged it into one glaring feral eye.

Long was the blade, and deep he drove it.

Steel point sundered eyeball and drove back

37

within that vulnerable hollow to pierce smallish animal brain. Reflexively the beast hurled its foe from it, for it was sorely stricken enow to give over battle in favour of sensible flight. The valiant youth was propelled mightily backward against Bran. Both fell. Past them stamped leather-shod feet, and Midhir drove the dagger-long wedge of a spearblade solidly into the brute.

The leaf-shaped blade of iron directly pierced the beast's heart.

Bleeding in a dozen places, the brown bear fell, rolled, clawed snarling at itself and the earth and air. Its roars and snarls diminished in strength and volume. And then its legs were kicking loosely, aimlessly. It died.

"Th-thanks be to ye, Midhir mac Fionn!" the youth gasped in a strained voice, when Midhir helped him to his feet.

"Thanks to *me*! Was yourself attacked the monster, Cormac! Be ye hurt?"

"Uh—" The youth swelled his torso in a brace of deep breaths that brought winces on him. "Hurts a little . . . it's terrible pain I'd be feeling an my ribs or back were broke or cracked, would I not?"

In the aftermath of the attack and the prodigious fight, Midhir's chuckle emerged as a giggle uncomplimentary to himself. "Aye, lad," he said, clapping the youth high on the back. Leaving that hand there, he looked at Roich. "Roich?"

"Bruises. Naught more. First the waggon caught me, then Cormac fell on me—small wonder ye prevailed, son of Art: methinks ye outweigh yon beast!" Roich was feeling over himself with hands that visibly quivered. "He— Crom's beard! My coat is *torn!* Torn, as if 'twere naught but linen, this stout coat of leather!"

"Aye, and so is the arm beneath," the druid said. "Come ye back to the fire and let me see to it, mac Lurchain. Cormac— it's sure ye be there's no hurt on ye? Let me have look at your back."

"No need," Midhir said. "I've seen men slashed to the bone, but in the heat of combat they never noticed. But our Bear-slayer's all right, Druid. A triumph of the skill and steel of Taig the Armourer!"

"And Cormac's steel *ribs*," grinned Roich, speaking a bit loudly now the danger was past; his hands still shook. "Much thanks I owe ye, Cormac mac Art!"

"Morelike your worthless life you're owing to him," Midhir said. His hand on the youth's back propelled him to the fire on legs suddenly gone all aquiver.

The men moved back to their blaze, the youngest among them fair creaking from the crushing bearish embrace he'd endured. With herbs from his pouch Edar treated Roich's upper arm, and the druid insisted too on seeing to the few scratches on Cormac's hand; the hero had not noticed them.

The while, Roich and Bran were stintless in their praise of the bear-fighting youth or New-man. Was praise from Midhir that swelled the bearslayer's boyish chest, though; this was the man most trusted by Cormac's father, who called him even *Arbenn,* chieftain, and not in jest. And it was Finn's son Midhir too who was most responsible for the training at arms of his lord's son, as it was Sualtim the Druid who had trained the youth's brain.

"It's truly a man ye are, son of Art," Midhir said very seriously. He was carving their neglected dinner, now overly charred on one side. "Your slaying of those Picts on that day of shield-splitting and now this deed are the sort that birth legends,

39

and it's sure that ye've caught the eye of Connacht's good king. Cormac mac Art: Bearslayer!"

"And mayhap the High-king as well," Bran said excitedly.

"The day will surely come," Midhir said on, "when ye'll serve our lord king directly, and him with gratitude on him for it, and . . . peradventure, Cormac, weapon-man, it's yourself who'll be winning for Connacht the Championship of Eirrin, even at the Great Fair!"

"Aye, weapon-comrade!" Roich cried.

Cormac said naught, keeping his eyes down while he bathed in the good rich oil of praise.

"Were best not to be attracting the eye of the Ard-righ," Edar said quietly. "It is known that men have died, aye and with mystery on it, once they've caught the ever-roving eye of poor King Lugaid. For our High-king ever sees enemies alurk all about him, and snakes under his very bed."

"Snakes!" Bran cried.

And laughed, and so did the others laugh with mirth upon them.

For all knew that their fair land of green meadows and swirly mist and high blue-misted mountains possessed no slithering reptiles. Nor had it ever.

"Aye, and if told there be no snakes in all Eirrin," Roich said with high exuberance, "our High-king would surely be convinced 'twas a lie, and set a watch over him who told it!"

"Nay, nay, for his own wife would assure him was Padraigh drove all those doubtless-millions of creepy reptiles from our land, belike with that pointed stave he carried!"

And they laughed anew.

Edar was more serious still. "All that Padraigh brought us is a plague of serpents in human form, men who slither about the fens and meadows of

Crom and Lugh and Behl in robes of black, seeking to win all to the worshp of the gibbet of dying Rome!"

Midhir hastily returned to his bragging on Cormac, for none among them wished to give ear to a druidish lecture on the druid's deadly enemies. Was the biggest bear ever he'd set the gaze of eyes on, Midhir mac Fionn avowed, and the more courageous Cormac was in bracing the brute single-handedly.

"I was after trying to brace him double-handedly," the young man said, rather shyly amid the praise, "but he made such an objection to my sword that I threw it away!"

Again there was hale laughter, and a chuckling Midhir said, "Never would I be saying that it was a *foolhardy* act, son of Art!"

"Oh, *never,*" Bran cried, and they laughed anew, while the beat of their hearts slowed and the prickle faded slowly from their armpits and the tremors commenced to quit their hands.

"Admittedly," Midhir siad, half strangling on his chuckles, "had the subject ever arisen whilst we were at your training at arms, Cormac, I'd have been advising ye not to attack a bear taller than two men and outweighing four!"

"A . . . *bear,*" Edar murmured slowly, and his frown chased their laughter.

Blinking, thoughtful, the servant of Behl and Crom frowned about at the darkling woods. "Bears have not been seen in these forests for years, for here no caves lie near, to house them as they like it. Even so—were a bit early for one to be up and abroad after his winter's snooze . . ."

Edar looked at Cormac, and still his brow was creased and furrowed. The others were silent, stilling even their breath. The druid had spoke naught but the truth, and now it was called to mind, neither the bear's attack nor even its presence seemed . . . natural.

"It is an omen, son of *Art,*" the druid said, and his stressing the name of Cormac's father reminded them all that *art* in their tongue meant no less than "bear" even as it did over in Pretene or Britain, where one Uther had so named his son.

The sat unspeaking, impressed to the viscera, and only after several minutes did Roich break the silence with an enthusiasm born of nervousness.

"It's no son of *this* bear Cormac is!"

"Though he will soon have a great enveloping winter's cloak of its hide," Midhir said. "I and Aevgrine will soon be seeing to that."

But the youth looked dark with the shadow of thought on him.

"Omen?" he said. "An omen, Druid Edar? And . . . see ye it as good or foreboding, Lord Druid?"

Edar but shook his bronze-locked head. "This Behl does not reveal, nor does the Druid-sight that allows us occasionally to glimpse the time-to-come. Though in truth it is by night the beast came upon us, while Behl is absent from the sky and only the cold moon watches . . ."

Was then Midhir went again to the horses, which were still hardly calm, while Roich and Bran attacked the gloom by commencing the comparison of Cormac with the mighty hero Cuchulain in his strength and in his courage. Too high were the spirits of all to be affected darkly this night by the druid's words. Cormac beamed, seeming to glow from deep within him, and his unease passed. Nevertheless he kept his stare fixed on the fire, pretending to ignore his exuberant companions and their high compliments. They were after all men in liege to his father . . .

Midhir returned to the fire. "Here, Cuchulain Bearslayer, this night it's the champion's portion for yourself," he said warmly, bringing forth a dripping gobbet of meat larger than his hand.

The flames commanded Cormac's eyes, and his gaze was as if trapped by the dancing tongues and feather-shapes of yellow and orange, crimson and white . . .

The champion's portion . . . Cu-Chulain . . . the Hound of Chulan . . . Cuchulain of Muirthemne . . .

—and then Cormac mac Art was oblivious of the proffered meat, and the voices of these his companions, for he was no longer with them . . .

He stood in a fine shining chariot drawn by two horses with the spirit of spring breezes and springs. Mourning was on him for his driver just slain, his long-time driver and old friend Laeg, and he hurled again his spear of victory into the ranks of the gathered enemy, and its gleaming bronze point drove through a man so that he died and him behind that one was hurled backward by the point's bursting through the first and nigh entering his belly.

And then another of the gathered enemy leaped forward, and tore free that much-blooded spear, the *gau-buaid*, and hurled it even as Cormac whipped up his fine team of horses—

No! Not Cormac; no son of Art was he, with sword of blue-grey steel by side, but him born Setalta and later called the hound of the smith, Chulan—Cuchulain he was, and battling the enemy who had never forgot the terrible War of the two bulls, the Brown of Cuailgne and the White-horned of Cruachan Ai. And the spear drove into one of

43

his chariot horses, the finest in all the land, even the Grey of Macha, King of the horses of Eirinn, and him having served Cuchulain so long and so well. And he, he, Cormac who was Cuchulain, cried out, for it was another friend he'd lost this day, and life and time were closing on him the way that in his anguished mind he heard anew the druid's words of his youth:

"If any young man should be taking up arms this day, his name will be greater than any other name in Eirrin. But his span of life will be short." And the boy Cuchulain had immediately gone and taken up arms, aye and reddened them that day, and too he had sworn his oath of glory: "I swear by the oath of my people that I will make my deeds to be spoken of among the great deeds of heroes in their strength."

And indeed his name became thereafter greater than any in all Eirrin, in Emain Macha or Uladh or Laigen that was Leinster, or Cruachan Ai to become Connacht, or Tuathmumain that was become Munster.

Then, while in the midst of the enemy he anguished over the Gray of Macha that lay kicking before his chariot so that it tore free of pole and harness, he of the enemies of Cuchulain whose name was Lugaid hurled his throwing-spear of enchantment, and Cuchulain grunted and was staggered at feel of the terrible blow.

(By the fire in the wood of Connacht, young Cormac jerked and groaned so that his companions asked in concern if he had wounds on him that did not show.)

He looked down then, he who was not yet Cormac for centuries were in the way of it, and he felt the cold that came after the blow to his body, and he saw then that the spear had gone into him. In anger rather than horror he tore it from his middle, for it was long and did tug heavily at him. But then, liberated, his bowels began to coil out onto the cushions of his chariot. Down fell his arm that held Dubhan his shield, and he could not force his other hand to draw forth Cruaidin Calcidheann, the Hard, Hard-headed One, his great bronze sword of so many deeds, and the Hound of Chulan knew then that his life's span would indeed be short. For Lugaid had surely given him his deadly wound.

Then did his other horse and companion of so many battles strain, and find that his partner was loose of the chariot, and the Black Sanglain lunged forward into a gallop so that had not Cuchulain gripped the chariot before him he'd have been hurled free. Spears whizzed amid the cries of his enemies, who had stood silent as if in awe and disbelief that he could be so wounded. And the Grey of Macha that was the King of all the horses of Eirinn left there to die among his enemies.

Down ontoi the strand beside the loch galloped the Balck Sanglain, drawing the chariot alone in his bolting, and it struck a great rock at the water's edge so that it bounded high and landed on its side, and Cuchulain was hurled from it.

then did he put shame on his enemies that were shouting after him, and indeed on all men. For he set his teeth and gathered up his guts to himself, and with the aid of his other hand and the chariot, he dragged himself to the edge of the water, and Cuchulain drank and washed himself that he might not die so filthy with dirt and blood and sweat before his enemies. And again by the aid of the chariot, he gained his feet with a lurch and a grunt.

A great slashing cold pain ran all through him from where his hand clutched his entrails to himself, and seeped blood between his fingers. And his enemies stood hushed whilst they stared, for he walked, and with his death-wound on him.

Each time his foot came down on the sandy earth the jar seemed worse than had he leaped from the top of a mighty oak, but Cuchulain walked. His eyes stared only ahead, at the great standing rock rising from the sand, and Cuchulain walked. His feet moved, one and then the other and then the first again, the while he clutched himself the way that his bowels did not spill forth and trip him. And his blood leaked and leaked, and he walked.

He walked, in an agony of pain, and surely when they had gone a million miles, his mind on naught but lifting his one foot and putting it down, and then the other, he had paced along the lock to the standing stone that had been raised there, for it was a pillar-stone.

They see a dead man walk, he thought, and clamped his teeth against a groan when he paused at the stone taller than he, the greatest hero Eirrin would ever know, with his guts slippery in his hands. His head swam and the world was red-tinged though sunset was hours away, and he clung to himself, holding back blood and looping bowels with one hand while with the other he worked.

Hours seemed to pass while he leaned against the pillar-stone, and got loose his breast-belt with a bloody hand, and then his loin-girding belt. Buckled together, he looped them over the standing stone, and set his broad back to it, the while his eyes saw a darkening red fog that was somehow also a sound, a throbbing continuing thunder in his ears. And he made shift to fasten the belt over the hole in him, and secured himself thus to the pillar-stone beside the loch. A terrible grunting groan escaped even his set lips that ground powder from his teeth for he had tugged tight the belt and yet had not the strength to hold tight his jaws the longer. And his mouth came open, and leaked blood upon his chest that was like unto that of a bear.

Yet he knew his ribs would not hold his heart, for his great hero's heart was turned all to blood within him.

But he stood. He had bound himself upright against the stone, the way he would not meet his death lying down before his enemies, like the normal man he had never been. And though he saw only dimly, he knew then that the host of his enemies came down onto the strand, shields and spears ready, and he knew that he faced them standing erect with heels braced and guts bound up so they could not spill from within him, and even now they in their company were in dread of approaching him closely. Laughter he would have giventhem then, but he knew he dared not, for the strain of that laughter might sunder the straps of leather holding back the bowels that strained and sought to pour looping from him.

For he was Cuchulain of Muirthemne, and he'd die on his feet and facing his enemies. And a cloud and a weakness rose to come over him, so that his eyes were fixed.

"It is a great shame for us," said Erc who was the son of Cairbre whom Cuchulain had slain, "not to strike the head off this man, in revenge for his striking the head off my father!"

And Cuchulain saw Lugaid then, Lugaid who had done death on him, and he was reaching for his sword—though Lugaid in truth had gone all reddish and dark and seemed to pulse with the throbbing thunder Cuchulain heard; dusk must be coming on uncommon early this day. And he heard the pounding hooves that told him his beloved horses were coming to seek to save him, and them without Laeg to drive nor Cuchulain their lifelong master to shout them on. For he was beyond shouting.

And they did, the Black Sanglain and even the wounded Grey of Macha or so he thought he saw, both of them that slew many with flashing hooves and terrible warhorse teeth, and they were slain and died, his mighty horses, and Lugaid was coming for him with his sword up and his shield-hand rising the way it would lock in Cuchulain's hair that Lugaid might strike off his head.

And sadness was on Cuchulain to discover that his body that had served him so well no longer paid heed to his demands of it, for his arms would not rise to grapple with Lugaid, though he had killed ten tens and more of mightier men.

Lugaid's face came closer, and filled all his vision, and then it seemed to shimmer like the pool into which a stone had been tossed, and it was no longer Lugaid's face before Cuchulain, but that of the druid of his boyhood, Cathbadh.

"Your name will be greater than any other name in Eirrin," the druid said, and his face pulsed redly. "But it's short your span of life will be."

And this was the death of Cuchulain and this too was the first of the *Rememberings* to come upon Cormac son of Art.

Then Cathbadh's face, too, shimmered, even as the bright sunlight of summer off a thousand fine shields or off the broad surface of Loch Cuan.

And it was not Lugaid that he saw. And it was not

Cathbadh the Druid he saw, with his face somehow surrounded by flames so that he stared out from within those very flames. Aye, though in truth it was a druid, neither Lugaid nor Cathbadh. Was Sualtim he saw with his agonized eyes.

Sualtim! he thought. *This is not possible—that mentor of Cormac mac Art that I will be is not even born yet!*

Oh—I am Cormac mac Art! I was Cuchulain. I am Cormac. I am in the woods, not dying though I have died afore in lives other than this one . . . the woods . . . campfire . . . but that is Sualtim Fodla staring at me from the fire!

Aye. Amid the dancing campfire, now opaque so that their white-and-yellow glare was invisible behind him, now opalescent and wavering amid a ruddy glow, now transparent so that he was but a cloud and the flames were completely visible behind him and *through him;* there stood Sualtim of Wisdom Itself.

Thin he was as ever, gaunt of face so that his skin was as aged white parchment drawn over the bone. A band of soft doeskin two fingers in breadth circled his brow, binding his thin, straight hair the colour of June clouds on a sunny day or the sleek coat of a red-eared white calf. On him not his robe of oak-forest green, but the one of white, the white robe of ceremony that was the colour of the hair of his head and his eyebrows.

The quick, bird-bright eyes stared blue at Cormac mac Art. And the gaunt old face with its lines from nostrils to the corners of his wide mouth was drawn with anguish and . . . could that be fear? *Sualtim?*

From the flames in Connacht-Shield Woods, Sualtim spoke.

"Treachery, son of Art! Get ye to the house of

your father, you who are boy no longer, for it's dark treachery stalks the rath this night."

That was all. The image flickered with the flicker of the fire, and grew less and less substantial. And then Sualtim was gone.

Cormac would have fallen bvut for the hands of an anxious Midhir.

"Cormac! What is it on ye, lad? Tell me! Crom protect—it must be that he had injuries within from that great bear!"

"N-no," Cormac stammered, but still he was weak and disconcerted so that he reeled as he sat, and was held up only by the concerned grip of a weapons-compatriot.

"The boy—" Edar began, and interrupted himself. "Cormac has the look on him of a man who feels his other lives." Then Edar looked about, frowning, and there was confusion in his voice: "Sualtim?"

"Cormac—"

"I . . . I am unharmed, Mid-Midhir."

Cormac forced his brain to work. *Cuchulain—never mind that: later!*

Sualtim! Well he knew that the druid had been there, had spoken to him—yet he knew that it was not in the flesh Sualtim had come. In a Sending, a *samha,* he had warned, called . . .

Shaking off Midhir's solicitous hands, Cormac thrust himself to his feet like a big cat. He looked about at his companions. They were staring at him.

"I have seen Sualtim. He was speaking to me. Midhir! Ye must be coming with me—now, tonight. Two of the horses we will ride; two we leave to pull the empty carts on the morrow. Edar, Roich, Bran: when day comes, make haste. We leave ye now."

And none gainsaid the boy-man from Eirrin who turned now to ready a pair of horses; the boy-man of fourteen, who was suddenly a man in other than physical deeds, and to be obeyed.

Chapter Three:
Glondrath

The forest called Sciath Connaict debouched amid a sprinkling of alder and bilberry onto a fine long meadow that flowed out green, and planted in summer to a gentle rise on the leftward flank, as one emerged from the woods. Here Connacht defended herself. Two miles beyond the forest and this meadow lay the coast and the western sea. Just seaward of center on this ancient plain, a mighty mound rose on what was called Magh Glondarth: The Plain of Deeds, for in times gone by many a battle had been fought on these acres. The sprawling mound itself bore the name *lios*. When it was fortified atop so that there clustered what amounted to a warlike village or manor-estate as here, and ringed about with a strong defensive wall of earth, it became a *rath*.

To Comal's son Art his king had given command of this key military post, which was both home and holding-for-the-king. Though many called it Rath Airt, naturally enough—Art's Rath—it remained not his, but a part of the kingdom's important defenses. For it bristled betwixt the dense forest east of which lay the rest of Eirrin and its kingdoms, and the sea, whence came occasional raiders from the Northlands and, unceasingly, the Cruithne; the squat dark men the Romans called the Old Ones: *Pictii;* Picts. And thus it was not Art's Rath at all, but a highly important outpost of the kingdom born centuries agone as Coiced Connachta; an outpost that took in all these acres and the land even unto the sea, and that for two centuries had borne the name Rath Glondarth, and more simply by someone's cleverness, Glondrath.

The Rath of Deeds. And many were the deeds done here by striving men at the game of the Morrigu and the shield-splitting, nor ever had Rath Glondarth fallen to attackers.

Just after dawn, two men on horseback emerged from the woods. To their right the meadowed plain rolled out and out like a carpet laid at the foot of the mountain that rose tall and tall—and gapless; to their left began the long gentle rise that gave way to highland farms and pasturage. Because of the forest with its myriad oaks and plentitude of acorns, many were the fine pigs that were raised hereabouts. Fond of pork, were the sons of Eirrin.

Nearly a mile straight ahead rose the *lios* and Rath Glondarth, the command of Art mac Comail of the western ui-Neill.

Comal's fifth son was Art, and little there'd been left for him on his father's death. Given this command because of his sword and his warlike brain, along with the failure of its previous lord, Art had proven so strong and fair-handed that men and their families had flocked to him. His command had become his estate, and good was the tribute sent by him to his king each year. Good too was

Glondrath's trade; pork fattened on these grasses and roots and acorns was known as far to the east as Carmen and southeast as Caisel and aye, even in Tir Conaill of Ailech to the north. And many were the lords' halls south and north and east of Connacht that dispalyed on their walls Pictish spears and shields and blades, for those there were in Eirrin who had never seen the Cruithne.

Picts were well known betwixt the forest called Sciath Connaict and the sea.

Both riders who emerged from the woods were cloak-muffled, furs up, for the dawn-chill had hardly dissipated. They sat their mounts loosely in weariness, and both beasts were winded, blowing with flanks atremble. For hours they had been urged with care through the night-blackened forest. Their riders had held their mounts to a walk while trusting otherwise to the instinct and surefootedness of the animals on the hardpacked roadway. The trail was broad, though, for reasons of defense and the slowing of any possible force of invaders, it wound about abominably.

Winded or no, the horses quickened their trot. One whickered and both strove to stretch reins and riders' arms to allow a lope. For with home, oats and stable in sight, they were no less anxious to reach that hilltop fortress than the men they bore. Yet despite the haste that had driven them to the long ride through the night, the men held their reins now in stern hands that drew skin tight over knuckles. Neither was anxious, this close, to have his mount go down under him in final weariness.

They but glanced at the apple orchard to the east; the guard that was ever posted there to surprise interlopers would not bestir themselves and betray their position to challenge only two

53

men. And besides, Midhir mac Fionn was at pains to display in that direction his scarlet-painted shield with its four sun-catching points of silver; a gift from his lord Art that shield, and known farther abroad then hereabouts.

The forced ride had been cruel in more ways than one. There had been the darkness and the danger of a stumbling mount. There had been the sleepiness that came on, with the growing ache in buttocks and thighs. And too the long silent hours of darkness had afforded much time for brain-meandering.

Nor had Cormac mac Art done aught else. His mind would not clear, nor would it consent to remain on any one of his several worries. Of no avail the years of words and mental exercises drilled into him by Sualtim whose counsel was ever that one should get to know oneself, and then to control him one thus knew, to make him the better—and no animal merely reacting.

There had been too much, and all at once. The thrill of bracing that huge bear had been enow. Sure and such a feat deserved to be followed only by a basking in the bright glow of praise, followed by earned sleep. Yet close on the heels of that encounter and that accomplishment had come the . . . the rune-sent vision, the *samha*.

Cuchulain! Sure and Cormac knew the tales, which he had heard far more than once. He had dreamed of those times, of those days of great and incredible deeds. But this—!

Had his mental state, the decline in mental and physical heightening from their peak following the slaying of the bear . . .had these and the eye-seizing, mind-dulling effect of the fire merely sent him into a sort of trance? Had he but seemed to see, to feel himself a participant in those tales of the Hound of Chulan the Smith?

Or . . . had Edar's words held the truth? Cormac, the druid had said, had about him the look of a man remembering his past lives.

Was that what I was about? Was I Cuchulain—or rather am I? Is it possible?

Certainly few in Eirrin questioned the ancient Celtic assertion of immortality by way of the return of the basic life force in a new body. Reincarnation was a part of religion and life. A man came onto the earth, and trod the ridge of the world for a while. The while was called a lifetime. Its length varied. Then he was gone for a time again to that Other Place, Donn's realm. Thence he returned to begin anew as an infant, the offspring of new parents, a new personality with a new name in a new body. Nor did he remember his previous lives, save in occasional snatches and glimpses. Thus was explained the inexplicable: genius in this or that trade, or at singing, or at any of the arts or skills.

Cormac's taking to weapons and combat seemed instinctive. Perhaps. And perhaps it was the continuing ability of another life, or lives. So had Sualtim suggested, and few argued with the druids.

Whatever the explanation—if one indeed existed— that strangeness of the "remembering" had been enough, of itself. For Cormac had felt the pain and pangs of dying, physical and mental, with him unable to prevent that death or even take one more foe with him . . .

And then had appeared Sualtim. To the matter of the bear and the matter of the *Remembering* was added still a third jarring experience.

Never before had the druidic tutor of his boyhood appeared to him thus, and the man himself not there. Yet Cormac was certain had been no trick of his mind. Illusion, perhaps—but of Sualtim's mind, of Sualtim's devising, of Sualtim's sending. All through the night had Cormac mac Art worried over the meaning of the druid's all too few words. And still he did, as he and Midhir allowed their mounts to pick up their pace to a trot toward the outer wall of Glondrath.

Aye . . . and Cormac had known fear, too. He still did.

Treachery, Sualtim had said. Treachery—by whom, from whom? Against whom? To what malignant purpose? For how could treachery be benign, or even neutral?

Even more troublesome to his youthful mind was the dread question: Had the treachery succeeded in its doing and its purpose?

He would find out soon enough. Around him bird sang their gladness of spring's coming,. and he heard them not. The horses were nearing the tall wall of oak and earth. Men gazed down upon the riders, men in armour and, under their helms, faces that Cormac well knew. Dour and drawn were the faces of the two weapon-men on Glondrath's eastern wall, showing little warmth of welcome to their commander and their chieftain's son.

Much of his earines left mac Art, then. A new energy of excitement came on him, born of apprehension and foreboding—and fearfulness.

The way was opened to the two, without a word. They passed within.

"Brychan!" Cormac called. "What's amiss?"

The two guards exchanged a look. One said, "Amiss?"

Cormac's stare was nigh onto a glare. "Ye heard me aright."

Brychan tucked under his lip; his companion made reply. "The druid will tell ye, son of Art."

Brychan could not help himself. "How—how knew ye aught was amiss, son of Art?"

Cormac but looked at him; Midhir glowered. The weapon man set his teeth in his lower lip and busied himself with the gate's closing.

The horses paced into the sprawling townlet that had grown up around the fortress-become-manor-house. There the main granary. There the other. There the stables. Near it the milk-sheds. There the creamery and buttery, there the cozy home of Midhir and his wife Aevgrine, and there doored mounds over underground storage chambers. Two large smokehouses. The barracks, sprawling, and homes of workmen and maids, drovers and churls, planters, the smith and armourer, the tanner and the horse-manager. Dogs yapped, wagged their tails, and some came running. Cormac's mount whickered. A woman lugging her wash looked his way, met his eyes, looked a greeting with what seemed embarrassment, looked away. Children were clamorously at play—or work, for that life began at six or seven and sometimes earlier. Yet they seemed subdued, and they hushed at sight of the two riders.

Taller, huger, somehow darker and more gloomily foreboding, loomed the old fortress itself, the house of Art; the fortress-house that had been the home of Cormac mac Art through his memory.

Other people avoided his eyes, or looked away. None smiled. A chill came on Cormac's very bones.

Something was sore amiss.

From the house of great oaken beams came Sualtim. Aye, and he wore his white robe as he had in his bodiless appearance to mac Art in the early

57

hours of the previous night. Normally Sualtim, and indeed druids in general, wore their robes of deep forest green; the green of the leaves of the oak sacred to Behl.

"Sualtim! Where is my father?"

"Within, lad. Midhir: I would take Cormac in. Will ye be seeing to the horses?"

Midhir glanced about, caught the eye of a youth of eleven or so. Midhir beckoned. Then he returned his eyes to the druid, even while Cormac slid from his horse. He alit with a clanky jingle of armour and the thwock of leather-shod, wooden sword-sheath against his leg.

"Cormac," Midhir said, and when the youth turned and looked questioningly up at him, "your buckler."

Cormac gave his longtime trainer a look—and came about to fetch his shield from the saddle. The two had left behind their spears, awkward and indeed dangerous in a fast-walk night ride through the woods.

"Druid," Midhir said, as he threw his right leg over. He slid from his horse without glancing to the ground. "Are ye saying that ye want me not with ye two?"

The boy came in response to Midhir's beckoning gesture; to him Midhir handed over the horses. "Give them good care, Curnan. It's weary and doubtless hungry they are, but too hot to turn free in this chill." And Midhir looked again at Sualtim.

Sualtim opened his mouth above the thin though very long beard of grey-flecked white. Ere he could speak, Cormac did.

"Nay," the son of Art said. "Come ye with us, Midhir." He started past Sualtim, to the great-house.

"My pupil," the druid began, from long habit, and paused to amend. "Cormac . . . wait."

The youth half-wheeled on the old man who remained straight though age was at work to fold his shoulders inward.

"Ye bespoke treachery, mentor," Cormac said, forgetting he'd not told Midhir of the words of his vision. "No one we've seen here has behaved naturally. It's ill or wounded my father is—"

"I but want to go in at your side, son of Art."

And so they went. Within, in silence, they walked past the mournful face of Branwen with her deep belly, and then of Conor her nigh-bald husband, and Midhir followed them through the fortress-house to the door of the chamber of Art mac Comail. Was then a hand from the cold bed of a winterbound loch grasped at Cormac's heart, for Sualtim did not knock.

Not even the druid, not even Cormac, entered the presence of the stern military Art mac Comail without knocking.

Cormac knew then, with his belly going light within him, that he'd be finding druids within the room, and Art lying still and cold in death, and he was right.

His eyes swam—and it was as if they sent a signal to all within Glondrath. Throughout the house and the entire rath then the keening began, for such was the way of Eirrin, and all had but awaited the arrival of the son to begin their clamorous mourning of his father's death.

Some sons hated their fathers, often with reason. Some loved those who had sired them, equally with reason. Some sons were like shadeflowers all their lives, pale and as if delicate in their lack of force-

59

fulness and accomplishment. Those were indeed sons all their days; sons of fathers, as opposed to men, who were also sons. Aye, and shadeflowers they were indeed, for the great light-blotting shadows of their fathers lay long and oppressive over them. Of these some sought to emerge into the light; others, like fearful rabbits, did not. When those fathers died, many of those sons, those permanent *sons,* subjects, were so unaccustomed to the light of freedom and decision and deeds that they were as blinded. Unequipped and unable to cope were they; such "men" became never men and were useless. Others kicked up their heels in the sudden freedom of the father—to which they were unaccustomed, and with which they were unable to cope. No longer controlled, they were unbridled. And they too were useless.

The sons of other men somehow emerged from the shadow naturally, perhaps realizing that they had been aided by their fathers and perhaps not. They became men.

And for some the shadows were foreshortened, removed; the great oaks fell before the coming of their time. Many of them sought the father, Father, all their lives. Religion helped; the religion of the Priests of Rome was for them, as it was for all who sought slavery or indeed were slaves, for among them had it been born. Some few of these sons who were early rendered fatherless became men. Perhaps they realized they were fortunate never to have been overshadowed, or to have joined the ranks of the seekers of Father. And for them and their presence in it the world, too, was fortunate.

It remained to be seen into which category Cormac mac Art would enter. Mac Art he was and would remain, though there was no longer an Art.

Art was dead. His son was alive, very alive.

He wa not one with those who loved their fathers to fault. He was not one of those consumed with love for the father. Nor was he one of the many who hated hte man who both sired and tyrannized— or ignored—him. For Art had been neither ineffective nor tyrant; each bred hatred. Consummate respect had been on Cormac, for Art; his fourteen years of life and his deed had reflected it. He'd He'd had much to prove; Art was to be respected, and to be impressed; he was worthy. And too his son was not the sort to be a basker in the light of another—or a delicate flower either, to dwell tranquilly in another's shade.

Cormac would not exult in Art's death. It did not occur to him that a son were the better for breaking free of the shade or having it removed from off his life.

Nor would he grive to excess and know despondence. It was not in him, and respect and love were never the same. As Art had been stern, and military and gruff, and busy so that Cormac had spent much time with the weapon-man Midhir and the sage druid Sualtim. Cormac had indeed respected more than loved his father; sought his approbation more than his attention and demonstrations of paternal love.

All of which was to say that Art's son Cormac had had a quite normal relationship with his father, though he was blessed in having one worthy of respect and who did not generate hatred. Few such peopled the ridge of the world. Siring sons, as Sualtim had pointed out in warnings to the boy as he approached puberty, were a simple matter. Being father to them was something else again.

Cormac had wept, but not in despair. And he had put by his weeping; there was not time for it just

61

now. Such luxuries must be deferred. Just now . . .

Art was dead and laid out white on his bed, as had been his wife but two years agone. But was no disease or accident that had laid low Art son of Comal and called him hence to await rebirth and return.

Sualtim had found him yester eve, on the westward side of the barracks. The throat of the master of Glondrath had been slashed open. Nor were there footprints, or other traces of the slayer.

The druid and the women of Glondrath had washed the dead man, and his hair, and had dressed him in his cerements. So he had lain until the arrival of Cormac and Midhir. And Midhir had made a weapon-man's pronouncement; Art's throat had been cut with the blade of a dagger, not a sword or broad blade of a spear.

These few facts the three exchanged and mulled over now, in a dim-lit room within the greathouse. Cormac's tears had begun to seep again, though he made no sound. Outside, the death-keening rose loud and eerie. Was the way of Eirrin.

"Was someone he knew and trusted, sure," Midhir said, the words emerging between teeth that were set together. "For no enemy would have got so close as to slit the throat of such a warrior!"

"Aye," Sualtim said. Catching Cormac's eye, he looked pointedly at the young man's beer, that made of wheat and honey. "Aye," the druid repeated. "Aengus mac Domnail bethought him that he saw a man clambering over the rath-wall a short time before I discovered the bo—discovered the lord Art."

Midhir's head jerked up and his face was instantly alert. "Ah." Aengus was his second, as Midhir himself had been second to Art.

"Aengus is after taking out a company of men yester night, to search. Nor have they returned."

Cormac sat in silence whilst he gave listen, nor would he use the beer to dull and ease his mind. The while he thought of Art, and of the past, and of himself, and the tears flowed down his cheeks. The sons of Eirrin were men, and sureness of it was on them; they'd no need to hold back or disguise their tears.

Cormac knew himself to be alone now. These two discussed a dead man. He was—he had been Cormac's only kin. He had not known the sister who died, at less than a year of age, a year before his birth. He hardly remembered the brother on whom illness and death had come, in his third year, when Cormac was but one. His mother was two years dead; in winter she died, as so many did. He was alone. He felt that alone-ness, and knew it would become loneliness.

Despair he would combat, and reject, for he remembered the words of his father on that subject, after the death of Cormac's mother Sobarche. Despair was not worthy. That he had of his father, and he would keep all that he had of that good and noble man. Was Art too had told him that Eirrin had need of weapon-men, that Connacht did, and so he must observe Midhir, and listed to Midhir, and practice with him. Too, Art had said that the world had need of men who *thought*, and particularly of such men of weapons, so that he had bade Cormac listen to Sualtim, and made the boy subject to the druid who had earned the sobriquet *Fodla* for his wisdom. A man should not draw blade and leap, Cormac had been told, and told. A man should think, and consider, and let his own self decide, rather than his glands. And then were it

63

called for, he should draw blade and leap—and if possible with the absolute ferocity of a hungry and cornered wolf. Were best not to kill, he had been told, unless it were necessary. If it were—then kill, and kill swiftly.

Someone had thought, and considered, and drawn blade, and slain Art, swiftly.

On this Cormac was reflecting when they heard the horses outside, and then the voices and tramp of men.

Was Aengus, with all his company. They had found naught. In the noonday sun he looked worse than unahppy, for all his freckles that vanished not with the winter; shame was on the face of Aengus Domnal's son, as for some failure of his own.

Midhir allowed himself to well into a rage that would build to loud railing against his second; Aengus's face and downcast manner helped, of course, for they were all of them sore in need of an object for their wrath.

A very young man put his hand on the shoulder of Aengus Domnal's son.

"Thank you, Aengus," he said, and his eyes were on Midhir, and they were clear of tears and blue-grey as sword-steel.

Aengus looked both sad and grateful. Midhir subsided. They stared at mac Art then, the two stout weapon-men and the long-gowned druid. They saw him anew, and his words now heightened their new feeling for him.

"Sualtim: my father is dead and the slayer escaped. The rath mourns. Prepare him for burial, on the morrow. Midhir: send messengers throughout the land about, and to the king in Cruachan, that Art is dead and his son burying him on the morrow. See that none of those with Aengus go;

they have done their best, and are weary."

He looked at them a moment, and then Cormac turned and re-entered the house.

Sualtim nodded. "I will prepare Art, and prepare for the funerary rites," he said, though not for the ears of Cormac. "No need for the couriers, Midhir; that I was thinking of this morning and I saw them dispatched." He gazed solemnly on Midhir and Aengus. "See that no mention is made of this to Cormac. He too thought of it; let it be his word."

The two men nodded, but they were gazing after the youth-become-man, not at the druid. So big and accomplished Cormac was for his years, and him coming to manhood so suddenly, and his hard encounter with the bear to be swallowed up by this tragedy, the way that he'd never feel the good glory of it was his due. And now, now he was master of Glondrath, and he both knew it and had shown it.

And, they all realized . . . surely he was in danger.

Amid the keening and the intoning of words in a language far older than Eirrin, Cormac remained silent. Solemn, stern, their life-symbolizing robes of forest green laid aside for the pure colourlessness of white, Sualtim and several assisting druids said the ancient words, their voices rising from mere murmur to volume that was nigh-shouting, and descending again.

Cormac stared dully, stricken, while his father was buried. The belief that Art would be back was a sustaining comfort, but provided little relief for grief and its normal companion, self-pity. Art would not be Art again. He would return as an infant and would bear the new name of that father. Even should his and Cormac's life-paths cross, they'd know each other not.

Midhir stepped forward, for custom prevailed and was time for personal statements of loss.

"O Art my lord, you were betrayed to your death; your end is sorrowful to us all. You to die and we to be living! Our parting is a grief forever." His voice caught and trembled as he said, "Farewell, weapon-companion; farewell, my lord."

And Branwen said, "Dear to me O my lord Art, was your beautiful ruddiness, dear to us all your manly form and your kindness; dear to us your clear grey eye that saw so much and held such wisdom. Dear—" The housekeeper broke down weeping then, and her husband drew her away, nor were the eyes of Conor dry.

Was Aengus moved then to the fore, nearest that which had been Art mac Comail.

"My lord and my commander," he said quietly. "There has not come your match to the battle; there had not come and been made wrathful in combat, there had never held up shield on the field of weapons the like of yourself, O Art of Comal!"

As Aengus stepped back, Sualtim switched from the Old Language to their own Gaelic: ". . . for had the world been searched from Behl's rising to sunset, Art mac Comail, the like would not have been found of your valiant and wise self. And it is breaking my own heart is in my body, to be here speaking so and listening to the sorrowing of the women and men of Glondrath of Connacht, and Connacht to be in its weakness, and without strength to defend itself, for Red Comal's son is gone from among us."

Exaggerations all, as were the loud cries of lament and the wringing of hands and beating of breasts.

Was the way of Eirrin, and none was hypocritical of lament or plaint for well-liked had been Art Comal's son. And when all others had spoken their last to the man to be received by the earth and by Donn, Lord of the Dead, his son came forward. Tears shimmered like dewdrops on Cormac's face.

"I am a raven that has no home," he said, little above a whisper. "I am a boat tossed from wave to wave; I am a ship that has lost its rudder; I am . . . the apple left dangling on the tree alone, and it's little thought I had of your being plucked from beside it. Grief on me! My sorrow, my father! Ochone! Grief and sorrow will be with me from this day to the end of time and life."

After a long silence Cormac added, "May the gods make smooth the path of Return for you, Art mac Comail, *athair na Cormaic Aenfher!*"

And he who had been called Cormac Pictslayer and Cormac Bearslayer and who now called himself Cormac the Lonely turned away of a sudden. He would not watch whilst they poured dirt over his father, but returned alone to the rath-house whilst those others completed the funerary rites of the murdered Art mac Comail of Connacht.

Cormac mac Art had sat alone in his father's command chamber all the morning. Outside birds twitted and a jay shrieked his raucous cry, as though angry. Otherwise there were only the somewhat muted sounds of the rath's going about its normal business; the mournful, ear-grating keening for the dead warrior had ended. Art was in the ground. His son sat in the chamber wherein the master of Glondrath had spent most of his last eleven years. This day Cormac gave to grief, and memories. And there was the encroachment of some bitterness.

His father had been a weapon-man all his years, a man with the blood of conquerors and kings in his veins. Yet he had held little power, little land that was his own. A few acres, well away from here, in stewardship. He had known that his wife was far happier there than here; she had said naught, and he had striven for her peace whilst he kept the king's.

Among those subject to him, the pigs for which

Glondrath was well known were more numerous than human beings. The finest pork in Connacht, any agreed; the finest in all Eirrin, some said. And for this was known the descendant of Niall!

Companions most of their adult lives, Art and Midhir had served the King of Connacht willingly and well. The counsel of Lord Art, however, was seldom asked. Nor was he asked to come up to the capital where lesser men glittered. No war came on Connacht, and the constant necessity of beating off the incursions of Pictish raiding parties brought Art mac Comail no great fame or honour. Wealth and power avoided him—or rather were denied him.

Even Art's command of this southwestern keep came not by birthright or even as result of his strength, but because of the weakness of another.

Gulban mac Luaig had commanded this rath and its people until eleven years agone; was then Gulban embraced the New Faith and commenced to wear the cross rather than the torc and sundisk or lunula. Too, he began to talk of peace with the Picts. With the Picts, who were not considered even so much as men! For the New Faith changed men, as it was changing all Eirrin and thus history— else the sons of Eire would have taken half of fallowing Britain erenow, rather than allow it to be sliced into pieces by pirates from oversea after the Romans' departure. Battle and slaying were not "right," Gulban began to say. Honour did not lie therein, as his people had believed for centuries upon centuries. One should turn the other cheek to him who slapped, and do all in one's power to embrace peace, to spread and maintain peace— without point and edge. This whether the Picts gave heed or no.

Was all well in theory, Cormac remembered Art and Sualtim as saying, despite the obvious fact that the natural state of humankind and that which led it on, ever on—was striving. That striving frequently led to disputes and even war betwixt two strivers or striving peoples. And that led to the survival of the strong over all the ridge of the world. It was hardly unkown that in what remained of the two-headed wolf that had been the Empire of Rome, Christians slew each other with no less zeal than those they were arrogantly pleased to call "heathen" and "pagan."

Besides, the Picts did not subscribe to such views, either in theory or practice.

Those dark savages would as lief slice the stones off a priest—and later his throat, an they were in a merciful mood—as of a weapon-man. These things Gulban, lord of Glondrath, knew well but seemed to have forgot. Connacht's king knew, too, and no forgetfulness was on that wise monarch.

Indeed, as reminder, a hideous trophy hung ever on his wall amid the painted shields and flint weapons taken from slain *Cruithne,* Picts: a pouch stripped from the belt of one of those demons in semi-human guise. It was a hand-made pouch, threaded with drawstrings, made of the breast of a Gaelic woman of Connacht.

Connacht's king's reluctance was overcome by his wisdom and concern for his realm; he had Gulban stripped of rank and power. Indeed was said he had bade the man seek employment among the blackbirds, as he called those Romish priests, or at the court of the High-king, who was reportedly leaning in a crossward direction.

Was then that the *Connacht-righ* handed over command of his important rath to his captain of

deeds and strong will and arm, Art, son of Comal.
With his wife and very young son, Art mac Comail
moved to Rath Glondarth and took command.
Even with the resentment that was on many because of the fall of their former lord and commander, Art had these peoples' respect at once,
their loyalty in a season, and the love of most
within a year. For such a man was he.

Cormac well remembered the shame and dishonour on Gulban.

Gulban was changed *aforetime,* he mused this
day after the funeral, *and him a good man formerly.
It's no friend of the New Faith, the faith of the
Dead God I'll be, ever, with their carpenter-god
who makes sleeping dogs of men and would as soon
that women were slaves.* For such had never been
the way of the daughters of Eirrin!

In his father's chamber, Cormac sat, and he
reflected on his growing to youth and manhood
here, under the tutelage of Art and of Sualtim and
Midhir. Advice he gained, and example, and on
some occasions his lessons were accompanied by
anguish and grief. Advice in the way of a man he
gained, a man of *Eirrin;* a man of weapons.

Aye, and so he was become, a weapon-man of
Eirrin.

First there was respect and later deep friendship
with Midhir, his father's close friend to whom Art
always gave listen and whom he trusted to make his
son a surpassing warrior. Cormac well remembered
that aspect of his life; their practice and practice,
their telling of warlike tales at night by the fire,
quaffing weak ale often no more than barley-water.
For ale was a staple, and children began early the
drinking of that which all adults quaffed as a matter of course. And Cormac remembered how he

71

and Midhir had lied shamelessly in those tale-tellings . . . each with the knowledge of the other.

Within his head the grieving mac Art saw the face of Midhir that day two years agone, and astonishment on that face. Cormac had watched the expression give way to happiness, and pride.

"Ye've won, lad! It's death ye've just done on me, Cormac!"

And Cormac recalled with what delight and pride Midhir had conveyed that information to Art mac Comail. Art watched them next day, at their practice. And of course Cormac lost under those eyes, was "slain" three times by Midhir, and when he looked up after that third defeat, Art was no longer there. Naturally within ten minutes the lad had put defeat on the experienced weapon-man, and his father not there to see. But Art knew, and was proud.

Art continued to give his son word and example in the ways of leading men, and Cormac stored away that knowledge. Again he heard within his head the words of Sualtim the Wise:

A sharp mind, that truly brilliant servant of Behl and Crom was fond of saying, weighs a hundred stone heavier than a sharp sword. And Art had bade them both that the word "swift" could be substituted for "sharp," and he exchanged a long look with Sualtim, who was his friend of mutual respect.

Then Cormac had begun defeating Midhir again and again. The lessons ceased. They became workouts, to keep both men ready and sharp of brain and reflex. Aye, and Cormac remembered his father's pride-in-son. More than once had, Art recounted the history of their land, enumerating the kings of Connacht and the High-kings in Meath.

72

And Cormac remembered the quiet words of a man who showed no bitterness, though he had cause.

"Perhaps Ailill Molt was the last son of Connacht to sit enthroned on Tara Hill and preside over the assembled kings at Feis-more," Art had said, gazing on his stout and clever son, "and . . . perhaps not."

For Art the Bear had seen his own ancestry and high promise come to little, and held far higher hopes for his son, who would be more man, surely, than himself.

Thus with his brain full of manifold and multiform thoughts of the past did Cormac mac Art sit and wallow in days gone by, and avoid thereby thinking of the present and future. And afternoon came, and deepened.

Gods! But two nights agone he had felt strapping big and mature, much the man!

Now he was aware only of being young, with no sureness on him of either his present position or of the time-to-come—even the morrow. There was little to inherit. Nor would his king be handing over command of this important outpost to one of Cormac's years, no matter whose son he was.

His mind continued to seek pleasant memories. He was undisturbed as he had requested; not even Branwen came to press food on him. He relived in his mind that battle with the Picts, and him alone against their four, dark and squat with blue paint on their powerful bodies. He remembered his fear that day—and how it had gone, vanished, so that he became what Midhir had so long counselled and demanded: a pure weapon-man. A creature of lightning judgment and reflex—and muscle. Thus had he fared, until four Picts lay dead, the last as surprised as the first. And their conqueror was hardly scratched, the lad they'd sought to make

73

easy victim.

And . . .

Afternon deepened the more. Light had long since ceased to find its way into the command-room of Art. At last he who sat there seemed to come awake, as though he'd been asleep or away. He sighed in the manner of an old man. Realization came on him then; he had accomplished naught by sitting and mourning. Naught would ever be accomplished by wallowing in the past. There was much to be accomplished. Questions wanted answering. Art was dead. Cormac lived, and must live.

No questions will be answered by my sitting and mourning, dwelling in the yester days and mooning for a time that was happier! He gave a few seconds to that thought, and he never did it again. Once again Cormac mac Art began to live for today and tomorrow.

He rose, and frowned at the twinge in his back, at the kinks he felt. On impulse he pounced across the room. That was of some value; he paced, lifting his legs exaggeratedly high while cranking both arms, swinging them in half- and then in full-circles, meanwhile dropping occasionally into a squat or bending from the waist, stiff-legged.

Then Cormac left that chamber of memories.

It was not Sualtim's quiet counsel he'd seek now; let tomorrow be put off a bit longer. He'd find purpose and some release in the lighter-weight company of Midhir. A moment's reflection put another thought into his head. He'd ask Midhir for a working out with arms.

With that thought, he went to his own quarters. There he donned quilted long jerkin of leather, with its pendent crotch-protector. With his strength he could get easily into his coat of chain, without aid. He spread its oiled leather wrapping on the desk with which his father had surprised him on a birthday five years agone On it he laid his coat of linked circles of chain. Bending to ease it up his arms, he mused on his growth. He had reached his father's height seven months agone—and had not stopped growing.

Was his fourth coat of armour, this one that had been Midhir's. The making and linking of slim steel rings into armour was a lengthy process of painstaking labour and considerable skill, his father had impressed upon him. Grow more, Art had said, and he could have a new coat next year, made for himself. Cormac swallowd. Would he ever see that promised mail?

At present, Midhir's chaincoat fit. Midhir was thick and brawny; Cormac was built more rangily, with muscles like those of a cat. Already Midhir's coat fell not so low on the youth as it had on the man of twoscore and one. Having pulled it up his arms and, with a little grunt, over his head—the while being careful about his ears and face—he let it jingle down his body and moved his shoulders under its weight, nigh twoscore pounds. He strapped on his scabbard-belt with its huge clasp of shining brass, pulled his buckler from the wall. Brass-faced and leather-backed it was, over the thick circle of wood, with both its bracer and grip padded with leather over wool. Sliding his hand through the bracer, he fisted the grip and departed the room. His cloak was heavy on his shoulders; the bearskin collar extended halfway down his back.

His stomach snarled, and he made Branwen relatively happy by stuffing his mouth with ham and his hand with pan-bread. Was not enough, she scolded; but he pointed to his overfull mouth, made a few wordless sounds, and left.

Outside he was greeted with restraint, the way that he durst not smile had the urge come on him. Midhir he found armed and wearing a leathern armour-coat, watching two youngsters. They worked away with smallish bucklers and leather-covered swords of wood. The warrior was happy to have his company sought by Cormac, and happy to be drawn away.

They walked in silence to the gate. Midhir gestured; they were passed through and set out across the broad plain. They talked, now.

The fact of death was one thing. That it had been murder was another. Who had slain Art mac Comail? Why? Could it have been an act of the moment, an act of rage, or . . . had someone wanted the man dead?

"If so," Midhir said, "then it's yourself's in great danger, Cormac. For he'll want the son in the earth with the father."

"I cannot believe it. *Who?*"

"That," Midhir said as they walked toward the woods, "we must learn."

Cormac's brain churned. Aye, And—*how?*

"And then it's vengeance ye must have, lad. It's a matter for blood-feud."

"Agreed, Midhir. And—"

"Know that whatever the situation may be or become at Glondrath, Cormac, Midhir mac Fionn will ever be with you." Midhir slapped his sword-hilt. "Vengeance, Cormac! Vengeance for Art!"

"Aye, and I'm thanking ye, Midhir. But—"

"Gods of my fathers—Art *murdered!* Vengeance I say, blood-feud and vengeance I vow, friend of my life!" And Midhir's sword scraped partway out of his sheath in his passion.

And of a sudden Cormac mac Art grew older still.

Of a sudden he was aware of a great difference between himself and this pure man of weapons. Cormac had been trained by him, aye, until he was the equal and then the better of the master. He had also been trained, though, by Sualtim Fodla. Trained not to go thundering-blundering ever forward without taking careful stock, and counsel with himself. True, that thinking was to be done with all swiftness. Consideration and planning, these he had been taught—and to seek the answer that was not so obvious as a gnat perched on his nose.

"We have no name, Midhir. Whom shall we suspect? We—"

"We shall have a name!"

"Aye," Cormac said, with a long aspiration. "Nor do we know whether it's a plotter we seek, or . . . someone who . . . flew into a rage." He was only just able to govern his voice then, and he paused a moment to gain control. "There is much to learn, Midhir, and more matters to be considered than we have knowledge of."

"What matter? We find him! If it's ten of them there be, we find and do death on ten then, Cormac Bear-slayer! Here—this path. 'Ware that fallen branch."

The coolth and dimness of the woods closed about them. Cormac strove to explain. He had no notion of his own future, much less of his father's slayer. He was glad he would at least have Midhir for companion, that he be not totally alone, now. Still, he had learned well his lessons from Sualtim and Art mac Comail. When there was opportunity, the two men of wisdom had impressed upon him, and the contemplated act merited action, it must needs be second to thinking and planning.

"And swift," the voice of his father intoned in his mind, "as the situation demands."

The pure man of action at his side hardly understood, and as they paced into the woods they were nigh to arguing. Midhir but stated that which to him was obvious.

"And shall I be taking spear and buckler and sword, then, and setting-out in quest of the slayer?"

Midhir slammed first into palm. "Aye! O'course!"

"And in which direction, Midhir?"

Midhir walked in silence.

"And what name shall we be putting on him, this man I go after this instant?"

In silence Midhir talked, and with a frown upon him. Cormac knew then that the man was alive because of his arms-expertise, his prowess and strength—and through good fortune. Nor did mac Art know that the time would come when he would team with another man of similar make-up and mentality, and him a huge flame-bearded Dane . . . and that mac Art's counsel would prevail.

"Midhir."

"Aye."

"It's no family estate Glondrath is, Midhir. On the morrow, or next week, the new lord and commander may come riding."

Midhir stopped dead still. He stared at the much younger man. "By the gods my father's people swear by! Cormac!"

"Just so, Midhir. My entire world is—ho, look there."

"Ah. A *sidhe.*"

They entered a little clearing among the thick-budding trees and brush. In its center was a cairn, though not a *sidhe* or fairy-mound. No, Cormac saw, this was a place of worship-rites for the common folk who yet followed the very old ways, as Celts did over in Gaul. Pacing over to the pile of stones, Cormac saw the ash of a recent bonefire. Midhir was just behind him when the youth, noting that the bones were those of small animals, bent to examine them.

He heard the harp-like twang. He heard the high-pitched bee-sound come, rushing through the clearing's air. And he heard the solid *thunk*.

Cormac knew the sounds. A released bowstring; a whizzing arrow; its imbedding itself in a target other than straw or wood. Heedless of the ashes, Cormac fell deliberately forward, thrusting forth his shield-arm. He rolled with difficulty, holding shield and wearing sword, and only then allowed himself a look.

Midhir, an arrow standing from his eye, limply bent at both knees and then fell, partway on his side. His left leg kicked twice, then a third time, more weakly—and no more.

Midhir! The thought was anguish and anger combined in Cormac's mind. Bloodlust and rage leaped up in him and his heart pounded so that his pulse was a drum in his temples. Yet his brain maintained control. Kicking himself half around, he hurled himself into the scant protection of the low bushes amid the trees at the clearing's edge. No fool of viscera and twitching reaction he, to give way to emotion and rush the supposed hiding-place of the archer; the man would but make good use of another of his goose-feathered shafts ere Cormac found his position, much less reached it.

The arrow had come from directly in front of him, beyond the cairn. He had dived leftward, tumbled arolling, and hurled himself into gorse and doebush. No more than thrice his body length separated him and the bowman, diagonally across a part of the clearing. Cormac scrambled, trying to make himself small behind his shield. Cheek against the ground, he peered around the shield's edge.

Yes; after a time he was certain he described what he'd not have seen had the season of spring been more on the land. No greenery obscured the man behind that split- or twin-trunked alder over there.

No matter how he strained his eyes, Cormac could not identify the bowman. Cormac was aquiver; not from fear did he shake, but with realization that this was surely his father's slayer—and that the murderer was surely bent on putting an end to the line. Only minutes agone Midhir mac Fionn had said it: "For he'll want the son in the earth with the father."

Aye, Cormac thought, narrowing his eyes. *That arrow sang its nasty bee-song over my head—had I not bent to the ashes, it would have found its real target—not Midhir!*

Cautiously, keeping the shield interposed, Cormac crawled and wallowed behind a thick old oak. He was able to keep it between him and the twin-tree then, while he backed, on his knees and slowly, to another broad-boled patriarch of the forest and then to a third . . .

Cormac rose then, and faded into the woods and its veiling shadows. He went silently as he was able with sword and buckler and jingly armour, and him on no path. The cloak caught now and again, though he held it close; a hardy, struggling redthorn fought him for possession. The lack of greenery made his passage both easier and more nearly quiet. At last he judged that he'd worked his way beyond the clearing of the cairn, behind the murderous archer.

Shield up and sword aready, he moved in.

His heart pounded and he was sweat-wet; Cormac had never before stalked another human. And then he was there, and disappointed with a feeling of weakness on him as preparedness drained; the man was gone.

Oh, he'd been here right enow. All about the double-trunked tree the new grass was well trampled, particularly here, on the side away from the clearing. Some slim green blades were still creeping slowly erect again, as though fearful of being trodden anew.

For a long space Cormac waited there, roving t e woods with his gaze until his eyes stung. He saw nothing. He heard only birds and insects. Yet it was with caution that he paced out to his fallen friend.

Midhir lay still, the arrow rising from his face. Midhir was dead.

Cormac had known it in the mind behind his mind, yet he had resisted the fact and set it aside. Now tears stung his eyes while he examined the arrow that had slain the man he had but minutes agone told himself he'd cling to. Now there was no one. Only Sualtim, a stern old man too wise and old to be a comfortable grandfather, much less a father-substitute.

The arrow was a long wand of ash, tipped with gray goose quill. Two blue stripes ringed the off-white shaft. That was the portion that counted for naught. The small tip that meant life or death, one more drastic change in Cormac's life and a far greater one in Midhir's . . . that tiny portion of the arrow was imbedded in Midhir's brain.

Cormac moved away from the dead man. Bent to stare at the ground, he paced slowly. Midhir. Dead, all in a moment. Dead. And this second death, this second theft of life that robbed Cormac, too, of so much, was a greater blow than had been his father's slaying. Not because of a greater feeling on him for Midhir than for Art; no, it was that he had turned in his mind to Midhir, pinned his hopes on this man.

And now both were gone. There was no one. All was gone. Anguish tightened his stomach; desperation swirled about him like murky fog.

Several times he jerked his head to rid himself of the tears that persisted in trying to blind him, though he was not sobbing. Cormac felt even more alone now than he had earlier this day. Now there was no one, and the thought came again and again. Now he—

He discovered the trail of the murderer. The man was afoot.

Cormac used his brain only a little, this time; it was cluttered and clogged and partially paralyzed by grief and sorrow for self. The day was late. Dusk was almost on the forest, and the treetops cut out much of the light of the low-lying sun. The air was becoming chill. The rath was but a few minutes away, with horses and good spears and men who'd be eager in the rage to accompany him in following a good trail.

Cloaked but afoot and without spear, horse, or companions, Cormac nevertheless followed the murderer's trail through the forest. He felt the weening necessity of taking action on his own, and he did.

After a time he realized that the slayer was angling around, moving in a tight curve, around the northward edge of the rath-lands. He surely could not be headed for the mountains. The coast, then.

Cormac followed, never giving a thought to the fact that now he could raise help merely by shouting out. Thereby though he would warn the murdering archer. Not likely the fellow would be expecting a lone youth to follow him, and bearing only weapons for close fighting. The slayer was moving sloppily, not troubling to avoid twigs that showed Cormac their fresh breaks, or loamy spots that held a footprint or two, or clumps of early grass that were still rising after the flatening by his foot. Here he had wiped animal excrement from his buskin. The trail was that for the following by a child; that of a man confident he had escaped and was not pursued.

Cormac's tracking took him from the forest into rocky coastal terrain where the archer was harder to follow. Cormac felt the cold sea-breeze that brought the tang of salt to his nostrils. He moved along the little runnel from a weak spring; found a footprint where the man had hopped it. He hurried on in the direction it indicated.

Now there were no trees, and little shrubs. Stones littered the sandy earth beneath his feet; here reared a great boulder or outcrop of rock, there clung a haw. He heard seabirds, screeking and mewling like cats. Steep cliffs formed over the sea that ran from Eirrin's western coast to—nowhere, so far as any knew. Here a foot had slid. Here the other had come down hard. Here lay stones partially imbedded; two had been freshly upturned by the passage of a foot.

The trail led the youth down a steep incline created and then scarred anew by erosion. It was only just walkable, and here the archer had fallen.

Cormac did not.

It was down onto the strand the man had gone, Cormac thought, and he ran down the long hill to keep from falling. Intelligence and craftiness, now, were submerged in a red rage.

The sound of the battering of water against rocks rose in volume; the tangy scent of brine intensified; the chill grew as his cloak billowed about him. Now great boulders rose round about rearing up like strange plants from the sandy, rocky soil. Coming onto the talus at the foot of the incline, he slowed his steps.

Yet still he pressed forward intently; too intently; he was completely unaware of the possibility of a trap until it was sprung.

They were Picts, and they were three.

With the shrieks that were designed to terrify their prey whilst heightening their own courage and ferocity, they leaped at him from behind a flanking pair of towering boulders whose surfaces were smoothed from long exposure to the salt-gritty winds from seaward.

Short men they were, and dark and broad, with black eyes under heavy brow-ridges and stringy, straight black hair caught by bands of leather beaded or decorated with coral. Two wore buskins and leggings of filthy, greasy leather, and naught else but bronze bracers; the third was doubtless proud of his blue Celtic tunic—still stained with the blood of its former owner. This Pict wielded a shining sword of steel, hardly made by his kind; his companions brandished flint axes and had flint daggers girt at their sides. Huge-bladed things they were, against their chipping and snapping. All three attackers were heavily muscled, massive of arm and shoulder and leg, long of coal-black hair—

and ugly. Blue paint rendered them the more savage and hideous; one had added ruddy stripes traced diagonally down his forehead to give him a permanent scowling appearance.

They came fast and yelling, and Cormac did indeed freeze.

Only the thick bearskin collar of his cloak saved him from the running stroke of a flint-headed ax. The blow staggered him—and was pure reaction that jerked his shield-arm so that the second attacker, him with the sword, was struck hard. Running, he was hurled windmilling twice his length.

Only just was Cormac able to dodge the ax-stroke of the third Pict. Sword-sharp, the flinty edge whined venomously past his nose.

And then, happy to have foes on whom to vent his sorrow and frustration—on *which,* as the Cruithne were not considered men but only semi-human—Cormac met their return with full skill and a savagery that matched their own.

An ax slammed down and banged on his bronze-faced buckler. While it was still sliding off, the Gael's slash caught that savage at the waist with Cormac's edge. So vicious was the side-swiping blow that the Pict was cut nigh in half and Cormac had to twist his arm and jerk, to free his blade. His sword-arm jerked up under the wrist of a second wielder of short-hafted ax, so that it only just touched his mailed chest. Cormac's muscles bunched and his shield came around as though weightless. It bashed into that man's upper arm. The ax fell while the Pict toppled sidewise. The sword-armed one was coming back, and Cormac ignored the man he'd unintentionally disarmed. His eyes glared at the coming Pict like nuggets of frozen starlight.

the Pict should have foregone use of his trophy and held to his familiar ax. With his buckler Cormac easily met the sword of a slain Celt, and his thrust sank a hand's length of his own brand through blue Celtic shirt and dusky Pictish abdomen —and bone, and blood, and organs. Huge-eyed the man staggered back off the point. He dropped his sword; his mouth burbled blood. He fell kicking.

The third remaining Pict was without ax, though he had drawn his long stone dagger. He stared at their intended prey. Sore of wrist and upper arm, armed with a short blade against a long one of steel, seeing that their ambush had resulted in the horribly swift death of his fellows, the Pict turned and fled.

Cormac, battle-lust soaring in him like a fire in his blood, followed the savage downward amid a maze of boulders and rocky outcrops.

He halted just after rounding a rearing chunk of rock half again taller than himself. He stared down at the bloody corpse. Ax-hacked, it was Aengus mac Domnail, Midhir's second-in-command and thus Art's third. He lay in a soaked muck of scarlet sand.

All three dead, was Cormac's first thought—and then he recorded the evidence of his eyes. The swirling red chaos of rage and headlong pursuit fled his mind, and he stared in agonized comprehension.

Chopped in several places and no longer bleeding, Aengus still clutched a bow. His hip-slung quiver had spilled its arrows, and so rapidly was the third Pict fleeing that he'd not tarried so long as to snatch up the fine shafts . . . shafts tipped with gray goose, and each bearing two woad-stripes of blue.

It was impossible. It was unbelievable—and Cormac had to believe. Here was clear evidence: Here lay his father's and Midhir's trusted aide, and the man had slain them both, and had sought to do death on Cormac as well. Mac Art had no notion why this man had done such treachery on his longtime companions and friends, and his lord commander. His brain had been sore afflicted all the day; now his stomach twisted.

Cormac stared down at the hacked mass of mangled flesh, and on him was as much sorrow as shock and anger.

Oh, Aengus!

He was given no time now to contemplate the dead man's treachery. Weapons clinked. A Pict called out from up the beach; another answered, and then a third voice rose. Cormac went instantly alert again. There was no puzzle here. A party of the Cruithne, several of their skin-boats full, must have made landing here. By coincidence had they run full onto the fleeing Aengus; mayhap he had a boat waiting, and they had found it. Thus they had taken Cormac's vengeance for him. They had heard Cormac's precipitate descent of the long declivity—or thought that Aengus might have others with him fallen behind—and set their trap. Cormac had destroyed it, and two of the ambushers. Now the third had summoned aide.

Their voices told Cormac both that they were hurrying his way and that they formed a goodly number; too many for a sensible man to face alone.

Swifty wiping his sword on Aengus's leggings, Cormac sheathed the blade. He dragged the corpse behind the tall boulder. Taking up both bow and arrows, he raced back up the slope. He kept his footing and made headway through sheer deter-

maintain and the strength that hurled him upward. At the top, he turned and loosed one of the traitor's arrows; perhaps its keening and sight of it would force the Picts to take cover for a minute or two.

Whirling, Cormac followed his own and Aengus's trail back for many yards. He leaped the runnel to leave a deep footprint, stepped back and splashed down it for a dozen yards. From the little stream he pounced onto a boulder whose colour was all too dark to show a wet footprint to any other than close-searching eyes. And he leaped thence to hard ground, and sprinted into the forest.

Here was no trail, no path. Here stumps, fallen branches and bushes slowed him. A vermiculate mass of last year's honeysuckle sought to trip him. Swiftly as he dared—and at that falling once—he made his way back to the edge of the same trail. He ascended a tree that overlooked it. With care not to fall, he hurled one of the arrows—ahead, along the trail, as though he'd dropped it in headlong flight. Then he crouched, almost in darkness. The sky had gone a deep slate, save to the very west, where it had become all bloody—*like the land here below,* Cormac mused grimly.

He breathed as Sualtim had taught him, and thought the thoughts that Sualtim had taught him, to still his panting and his racing pulse. And he waited. Like a great cat crouched in a tree where he had no business being, he waited soundlessly and without the slightest movement save his breathing.

They came. Quietly they came-, these woods-wise devils, so that he heard them only seconds before they were passing beneath his perch: He held his breath. Sword-grey eyes full of malign intent glared down at them, and the Picts knew it not.

They passed like shadows beneath him, squatty

broad men numbering a score and more. They went on, moving inland. In the darkness below, they became invisible almost immediately. Cormac heard a cry of delight; they had discovered the arrow. He heard them break into a trot. He released his breath very slowly, drew in another, just as slowly and quietly. He heard nothing. He waited longer. The Picts passed from earshot, and no others came; why post a rear guard when they came from the sea and were pursuing one who fled afore them so precipitately that he dropped an arrow?

Cormac clambered down. He took a difficult, necessarily circuitous route back to Glondrath.

The long march at least served to keep him warm. It was dark in the forest; darkness cloaked the sprawling meadow of Glondrath when he emerged from the woods and took up a trot. As he passed a low house, a dog barked. Others joined that one, as dogs would in the night, whether or no they smelled or saw aught. Lights began to appear. Trotting, Cormac called out his own name, again and again. He heard the people that had been his father's charges calling back and forth, repeating the identification—with relief. Grimly purposeful, spattered with blood that was not his, he strode past without making reply.

"Cormac! All good be with ye! Nervousness has been on ust that—"

Cormac interrupted the speaker ere he'd finished voicing his anxiety; he recognized Fedelm, called Iron Jaw after a horse's kick had but bruised his face.

"Be fetching your weapons, Fedelm! Picts are well inland."

Fedelm blinked. the cloaked youth strode on, a

great stalking cat full of purpose. Never had Fedelm mac Conain had words of command from mac Art. Yet there was that about the grim young face, the way the words were spoken . . . Fedelm turned and set out for the barrack at a run.

Cormac approached the rath-house. There a great ring of black iron swung from the branch of a centuried oak, swung at the end of a rope thick as a man's wrist. From a peg formed by a broken-off branch hung an iron rod by its rawhide tether. Cormac's feet had not stopped moving when he had snatched the rod and struck the hoop a mighty blow. Then he thrust the rod through that ring of iron, within which two men could have stood, and began circling his arm.

The clangour of Glondrath's alarum shattered the night with iron sound, so that even the dogs were shocked into silence.

Cormac paused in his clanging: "PICTS" he bellowed, and clanged the signal-hoop the more. Other voices took up the cry, and others, and ere he had ceased tormenting the iron ring men were running, some mayhap bright-eyed with the rosy haze of ale fumes, but all bearing arms and armour.

Soon he was surrounded. Weapon-men aided each other into armour of chain and leather whilst they waited with scant patience for the arrival of others, and the words of the son of their dead lord. Some had brought torches, and none failed to perceive that there was blood on the big youth.

"The bow of Aengus Domnal's son," he shouted, holding high that weapon of treachery. And then Cormac mac Art told the first of the expedient lies he was never to hesitate to use, throughout his blood-smeared life. Was only a slight omission of fact, this time. "SLAIN, is Aengus! SLAIN, is

Midhir! Pi-i-i-ictssss," he bellowed, turning three-quarters of a circle the while he called out the hated world. "Two I slew, and one escaped—and it's these eyes saw him come up from the strand with a score and more of his ugly fellows. Armed to the teeth they be and tramping through the wood as though they own it—or intend to!"

Cries of horror and anger rose, and he had no more need of words; the men of Glondrath but waited to be led to the enemy that had plagued them for many tens of years.

"Fergus!" Cormac shouted. "Well I remember your injured arm, and cease your striving to hide it! Pick ten men to remain and defend, light torches and arm every woman and child lest the Picts double back! Hurry, man!"

Few were anxious to be chosen; Fergus looked about and about, and called ten names, one by one. He was roundly cursed more than once.

"Fergus the Horse is in command here—keep ye a close watch! We others will not be after returning till we've hacked them with point of spear and edge of blade!"

And ten remained, and the rest followed him in a mob, and Cormac mac Art was a leader of men.

The blood thirsty thrave followed the son of their former lord through the nighted wood. Raging like wolves they were, eyes aglitter with rage and malice under the twinkle of the ever-restless starshine. Once they'd come upon the Pictish trail, it was easily followed, and they fair loped through the dark forest until they came to the low-built house of a woodcutter. Then their cries rose higher with their ire, those men of Connacht, for the house was splashed with gore and the door stood open to the night.

Within, the family had been slain as they sat at table, and horrors had been perpetrated on their bodies. A dread silence fell upon the weapon-men then, and all heard the voice of the youth they followed without question. for Cormac mac Art stood in that house of gore and atrocity and swore by the earth beneath him, by the heaven above him, and by the sun that traveled daily to the west, that he would seek no rest by day nor sleep by night until this peaceful family of innocents was avenged.

A man called out from behind the house then, and once again they were on the trail he had found, a blood-trail now, for Picts were wont to let their axes drip where they would.

Farther into the woods they rushed abristle with spears. Cormac and some few others strove to hold them silent lest the quarry hear, and lie in wait, to set upon the hunters.

But no. The Picts were blooded. The scent was in their broad nostrils, and they sought more. Another house the pursuers found, with its door torn half from its leathern hinges the way that it swung drunkenly. Bright blood splashed that door. Blood splashed the floor within, and ran down the walls. Here again had there been slaughter, and only the good wife of this murdered man was armed; she lay ax hacked and deliberately mutilated, with a carving knife in her fist. There was no blood on it, only on her and round about her. In a lovingly-wrought cradle lay a babe; its face was dark and its neck broken. The marks of powerful fingers were still in the fair skin of its throat.

On through the cloud-haunted night rushed the Gaels of Eirrin, baying the Pictish trail.

Even at the forest's eastern rim they came upon a third house—and here battle raged. Yelling dark men sought to do massacre on another family. Amid torchlight and blood-chilling Pictish shrieks, a farmer and his big-built, deep-bellied wife battled the yelling savages, and with them their two slim sons. It was farm tools against knife and short-helved ax and flint-tipped spears, and the outcome was inevitable—though the Gaels fought valiantly to set a high price on their lives.

The men of Glondrath broke from the woods like the slavering pack onto the fox they'd long chased.

No less than seven Picts were down in their blood ere their fellows knew they'd been counter-attacked. The others turned then, beset by well-armed warriors rather than untrained farmers—and two more Picts went down in seconds. One fell prey to the long handled hoe wielded by a lad of no more than eleven or twelve; the other was opened by the adze of the youth's father.

"Into your house!" bellowed a man at Cormac's side.

Good advice for the farm family, with a boiling knot of stout warriors come to their succor. Yet none of the four obeyed, but held their ground before their besieged home while steel blades flashed like streaks of liquid silver in the starlight and carved out a path toward them.

The dusky men of Pictdom pressed back one upon the other; they gave ground toward the house; a good sturdy farmwife swung her scythe to open up one of them, all across his muscular back. A huge-shouldered savage lunged at Cormac with his spear, a Celtic staff with dark iron point. So savagely did Cormac chop down that weapon, just behind the head, that the butt came up hard into the wielder's armpit and like to have lifted him clear off the ground, for all his muscular weight. Beside mac Art, Dungal Big-head drove his own spear into that Pict and through him, so that Dungal had to let go his haft and draw sword. A spearhead scraped across his buckler and sparks danced; like a ravening wolf Cormac slashed sidewise. In a flash of steel the attacker's head was made to hang only by a shred of flesh and a twinned fountain splashed both Dungal and Cormac with scarlet.

"It's a fine team we are, Cormac!" Dungal cried, grinning.

94

The young son of Art said nothing, nor did he smile.

It is what had happened, that the battle-rage had come upon him. He hacked and slashed and stabbed, even half-braining a foeman with his buckler's edge. No man should have been able to jerk and slash with the heavy shield in that wise; Cormac in this combat was no normal man. Nor did he smile even in triumph, for he thought only of slaying Picts. On them he laid his needs for blade-reddening vengeance, for he could not slay him who had done death on Art and on Midhir.

A chance use of his sword sent the blade girding deep into the vitals of a dark ax-wielder, and in the back of his mind mac Art recorded the fact that a stabbing thrust was efficacious indeed when all about him were swinging their weapons. Was a lesson learned long and long agone by the Romans, though few others on the ridge of the world used their blades as stabbing weapons.

Around him men groaned and toppled, spitted and hacked so that blood bespattered wounded and dead, dying and unscathed alike. Indeed men with no wounds upon them looked sore blooded, whilst others who had taken severe cuts knew it not in the mindless blaze of battle-lust.

About the farmhouse the night-battle whirled and eddied, blades of steel and iron and flint flaming and flashing.

No Pict escaped. All were slain, with edge and point of sharp-edged steel. A man of Glondrath died cursing like a madman with his last breath this side of Donn's demesne; two others were sore wounded and a third bore a woundy cut that would be a long-time ahealing; scratches and minor cuts were widespread among the company. Cormac, having suffered only a couple of scratches, had no idea how many apelike savages he'd laid low; he was told he had downed four and wounded a fifth so that another's ax slew him easily, but mac Art had been as if in a trance and could not swear to so much as one.

Seven and twenty Picts bled their last on the grounds of Labraid mac Buaic, and afterwards weeds grew all too well there. None of Labraid's family was slain or sore wounded, though the older son had sustained a cut he loudly hoped would leave a scar there on his forearm, and Labraid's wife Uaithne had wrenched her back—in swinging the curved scythe with which she saved her life from a short-hafted ax. With cloth from their scantling supply the farmfolk tended the wounds of their rescuers, the while they learned that the band of weapon-men was led by the son of Lord Art, and him dead these two days.

Food and ale offered Labraid, though in truth he was no man of wealth. While his men loudly accepted, the new temporary lord of Glondrath made mental note to send both a cask of (better) ale and a fresh-slain boar to this house.

Loud were the cries, and cups were lifted high as Celtic spirits. New and noisy praise was heaped upon the youthful battle-leader. He heard new comparisons of himself with both Cuchulain and that great Cormac afore him. But on this occasion there was no adolescent swelling of the head and chest of Cormac mac Art. On his mien was the stern-set face of a man; in his mind were only two slain men: Art mac Cumail and his friend Midhir.

And still was he quiet when he led his company back through Connacht-Shield Wood, having reminded them of those who waited at Glondrath, and knew not whether to keen or cry joy. Behind them along the broad path they followed this time, those triumphant men of Connacht dragged seven and twenty Pictish corpses. And two men bore Eochu Fair-hair, to present to his sorrowing parents and sweetheart.

Though weariness was on him, mac Art detoured to take up himself the body of Midhir, that no forest beast might feast on the man.

Joy at the triumphant return outweighed sorrow in Glondrath, and was long afore many were asleep, and in truth the result of that undertaking was a rich harvest of babes, nine months thence.

Wounded Eber and Curnan survived the night, and druids and attending women announced that both would live to fight another day—though the former would most probably limp. Early on that morning of the morrow, a white-bearded druid and a beardless youth went to the house where Midhir's wife Aevgrine keened her grief. When they emerged the tall, rangy youth bore the arrow he himself had drawn from Midhir's eye.

Sualtim Fodla had watched the boy-man steel himself to that unahppy task, and he saw now that Cormac was not ill of his night of bloodletting, followed by this ugliness. And Sualtim frowned. For men who never knew illness after battle, and were not nauseous at such as the drawing of an arrow from the eye of a dead friend, were to be feared. Cursed of the gods they were said to be, and destined thereby for lives in which blood ran in scarlet rivulets. In a flash of *manadh,* or druidic foresight, Sualtim saw that indeed so would it be for Art's son. He knew too in that instant that the youth must not tarry here.

"Cormac."

Cormac looked at the druid.

"Glondrath holds your doom, Cormac mac Art."

Cormac blinked, though he did not pale. "It held my father's," he pointed out.

"Remain here and it's no other birthday ye'll be seeing, mac Art. It is what I see for you, an ye remain in Glondrath, that nothing of your skin or your flesh will escape red doom, except what the birds will bring away in their beaks and claws."

Cormac compressed his lips. "Walk with me, mentor."

They walked, and in the meadow's northern end Cormac drew an arrow from beneath his cloak and handed it to the druid, along with that which had slain Midhir.

"What see ye, mentor?"

"Call me Sualtim, Cormac; ye be boy no longer. Hmm—I shall not be saying that I see two arrows." He studied both shafts. "I see two arrows made by the same hand, from the wood of the same tree."

"So."

"An ash. Aye, and feathered by the same goose, or I miss my guess and these eyes are become older than I'm thinking."

"Ye see well, mentor. Two arrows from the same tree indeed, and from the same goose their fletching, made by the same hand. And—from the same quiver."

"Aye. Those two stripes, now, are no emblem familiar to me."

"Nevertheless, m—Sualtim, it's these arrows will lead us to the slayer of Midhir."

"Aye."

"And, most probably, of the slayer of my father as well."

"Probable."

And Cormac led the durid through the forest, and Sualtim made no plaint at the length of their trek, nor even the difficulty of its other end. Then they stood over the body of Aengus Domnal's son.

"One of these arrows ye saw me draw forth from Midhir, Sualtim Fodla. The other I took from that empty quiver there at Aengus's hip. Here be Midhir's murderer."

The druid stared at him, and then his shoulders drooped with his sigh. "Aye," he said, and it was a whisper. "And if I must believe that, and I must indeed, then I believe too that Aengus slew the Lord of Glondrath."

Cormac said naught.

The druid stooped by the corpse, found before them only by the birds they'd frightened away; was why Cormac had on yester eve covered Aengus's face. The dead man wore a sundisk of bronze, on a beaded cord of leather. It flashed in the druid's hand. Surely for no particular reason unless it was a flash of prescience or intuition, Sualtim turned over that sigil of the Old Religion of the Celts. He made a grunting sound of surprise then, as if struck. He looked up at Cormac. The latter bent, and stared.

Scratched into the back of the sundisk of Behl was . . . the cross of Iosa Chriost.

Slowly Sualtim straightened, and Cormac heard the old man's joints pop. He looked at Cormac, and his usual solemnity of mien was clouded over with deep concern.

"This bodes no good, son of Art. None. It's more there is to the murder of Art and the attempt on his son that mere murder of a man or two. A lord has died; the lordling has narrowly escaped, and think not that it was pure accident and your own whim

99

made ye bend just as that arrow was loosed, Cormac."

Mac Art stared at him, saying nothing. Gulls wheeled and screamed against a sweet blue sky, the birds jealous of these men who had chased them from their morning find. Aengus had after all eyes for the pecking.

"More here than a simple blood-feud, surely," Sualtim said. "Where the New Faith is involved, there are seldom simple motives."

"The *Dead God,*" Cormac said, his teeth set and his lip curling.

"Aye. But so long as he has followers, and Romish plotters every one—even those of Eirrin— he lives, Cormac."

"Was known my father was no friend of him or his priests!"

"So it was, and is. Nor is that all of this matter; I'd vow on it." Sualtim looked down at the corpse. "Disguised, but he wanted his god by him and so marked the symbol on the back of his sundisk— sacrilege! He dared much." With a sigh Sualtim added, "He accomplished much. Well. There is naught I can do for this man I thought I knew, who turned his back on the faith of his followers and followed the foreign god—even to murder. Will ye be doing aught for—"

Cormac interrupted his lifelong mentor. "I will not! The birds covet his eyes; let them have those orbs of Aengus *Bradawc*—Aengus the Treacherous!"

"It's bent on a vindictive path ye be, my pupil?"

Cormac met the soft grey eyes with his own suddenly icy-hard ones. "I am. It is what is left me, Sualtim. Come. I have shown you what I must, and it's a long trek back we must be making."

Cormac turned away to go. For a few moments

Sualtim gazed most thoughtfully at the young man's broad back. Then, with the tiniest suggestion of a smile twitching at the corner of his mouth, he nodded and stepped forward past the youth-become man. They set out to return to Glondrath.

After a time Sualtim said, "Ye spoke to me just now as though ye were Lord Cormac, my..." he swallowed the word he'd have uttered—"pupil"—and said, "son."

"I meant no offense to the mentor of my youth and life."

"None was taken, Cormac. Indeed, in some ways you have been as son to me, and to a man with maturity on him, it's prideful pleasure he feels when the boy becomes so obviously a man."

Cormac went on for a time in silence. Then, "Men followed me last night, mentor, as though I were Lord Cormac."

"And—"

"We both know I am not," Cormac said, and heard Sualtim sigh with relief. *So he was worried I had big notions, was he?*

"And you know you can never be lord of Glondrath," Sualtim said, very quietly, and far from happily.

"I know," Cormac said, as easily as he could sound; it had been but a brief dream. "Today or tomorrow or the day after, someone will come from Cruachan, with fine skirts and jewels on him. And he'll be telling all in Glondrath the name of the king's new commander. Nor will it be anyone here."

"It was no idle word I spoke, Cormac, when I told you you'd not live out a year an you remain in Glondrath."

"So I felt. A fell strangeness was on your face
101

and voice, Druid. Foolish is he who believes not druids in their saying of the time-to-come, and that look on their faces. Foolish is he who believes Sualtim Fodla not, in any matter! I do not misdoubt you, Sualtim Fodla."

They walked for a time in silence, and then Sualtim's age forced them to skirt to the edge of the declivity down and up which Cormac had yesterday run, so that they added to their journey. Even so, when they were on level ground once again, Sualtim had need of rest.

"I'd fain hold further converse in the matter of myself, Druid."

"Sualtim," the old man corrected; they were awalk again, entering the wood.

"That comes not easy on me, Sualtim. Is no easy matter, this being a respectful boy one day and a man the next."

"I know, lad. Many things have happed, one tumbling over the other."

"Too many. Too swiftly."

"I'll not be denying it, Cormac."

"Aengus," Cormac said, with a sad and uncomprehending shake of his head.

"If such was indeed his name. Surely he was only a minor peg of others in a game of Brandub, Cormac. A follower of Iosa Chriost—in disguise! Peradventure he wore his real name, too, under a hooded cloak?"

"Then who?"

"That," Sualtim said, "is to be learned."

Cormac said nothng. He walked, trying to make his chaotic mind concentrate only on keeping his strides short.

"Cormac—"

"I've none to seek blood-feud with. And naught

for me here but despair, and bitterness and . . . death, as ye've seen for me."

"I can deny none of that, Cormac. Your life has been changed. Like skeins taken up by a new blind weaver, the threads of your life are different, all at once. Nor can the same pattern be taken up again."

"*Why?* Why am I singled out, Druid?"

"Perhaps for something else. Perhaps the gods put *geas* on you to do that which ye've yet to learn. And perhaps not, but only that you may weave your own life, become truly a man."

"Alone."

It was an ugly word in any language; Cormac's tone made it the uglier. The druid had no ready reply, and they trudged in silence through the forest.

"In truth," Sualtim said after a time, "methinks Behl has no personal interest in any individual. There are too many of us to be overseen."

"The—the followers of the Dead God say that His father has personal interest in each person, and animal, and each happening on all the ridge of the world."

"So they do."

"Methinks Behl is the wiser," Cormac said, after a time of mulling. "A god must have better things to do and think on than to be interested in Cormac mac Art."

"Or should, indeed."

"It's more alone I am than any of those who believe in the Dead God, with His personal interest in them. It's little praying I'll be doing in this life, Druid."

Sualtim made no reply. They walked, enveloped in woods budding into spring and each man deep in his own thoughts. Though in truth each of them

103

thought on but one of them.

For a long while they moved thus in silence through the forest, until at last Cormac forced himself to say that which had come to the fore of his mind, again and again, to be thrust back in something approaching horror.

"I leave, Sualtim."

"Cormac—"

Cormac had said the words; was easier now to say the rest. The decision was made; remained but to make it true, first with words and then with the deed: "I leave at once."

"Cormac—" Sualtim trailed off. Then, "I understand. Aye. It is a man's decision, Cormac."

"Sualtim," the youth said with what was nigh onto sternness, "I do not need that."

The druid's robe-sleeved arm moved, reached out to the tall youth. It dropped without touching his mailed arm. Great sympathy was on Sualtim, and nervousness, too. Yet there was pride, for was he and Art mac Comail—aye, and poor Midhir —who had trained and created this youth who was so strong both in mind and body—and now was forced to prove it.

"The best horse in Rath Glondarth, Cormac. Art's horse. You will fly for safety to the northern kingdoms?"

"It is best, surely."

"Methinks it is. And with a sumpter horse behind, and gold in your pack. Cormac. Attend me. I vow to yourself and to Behl that I shall give myself over to discovering the murderers, the identity of the plotters. And when I have information, I'll be sending for you. Cormac—here. Tarry a moment."

They paused amid the trees while Sualtim removed the plain lunula he wore on other than ceremonial occasions. Borrowing the much younger man's dagger, he scratched a simple rune on its back. The druid returned the knife and bade Cormac note the mark, and commit it to memory.

"Should one bring this lunula to you, know that Sualtim has learned somewhat and has information and has sent for you. Even so, Cormac—come with care."

Cormac nodded wordlessly; in truth just now he trusted not his throat to speak. They walked on through the wood, and Sualtim talked, and talked; his words held advice for a man now, and him alone, without family or land amid strangers. Cormac essayed to be attentive though his mind strove to wander off along the murky and fear-fraught paths of might-be.

When they reached Glondrath, the two had agreed to tell none others of the decision and plan. Cormac took that which was his: his father's sword and its sheath though he left behind the well-known buckler. Art's great bearhide mantle he took as well, and a few trifles. None would question Sualtim; he it was who loaded himself with salable treasures and supplies sufficient for several days' travel without hunting. With those packs Sualtim entered the wood until he was out of sight of the rath. Cormac, on his father's fine black horse, rode along another trail and turned to wend through the trees only when he too was invisible to the people that had been his father's.

The two came together in a little glade nigh in the little-used trail that led northeastward through the trees to the northern kingdoms of Eirrin: Ailech where lay Tir Connail, and Airgialla, and Dal Ariadi wherin lay both Dalriada and Ulahd that was Ulster, site of the New God's main bishopric in Armagh.

Supplies and wherewithal they transferred to the broad back of Dubheitte: Blackwing, with Sualtim muttering that it was past time the sons of Eirrin emulated even the Romans in *some* things, and struck coins to simplify trading. The two gazed upon each other, and then Cormac remounted the big black horse that was ever anxious to gallop. Again the two men gazed one upon the other with misty eyes, until the younger suddenly set his jaw very tightly and rode away along the trail that would take him around the mountain that was Glondrath's northern border. Nor did he look back.

After him Sualtim called words Cormac had heard from afore: *"Cum do ghreim, Cormac,'s chan eagal duit."* And Sualtim Fodla repeated the injunction: "Keep your calm, Cormac, and there is no fear on you."

Cormac heard, and rode, and did not look back.

Pehaps an hour later he drew restless Dubheitte to a halt. He sat, staring at naught, easing the rein so the horse could worry the short new grass and taste its sweetness. Frowning, Cormac reflected.

Gods, what thoughts! Behl protect and Crom defend—that it's to this I've come!

The ugly thoughts persisted. He had trusted Sualtim all his life. Aye. And so had his father, and Midhir. As all three had trusted Aengus.

Now, his life shattered at the bloom of manhood and all three men torn from him by treachery and murder, he was no longer certain of anything . . . or anyone. Dared he trust even his lifelong mentor, a druid of the gods themselves?

Sualtim would learn nothing, Cormac mused. Sualtim would never send for him.

And if he did . . . how could Cormac be sure that he was not thus summoned into a trap?

O ye gods and blood of the gods! Surely not Sualtim . . .

But he could not be certain.

And only Sualtim knew wither he was bent.

Nay, he dared trust no one he knew, and no one in this land at all, or in the northern kingdoms; Sualtim knew he was headed thence, and others would guess.

In an agony that had been unremitting for days and was far more than any youth or man should have to bear, Cormac decided. He would ride not north, but eastward, to Leinster. That southeastern kingdom was shrouded by a long history of rivalry with both Connacht and Meath where lay Tara. Aye! And there would he keep open his eyes and ears. Leinster was full of priests; priest-ridden Laigen, Art had called it. There he would seek—with care!—to discover hint of the identity of those who'd ordered his father slain, those who had subverted Aengus mac Domnail.

And when he learned the name or names, found the men, whether they abode in Leinster or Meath, Munster or little Osraige, Connacth or Ailech, Airgialla or Ulahd or DalRiadia to the far northeast . . . then would the son of Art take his revenge. Aye and with Art's own sword, and none would deter him.

With his youthful face set as granite, he tugged at Dubheitte's reins, jerking up the horse's head so that the beast snorted and half reared, eyes rolling for enemy or quarry. Then Cormac clucked and loosed the reins a little, so that Dubheitte set off eastward, toward Leinster, and a new life—and the unknown. Thus did Cormac mac Art depart Rath Glondarth, and Connacht, like a thief in the night. Nor did he glance back.

PART TWO

THE KINGDOM OF LEINSTER

Chapter Six:
Partha mac Othna of Ulster

The sky roofed the Leinsterish coast with a deep blue shot with fingers of gold and grey. Along the strand rode a weapon-man. With a low curse of exasperation, he reined in, dismounted, and stepped away from his horse to answer a call of nature grown urgent. He moved overly far from the animal and his booted spear, as it turned out; appearing as if from nowhere, two savages surprised the Gael.

Dark, squat, half naked, they shrieked awful wolf-howls designed to freeze the very marrow of their prey. The man in the sleeved blue tunic under armour-coat of black leather proved no blood-frozen rabbit; he defended himself with sword and buckler. The flinty heads of axes clashed on wooden shield and steel clove the air with malevolent whines. Sparks flew from the clash of ax-head and rim of shield.

Above the strand and a few yards inland, another Gael was peering about in quest of a spot for night-camp. Without cheer he seemed, and on him the look of one weary of the saddle. Yet at the hounds of armed conflict he straightened and twisted his head about on a thick neck. Erect, rangy and tall in mailcoat and helm, he listened. Then he reined his mount about and cantered to the lip of the promontory. Below was beach, and the sea separating Eirrin from Britain. It shimmered out to a slate-hued horizon; the dying sun hovered at world's edge behind him.

Moving his great black horse closer to the declivity that ran gently down to the strand, he surveyed the water's edge.

He saw the man beset by two Picts, and he saw too what they did not: five more *Cruithne* were running toward the scene of battle. In a few seconds they would arrive; in a few more the lone Gael would surely be dead—or worse, hacked down and not dead.

The youthful rider of the black horse did that which he would pause to consider, in years to come: Cormac of Connacht spurred down the slope to the aid of a stranger, presumably a weapon-man of Leinster. He made another decision:

An old warrior had once come to Glondarth, and told Cormac's father of his years as a reaver. Once he and his fellows had taken a Roman ship, up north of Britain. Amid the spoils was a handsome vase, of Greek origin. The man swore that it depicted mounted Achaians spearing enemies. This, he and Art of Connacht had agreed with laughter, was why the Greeks were governed from Rome! True, such a maneuver was not guaranteed to drive a man straight back off his horse on impact of spearhead with shield or armoured flesh, but the probability was akin to that of a black cloud's bearing rain. Art's son watched Midhir and others

109

practice the tactic. They soon decided that were a man not afoot or in a chariot where he belonged, he'd best use ax or sword and consider his spear either as a throwing weapon or excess baggage. Nor was Cormac trained much as a horse-soldier; his people were hardly known for mounted combat.

Thus he left his spear in its long boot as Dubheitte started his plunge down the slope to the Leinsterish shore.

That charge nigh cost Cormac his seat and perhaps more; on a horse without stirrups, a precipitate downhill charge was unwise indeed. He was forced to rein back a bit and do his best to lean against gravity. Clamping his mount with all the strength of both legs, he braced hard against the beast's neck. Cormac knew a hollowing sensation in his stomach and the feel of being purely a nigh-helpless passenger on a juggernaut unmindful of leaving him sprawling behind.

Below, the battle continued. The five Picts raced to join it.

Forced to slow, turning his mount, Cormac made another decision. He must forego the element of surprise, else he arrive only in time to avenge—and likely to die, one against seven. For the five would be upon the two battling the man in the blue-plumed helmet before Cormac reached them.

Cormac bellowed out a long-drawn "HO!"

The beset Gael did not look up. Neither did his two assailants. All three were well occupied in activity requiring their full attention.

The five *Cruithne* took note, and froze, half-turned to stare at the huge black beast that now reached the foot of the sloping hill. Dubheitte lengthened his stride immediately he felt level soil beneath his hooves, however sandy. The horse

110

charged as though he'd been weaned on Picts. Having taken no time to think and with no better tactic in mind, Cormac gave the beast his head. With shield on left arm and sword in hand, he let Dubheitte gallop free. Blackwing sped as if he did indeed possess wings.

The dark warriors seemed unable to believe the horse would not swerve. Dubheitte had no such intention. At the last possible moment his quarry began to scatter. A vicious sidearmed upstroke opened the dark-skinned back on Cormac's right, from hip to shoulder To the left a Pict moved an instant too slowly, and Dubheitte's forehoof destroyed the stocky man's ankle. Then the animal was through them, galloping on.

Straightened from his sword-slash, Cormac had to tense and lean a bit leftward; with nothing against which to brace his feet, he could only grip the horse's sides. Fifteen pounds of shield on his arm aided him in righting himself. Then, awkwardly, he used his sword-hand to drag at the horse's reins.

The excited animal was unwilling to halt. He fought his rider's tug by leaning into it, slewing leftward. Ahead, one of the two Picts hemming the other Gael heard the drum of hooves and glanced around. Cormac had a fleeting glimpse of the blue-shirted man catching the ax-blow on his shield while he danced one-legged: he groin-kicked him who had been unable to resist looking away.

Dubheitte made a turn that was almost too tight on itself and his rider hung on with legs straining powerfully enough to interfere with the beast's breathing. Cormac was dismayed to see that his charge had not downed the enemy whose back he'd opened; that Pict was on his feet and braced for the Gael's return charge for all that blood washed

111

down his dark back and leg.

Damn the training that spoke against sheathing a blooded blade! Cormac had a spear and knew how to throw it. Surely a good cast would remove one enemy.

Dragging his complaining mount to a pause long yards from the five *Cruithne*, Cormac committed the reprehensible act of sheathing his blood-smeared sword. He unlimbered his spear and raised it. At the same time as he hurled it, he drummed his heels and grunted "Go!" Dubheitte lurched anew into a gallop. Again the youth was in danger of losing his seat. But with sword in hand and shield on arm he remained mounted—and unloosed another wild yell.

Matters still went less than superbly for the weapon-man turned horse-soldier. The five *Cruithne* had scattered. One lay grimacing, with his splintered ankle; Cormac had made his cast at the two who stood close together. The cast missed. Nevertheless their dodging insured that neither of them would make a good return throw at once, and Cormac twitched Dubheitte toward two others: a spear-wielding Pict stood over his companion of the crushed foot.

The big horse bearing down on him must have looked like a tumbling black boulder. The Pict launched his spear too hastily. The long ashen shaft went so high that Cormac hardly had to duck.

Moments later that savage's head was rolling on the sand and his downed comrade was blinded by the gouting blood. The headless corpse toppled over him. Again their foe was through. Now four *Cruithne* lived, and two of those were of considerably reduced menace. At least he'd kept them all from the other Gael.

112

Man and rider leaned through another turn. This time Cormac lengthened its arc, the while he took time to glance at the enemy. That proved wise: carefully leading the horse with a practiced stare, a silent Pict hurled his spear. His eye was as good as his arm. Cormac only just interposed his shield in time. With a great *bam* sound, the spearpoint struck his shield, drove into the wood—and stuck.

Dubheitte came about and lengthened his leggy stride into a third charge. His rider's shield-arm was dragged down by the long pole standing from the buckler's face. Managing to swerve his mount, Cormac made use of the liability: the spear-haft swept the wounded Pict off his feet. Another jabbed as Cormac plunged past and the youth's swordblade struck that spear aside. And again he was through them, at the gallop—and frustrated. Too, the impact of spear-butt with Pictish calves had torn the point free of Cormac's shield with a jerk that would give him an aching arm—later, when he had time to notice.

Though mac Art bent low to lessen the possibility of a spear in the back, none was hurled. He had at least disconcerted his chosen enemies.

Even then he smiled; the man to whose aid he'd come was yanking his sword out of the belly of his standing opponent. The other lay doubled from the kick he'd taken to his stones; the blue-shirted Gael plunged the bloody sword into his side and gave it a vicious twist. Two pair of Pictish legs kicked reflexively.

Dubheitte wanted to return to what he took to be his business. Cormac worked at slowing the animal and keeping him on a steady course of the other Gael. That man grinned and waved a dripping sword, then ran to his own horse. The chestnut-hued animal shied and flared his nostrils at the scent of blood. His master spoke low rather than cursed, while Cormac, grimly smiling, held Dubheitte in check—semi-check. The other man mounted.

"Forgall mac Aed!" he called, the man whose shield and helmet's plume were bright with Leinster's blue.

Cormac did not understand. He shouted "World without Picts!" and grinning, the two men charged.

Peradventure the gods ordain such things, as some have said; perhaps Dubheitte was over-excited and careless; perhaps his master was, in his inexperience and his pride—and assumption that two mounted Gaels were more than match for four Picts, two of whom were wounded. And perhaps a spear-cast was particularly good, or merely lucky. Whatever the cause, a hurled stave went low and buried its flinty head in Dubheitte's chest.

The horse screamed. Cormac was hurled to the sand as the big black animal fell. Even if he were not dead, he was surely in shock, and thrashed strangely.

His master's impact was painful and jarring, through mailcoat and padded underjack; worse was the slamming of his right elbow onto hard sand. His fingers sprang open. His sword made little *cling-ting* sounds as it struck the sand and skittered.

The spear-thrower was on him and he could but scramble, grunting when a stone ax banged off his shoulder. The mail held. Cormac meanwhile flailed head with his left arm. His buckler's edge caught the Pict in the leg, just beside the knee. He fell. Cormac daggered the dusky warrior before he could so much as turn over.

114

The youth felt hardly heroic; in four charges he had lost spear and horse and slain only two of the enemy. Better had he dismounted! Now a glance told him that the Leinsterman had somehow missed his intended foe and plunged on past. Well down the beach, he was turning the blaze-faced chestnut. The Pict Cormac had struck with edge of blade and haft of spear was sitting up. Though his back was crimson and one leg was obviously broken, he was awaiting the Leinsterman's return, weapons ready.

The fifth Pict was now rushing Cormac mac Art.

The youth retrieved his sword. He braced himself, knees bent, left side to the running savage, shield presented, sword out to the side, ready. Dark Pictish eyes glared into grey ones, over the shield's rim. The sword-steel eyes were just as malevolent, for all their youthfulness.

The Pict was no such fool as to continue rushing a man so prepared; he slowed and got his own shield up and between them. This savage had faced Cormac's kind aforenow, and learned caution — while gaining a steel-headed ax. His knotted arm swung the Celtic weapon as though it were a stick, looping, looping, watching . . .

Down the beach, the other Gael bellowed a wild cry. Cormac saw his own opponent's eyes flicker; the Pict knew he must die. He loosed a terrible swing of his ax. Cormac took the desperation blow on his shield. As he began a rising swordcut, he remembered what he'd seen the Leinsterman do. The Pictish shield whipped up and Cormac essayed the nasty tactic.

Aborting the sword-stroke, he took vengeance for the Gael whose ax the Pict wielded. Cormac crotch-kicked the squat, heavily-muscled man.

Then the off-balanced Cormac fell down.

115

The Pict's war-howl rose into a scream of pain and became a choking gurgle. Blazing black eyes bulged. His knees bent. His shield lowered as he obeyed the ancient, inarguable urge to clutch his wounded parts. He dropped to his knees.

That way the swishing, almost-circular stroke of the Leinsterman's sword took off only a little more than half the squat savage's head, rather than the entire skull at the neck. The Pict was just as dead. Cormac meanwhile was hurling himself aside; his ally's big horse was a great dark-brown mass as it plunged past, and the pound of his hooves was as thunder in the youth's ears.

"HA!" the Leinsterman shouted back. "Robbed ye!"

Cormac gave the man's back a dirty look as he got to his feet. He hurried to where lay the Pict with the broken foot; he'd not have the Leinsterman claim this one too. The courageous savage stuck up his spear; Cormac cut off its head and, on the backstroke, the Pict's. He whirled to run the doubly wounded last foeman—and watched the Leinsterman come loping up and urge his willing mount into a very thorough job of trampling the dusky form until it was scarlet.

The gazes of two pair of Gael-grey eyes met.

"Ho, ha, easy there, Taraniseach, easy! Ho there, my greedy friend! Seven Picts attacked me and it's yourself slew three of them!"

Cormac blinked and squatted, thrusting his sword into the sand to cleanse the blade of Pictish blood. "Huh! Calling that one your own, are ye? As well call that horse mine!"

The man came to him on his prancing, head-shaking mount. First glancing around to be sure there were no more foes, he flung his sword so that it drove into the sand. It stood quivering. Then he doffed his helmet, to shake out a shortish mop of hair as straight and black as Cormac's. Cormac saw that the fellow was good-looking, if button-nosed, and that he was surely in his twenties, though his hair was early departing his forehead. His eyes were like old stone, without the hint of blue.

"Aye; your mount I greatly regret, my friend." He looked at the downed beast; Dubheitte had snapped a foreleg in his fall. "But he be not dead . . ."

"Yes he is."

Cormac spoke very quietly. Steeling himself against his own misery at the loss of the fine horse, he used his sword to end Dubheitte's misery.

The yourthful Gael looked up at the older. "I do hope ye be wealthy, with many fine horses."

"No such luck," the man said. "I gave ye my name, weapon-man, and neglected to add that it's Coichtaigheacht I am, in the king's forces of Leinster. Ye be no Leinsterman, with that accent; what brought ye to this realm, to aid those so stupid as to be caught afoot by the enemy?"

"I am Partha son of Othna of Ulster," Cormac told him, using the name by which he had called himself these two weeks since he'd departed Glondarth. "A weapon-man in search of service, for it's my father's third son I am, and my elder brother took even my girl to himself. Nor heard I your name, Captain; I was distracted at the time."

The man who'd called himself Chief of fifty chuckled. "Forgall mac Aed, Partha mac Othna. And travel no farther. There's need in Leinster of sword-arms such as yours, aye, and your courage. It's hard-pressed times these are, friend Partha, with the *Boruma* nigh upon us and rumours too of Pictish restlessness." He glanced about at the

117

corpses. "Spies, possibly."

"Mayhap . . . and mayhap then we should not have done death on them all."

"We'll be telling none we could have taken a prisoner or two, eh? An ye be looking for weaponish employment, Partha mac Othna, my lord King Ulad has need of ye."

"Truth, I ate the last of my provisions earlier today . . . and am now without a horse, as well."

Forgall regarded the unfortunate steed. "A fine animal; again, sorrow's on me that he died because of myself. A fine animal..."

Forgall seemed a bit too thoughtful, on the border of suspicion. Cormac tried to seem both nervous and prideful, all at once: "My elder brother's," he said.

Forgall laughed and clapped a calloused hand to a mailed shoulder. "Good for yourself, Partha, for I am a second son myself, and my brother heir to but little! However long ye bestrode yon animal, I'd say ye had better service of him than your brother of a fickle maid—oh, I intend no offense, Partha; the words slipped out."

"None taken. She's what ye said, and more. Be there aught of food in that bulgy pack I see behind your saddle, Fifty-chief?"

In truth Cormac had not quite worked out his story, and had already added an unplanned embellishment with the allegation that Dubheitte had belonged to a nonexistent older brother. He preferred that there be no further discussion of his past until he'd had time to fabricate it. Besides, he was hungry.

Three fellows in the forest had caught him asleep but two nights agone. Two had held him moveless with nocked arrows whilst the third packed up the young pilgrim's belongings. They'd have taken Dub-heitte too, had not the animal thrown one of their number. Taking advantage of that distraction, Cormac had snatched up shield and spear. He caught an arrow in the shield, another, hastily loosed in the darkness, missed. His spear but grazed a man gone suddenly nerveless and running for his own mount. Another arrow made Cormac dodge so that he fell. The three men escaped into the darkness of a forest they doubtless knew. Dub-heitte they left; those gems and bits of gold that were all Cormac's wealth in coin-less Eirrin they took.

Armed and armoured, Cormac had ridden all that night lest those three thieving archers regain courage and return to slay him from well out of his reach.

Though his careful queries had brought nothing that could be construed as a trail to his father's killer, he remained undaunted. Mac Art was determined to give his life to the quest of those behind his father's slaying, and had made solemn resolve to that effect. Now he'd been on his way to Baile Atha Cliath, the Town of the Ford of the Hurdles. There he hoped to find some means of earning bread and meat. He had already resigned himself to sleeping on an empty belly this night, when he had heard and entered into Forgall's imbroglio.

He'd be happy indeed to share the Leinsterish captain's provisons.

Forgall however, had not been stopping here for the night. He'd but reined in and dismounted to relieve himself. That urge had nearly resulted in his death. He and Cormac solemnly vowed to devise a bag to hang on the forefront of one's saddle, that one need not dismount to make water.

Noting that Forgall glanced at a sky gone slate with only a puddle of molten red-gold to mark the sun's passage, Cormac assured him he could wait a while longer for viands. Forgall was on his way up the coast from the capital, he said, to collect men from a little fort just south of Atha Cliath. This troop must then go back down to Carman with him, to train and receive their instructions for the *Boruma*. Captain of fifty or *coichtaigheacht,* Forgall said, he was in need of five more . . . four, with Cormac joining his company.

Carman-on-the-Slaigne, Cormac remembered, was on Leinster's very northern border, at the estuary of the Slaigne—indeed, Carman's nearest neighbour was no town, but the isle of Beg-Eri. Munster's capital of Cashnel was but sixty or so miles west of Carman, and Tara less than a hundred miles to the north. Leinster—Laigen—formed a nearly perfect triangle, perched on one point. Munster and Meath bordered it, and, along the entire eastern coast, the Sea of Eirrin. Atha Cliath was only a bit south of Tara; the fortress Forgall was bound for, then, lay only five or so miles up the coast.

Neither man was interested in anything belonging to the *Cruithne,* and Cormac's pack, on his dead horse, was empty. They did gather the weapons of metal the Picts had carried, taken from slain *Erainn,* men of Eirrin. On a shared whim, with grins, each man took from a dusky corpse a little leather-strung Pictish amulet, black.

Twice Cormac said he would walk; thrice Forgall bade him ride. Taraniseach—Thunderhorse—he said, would carry another fourteen stone without noticing. Though tall, the rangy youth from Connacht weighed hardly so much—and Thunderhorse indeed made no objection to carrying them both. Cormac rode behind Forgall, whose pack was before him, on the base of Thunderhorse's dark-maned neck. Afoot Forgall was but a couple of inches shorter than his saviour; mounted, Cormac was easily able to see over the other man's head.

"It's a youthful terror with a sword ye be, Partha. That bit of mustache looks as though it's just coming in." Forgall spoke without turning.

"My height came on me early, but my face-hair is running several years late."

Cormac/Partha was not about to reveal his extreme youth. Others might make him their butt, and for all he knew Leinster allowed none of his few years on its weaponish rolls.

Forgall but grunted without pursuing the matter. They rode in silence for a time, whilst night closed down over the sea and Eirrin's eastern coast. Cormac bethought himself of the lies he'd told, of those he must tell. He wondered how long such a life must continue, with him wearing even his very name under a cloak of darkness. Had he realized that it would be a matter of years, his dismay would have been far greater.

He did not give thought to those he'd slain this day. They were Picts, only Picts, the enemies of all men. And he was a weapon-man, a warrior. Soon he'd be a professional, accepting the board and pay of Ulad Ceannselaigh, King over Leinster. A tiny smile drew at the left corner of his mouth, only a little and certainly not disarranging his unlined face. A professional! He squared his shoulders proudly and rode with hands on thighs, rather than hold to Forgall or aught else.

"Ah," Forgall said of a sudden, and Cormac jerked. "It's twice I'm after making mention of the

Boruma . . . do you of Ulster know of what I speak, Partha?"

"Aye. None in Eirrin but knows of Leinster's Burden, Captain."

It had occurred to Cormac that it might not be his place, his new place, to call a commander of weapon-men by name, and so he called him Fifty-chief. He'd have to be mindful of such niceties now; he was no longer son of a rath comander, and no longer in Connacht. He was only Partha, son of Othna; third son of a minor noble of northward Ulahd, or Ulster.

"Ah," Forgall said again. "And what do men say of Leinster's Burden, in Ulster?"

"That there be no justice in it," Cormac said, and he answered truthfully; so men said in Connacht, at any rate. "Whether there was when it was imposed none of us can say, across these three centuries—"

"Nigh four!" the Leinsterman snapped.

"But—surely there be no justice in it now."

"None. And all for a woman!—Two."

They fell silent again, with the horse named for the ancient thunder-god plodding stolidly through deep twilight. Cormac considered the Boruma, or Boru Tribute, and what he knew of it. He must know such things now; he was of Leinster. He might well soon be fighting because of the Cattle Tribute, Leinster's Burden . . . fighting Meathmen, the men of the High-king.

After awhile he said, "I am not of Leinster, Forgall. Tell me of the Boruma, and how it came about when Tuathal and Eochaid lived."

And Forgall did, as they rode through the cool night.

King Tuathal the Desired of the first century—as the Christians measured time—was sore beset by troubles. There was the usurper, Carbri CinnCait and his son, and his successor who returned from Pict-land, Feredach. Two daughters had Tuathal, though surely he wanted naught but strapping sons. His daughter Dairine he wed to Leinster's King Eochaid, the way that there was a union of the High-king and Leinster.

"She was a whore, by the blood of the gods!" Forgall said.

That part of the story was new to Cormac. Well, he thought, Leinstermen needed a good reason for what Eochaid did—and mayhap she had been as Forgall said.

"Yet she was the wife of a king and the daughter of the High-king, and Eochaid would not have her slain. Instead, he took her by night to a tower, and there locked her up, and let it out that she had died in her sleep of a fever. And after a time King Eochaid went a-mourning up to Tara."

All men understood death and the swiftness of its descent on even the most unsuspectingly healthy of mortals. Tuathal understood. Forgall told Cormac, and sympathized with his royal brother-in-law. Indeed, he solaced the southern king by giving him his other daughter, Fithil.

"Strange," Cormac/Partha said, "that she was not wed to another, by then."

"She was a harridan," Forgall said. And he told of how Eochaid, who was a king and knew the benefits of alliance, brought the "harridan" Fithil home to Leinster. And time passed, and one day Fithil discovered her sister, and her still living.

Cormac could understand the horror, the shame and humiliation, the cries of crime most horrible; both were daughters of the High-king, and both alive, and both wed to the same man!

"They died of broken hearts," Forgall said.

"Just . . . so? Of broken hearts."

"Aye," Forgall said with a most positive air, and Cormac was not minded to question the man. He did wonder how they told the story up on Tara hill . . .

Somehow Tuathal learned of the crime and the deaths of his daughters: treachery, Forgall said, foul treachery apprised the High-king. Then did the High-king gather together his men and auxiliaries and the members of his clanna and march on Leinster in sore anger and desire for revenge. Indeed Tuathal's army ravaged the land all the way the capital — where Eochaid humbly submitted. (Rather, Forgall said, than see another Leinsterman slain, for Eochaid wept daily for his murdered countrymen. Cormac said naught, and Forgall could not see his face. Well — it was Forgall's story.)

Tuathal then levied a crushing annual tribute: The *Boruma,* or cow-tribute. Nor had Eochaid power to resist, with Tuathal's army sprawled round about and, as Forgall had it, numerous mothers and children of Leinster as hostages.

Five thousand cows annually, High-king Tuathal demanded of Leinster, and five thousand swine, and five thousand cloaks of good workmanship, and five thousand vessels of good brass, well-wrought, and the final crushing blow: five thousand ounces of silver from the mines of little Leinster.

The fine was to be paid annually, and no period of years was stipulated. Centuries later, the High-king on Tara Hill annually continued to require that awful drain of Leinster. Most often the Boruma had to be gathered by force, with the men of the High-king carrying the bloody sword down into

Leinster. Those daughters of Tuathal's and the crime of Eochaid had given cause to more of Eirrin's blood-drenched history than aught else. Often the struggle was confined not just to Meath and Leinster, for others entered in because of empathy and alliances, even greed or unmentioned political hopes.

Whether Tuathal's daughters had been good and sweet or hideous and whoresome, whether Eochaid had been a monster or a man overly timid at telling gthe High-king of his elder daughter's liaisons—none of this now mattered. It was King Tuathal who had left the entire Emerald Isle this blood-soaked legacy. And now collection-time was again approaching.

"Will the tribute be paid, Forgall?"

Forgall snorted. "Not willingly!"

"Tara will come to collect with steel hands, then."

"Tara will. Meath will come. And Leinster will fight."

Tradition, Cormac mused, and the word was as a curse. He contemplated the stupidity and greed of men. Why had no High-king been big enow, man enow to dispense with that which was the prime cause of dissension among all the kingdoms of Eirrin? Why did each crowned Ard-righ sit on Tara Hill and leave the Boruma in force, that had cost so many lvies? Why did no man in high office, even the highest in the land, have the nerve and honesty to do that which was manifestly best for all, despite his contemporary detractors? Had a previous High-king caused the insulting, draining imposition to be lifted, he might have been damned by some in his time. Yet he'd be famous now, and beloved, for his courage and that great act, now and for many years to come. *Tradition,* Cormac mused sourly, and a bit more of maturity came over him like a mantle.

And the time was nigh. And here was Cormac of Connacht, self-exiled lest he be slain and the truth never be got at, bearing an assumed name . . . in Leinster. And Leinster would resist. That meant combat. The sons of Errin against sons of Eirrin, brothers of this isle, all, and no way to know them apart without the trappings of the very mortal kings who bade them go and die.

Cormac who was Partha thought on it, long and long, as Taraneseach plodded northward through the gloom of early nightfall.

So be it, he decided at last. *I shall join Leinster, then. I will fight for Leinster, and pretend it is Connacht!*

And Thunderhorse plodded through the first hour of night. Slowly his hooves clopped away the miles, and the mailed men on his back were silent with their thoughts: thoughts of war.

The fortress called Redrock was a small one, though ringed about with walls of earth and mud so thick that a chariot could have been driven atop them. Within was little more than garrison, stables and barracks, with a well and granary and a few other outbuildings round about the space for assembly and exercise. Forgall was greeted with great cheer, and Cormac knew the man was well liked by those he commanded. They entered, dismounted and swung their horse-weary legs while the big chestnut was led away to be stabled and fed. And Forgall led Cormac in to be housed and fed.

Forgall mac Aed was unstinting in telling the

garrison of the heroics of the tall youth beside him, "Partha mac Othna". Partha was immediately accepted as companion. Smiling, friendly Leinstermen offered food and ale to a fellow weapon-man, and one who indeed had saved their chief. The new comer's apparent youth was marked and remarked upon; Cormac said little, and laughed when he was called "Parthog," one of his new comrades attaching the word "youth" to his supposed name. He noted that there were those here but a couple of years older than he, and yet smaller than he. He would pass, a man in deed and a boy in age, among men some of whom were but boys in deeds.

Forgall's second came to him. This was a not-unhandsome, chesty man with reddish cheeks and huge hands at the ends of long, long arms. Bress mac Keth his name, Bress *Lamfhada*, Long-arm, his sobriquet. (Cormac learned only later that Bress was called Huge-feet, though not to his broad, reddish, and yet slightly equin face.) Mighty Bress the Warrior was not yet twenty. He wore his red brows in two horizontal arcs that ever gave him a perpetual look of superciliousness and disdain, as though all were less than he and it was condescension to speak of them.

"And how is it ye turn up so deep in Leinster, an Ulsterman none knows? Ah—pardon . . . an Ulsterboy none knows." And Bress let his face rearrange itself just slightly into a sort of smile.

"I have told the captain," Cormac said, and repeated his story with brevity. He forbore to comment on the use of the word "boy." Bress knew what he'd done this day, and Cormac thought he must be in a testing process. Bress was not a fellow-soldier; he was after all Forgall's second, and due some respect. And . . . unhappy?

"Ah. And what does your father up in Ulster, third son of Othna whose brother took his sweetheart?"

"He is the lord Othna, commander of the rath near the borders of Airgialla and Dal Ariada."

"Ah—is that near Armagh, then?"

"Less than a day north-by-west, afoot," Cormac said. He was not being tested as a man or a weaponman; Bress was treating him as if he might be some sort of spy! Cormac stood erect. Though longer of arm and thus of sword-reach, Bress was an inch or two shorter than the young man he braced.

"Ah. And ye come claiming to be a noble's son of Ulster, do ye?"

The barracks room had gone silent. Cormac's jaw tightened. He bethought him of Sualtim and his good advice, and he forced himself to draw and expel a deep breath through his nose. His gaze he kept on Bress's bluish green eyes.

"I come claiming to be naught but a weaponman proven, Bress mac Keth, with hunger and thirst on him, and a need of oil for his swordsheath."

Around them men laughed in a break of tension; Bress did not so much as show his imitation of a smile.

"It is a good answer," Forgall's voice called, and he came forward through his men after having conferred with sentries outside. "Nor need Partha mac Othna say more. I vouch for Partha mac Othna, who saved my life. Enough. *Arbenn-chatha;* no more questions. Our new man is proven and this very day, on the field of battle, not on that of practice." Forgall arrived at the side of the stiffly standing Bress. "The time is past for us to be abed—we've a long trek on the morrow, and daily training after that. Enough talk."

Bress gave Cormac a look that seemed to promise he thought it not enough.

Cormac wondered if *Arbenn-chatha* were Bress's military title. Or had his chief called him "Chieftain of battle" as a chide, since the big redhead seemed bent on picking a fight with the new recruit, or at least challenging him strongly?

What a little man he is, Cormac thought, despite his few years, *to be jealous unto truculence of his commander's attentions to a new recruit!*

A man whose name Cormac did not catch led him to a sleeping bench. He spoke quietly.

"Best ye be staying clear of Bress, Partha. It's a fine fighter the man is, with or without weapons."

"He does well with his mouth, indeed." But Cormac spoke just as quietly.

"—with a temper on him as mean as his sorrel-horse hair."

"An odd choice for Forgall's second in command," Cormac observed, wishing there were time to go over his mail-links once more.

"It is possible that Forgall be too easy-going," the other man said. "Bress is our tempering. He is not well-loved by any I know—but it's a fighting man he is, who has slain no less than ten times!"

Without comment on his own tally—all in Picts—Cormac nodded. He accepted both information and advice with a nod of thanks, and reclined for sleep.

He was so weary that, once his muscles had relaxed, not even the chorus of snores from his new companions or the ache in his shield-arm kept him long awake.

Chapter Seven:
Mesca and Mocci

The soldiers and new recruits of Forgall mac Aed entered Carman of Leinster under a pearl-hued sky lightened by a waning afternoon sun.

Though Carman was on Leinster's southern border and the stronghold of Redrock up near the northern, Meathish border, Forgall's company had spent but one night under the stars. The distance from Leinster's northernmost point to its most southerly was but forty miles. The kingdom was smaller than Munster, which sprawled to its west and south; smaller than Connacht, smaller even than Mide or Meath, which had been created of parts from the other kingdoms, as an expansion of territory around Tara of the Kings.

Carman was the greatest center of population that fortess-raised Cormac had ever experienced, and he saw little while trying to see everything.

To him the human throng was enormous and exotic. Merchants and close-crowding buildings; well-dressed nobles in pearl-sewn mantles, and yapping dogs; slouching rag-tags and bustling hawkers of this and that merchandise; all merely formed a backdrop. The Connachtish youth's eyes swerved this way and that to pick out women, and girls, more females in twenty paces than he'd seen in all his life. With fine clothes on them, and clean, curled hair, and paint or dyes to enhance eyes and lips!

The men tramped; Cormac tramped; Cormac stared. An occasional pair of bold eyes stared in return, and girls there were who imparted more swing to their hips, once they'd become aware of the big tall youth's grey-eyed gaze. Entranced and enchanted, he heard not the babble of a hundred conversations, nor noted the words of the loud-voiced hawkers of goods. He had seen cod and white haddock before, and pig's and badger-meat, and prawns and scallops and herring, and sloke and dulse, mace and honey, and fragrant little juniper berries his people used for flavouring and seasoning. He had not seen before so many fine-looking members of the opposite sex, and the Conachtish youth was at an age when his interest in females was passing high.

At the permanent military encampment outside the city—a bit too close, Cormac thought, to the city's main refuse dump into the Slaigne—forsaw to the entry of "Partha" into King Ulad's service, and to his outfitting. Yes, he could wear his own fine chaincoat in combat, when and if that became necessary. Otherwise, and for dress, the new recruit would wear the same sleeveless coat of boiled leather as his fellows, over their Leinsterish tunics of speedwell blue.

Cormac learned that he would be charged for both, against his wages . . .

The captain bade the veterans from Redrock be

at their ease and leave, so long as they were back in camp by sundown, for pre-dinner muster. Aye, Cormac could go into Carman too: the newcomer had earned his leave that evening on the beach. With Boruma time so nigh, Forgall warned, many and many a day might pass ere again they found opportunity to recreate themselves.

The veterans welcomed their leave, and most had already accepted Partha as a comrade. Some few of the other recruits, who must remain in camp, frowned; so, Cormac noted, did Bress mac Keth.

A burly farmer's son named Cas mac Con accompanied Cormac as guide; Cas was a score or so years of age, russet of hair and brown of mustache and called Bull by some of his comrades. Cormac willingly accepted the thickset man's guidance into and through a city about which mac Art knew nothing.

Cas gave little time for sightseeing, instead taking a direct route that soon led them into a section of the capital that Cormac realized was hardly the best. He followed without thinking, hardly noticing his surroundings apart from the many exemplary examples of femininity; he gawked and girl-watched. A mug of ale? Oh, yes. This place? Certainly. Lasrian's Blue Shamrock, eh? Noted for his own brew of beer from wheat and honey, with a secret ingredient Lasrian the *brughaid* would not reveal? Fine; Cormac knew not one place from another, and if Cas vouched for this one, why not? He was no expert as regards ale; an Cas thought Lasrian's special bew worth the trying, he'd do so.

The two men entered the little tap-room, which was also an inn, with a door leading to private rooms behind.

Places to sit were not hard to find. Neither, as they ordered mugs of ale, was companionship—for Cas. A few minutes later the farmboy soldier was gone; so was the black-haired girl he'd told Cormac was his cousin. The big recruit sat and drank alone, only sipping for he was not overly enamoured of Lasrian's vaunted brew. He strove to look as if he'd been wearing the blue tunic—over his own leather leggings—and long vest of black leather for years.

Cormac strove, too, not to be too noticeable in his watching of the most handsome girl nearby. Fiery of hair she was, and surely no older than he, though he saw that she was more sophisticated. That she was far from well dressed was of no consequence whatever; she was pretty and more, with a vivacious look about her. Her eyes were marvelous rounds of truly grassy green. Other patrons of the Blue Shamrock were no better dressed.

Indeed, the excellent young minstrel over in the corner wore a tunic of so faded a red it could be called pink. His hooded cloak was threadbare in more than one place and his leggings looked as if they'd been made of a carrion cow found a century ago. In a good clear voice, he sang quietly the while he strummed his lute.

Listening, enjoying the quiet music and verses-in-the-making of some love story or other, Cormac gave most of his attention to the girl. *(Young woman,* he thought, *for I am a young man!)* Naturally he pretended to be studying the brown liquid in his mug.

He was mindful of nursing his ale, that he might not empty the mug and have to suffer its refilling. Not so the two older fellows, who had obviously been here longer than he; longer, indeed than

133

necessary. The younger, perhaps twenty, made a teasing remark. It was directed at the girl. She continued to devote much attention to her nails, which she had dyed crimson in the manner of a lady of leisure. Berries had darkened her eyebrows, which Cormac assumed were lighter than her orange-red hair.

The fellow who'd failed to attract her attention with his remark now stretched forth a leg. He tried to toe her ankle. He could not reach. Slouching the more in his chair, he used his foot to tap the leg of her stool. She paid no mind. Her apparent interest in her nails was as deep as Cormac's in his mug of brew.

"High 'n' mighty li'l wench, huh? Nails like a lady—or a . . ."

She shot the young man a green-eyed stare magnificently notable for its coolness. When she disengaged that look, her glance flashed over Cormac, just in passing. He felt warmed by it. The man glanced his way; Cormac affected not to notice. The youth of Connacht was most aware of being well out of his element.

"It's mighty fine them nails'd feel digging into a man's shoulders," the older of the two drinkers said, grinning, staring at the girl. "The *backs* of his shoulders."

"Is it aught else ye'd be having?"

This from the Blue Shamrock's owner-proprietor, or *brughaid*.

"Only a room in back, Lasrian—with that pretty drolleen for company."

Lasrian shook his jowly head. "Och, Scumac, it's ashamed I am for ye. That wren as ye call her does not work here—and she's too young for yourself, sure. And yourself here with your

134

nephew . . . Scumac!" Again Lasrian gave his head a chastising wag.

The older man named Scumac imitated the action. "So I might be, Laz . . . but yon filly's not too young for Blai here, is she, boy?"

Blai laughed—a high-voiced giggle that Cormac thought ridiculous and nigh as shameful as the pair's treatment of the girl . . . the *young woman*. And them uncle and nephew! He saw her give Lasrian the brughaid a grateful look, which told Cormac what he'd surmised: she was a youth of tender sensibilities, better than those two, better than the Blue Shamrock, and distressed by the unwanted and lewd attentions of a pair of louts who should have been out slopping the pigs they doubtless slept with.

The minstrel strummed. Lasrian beamed on him. Then, looking at the door, he frowned. Cormac thought he could read the round-bellied fellow's mind: sure and the minstrel was good, and why then were none entering Lasrian's *bruidean* to give listen—having a cup the while?

"Sure and she prettier'n any filly I ever saw, Uncle," Blai said.

"Hush, stallion!" Scumac said, and he and his nephew guffawed.

Unnoticed, the minstrel had commenced softly singing about Medhbh, the Intoxicating One, and a *buachall* and a *bachlach*—cowherd and churl or herdsman and how they trampled blarhnad in their roughness and lack of sensitivity; blarhnad was a little flower. Lasrian was nervous, and Scumac and Blai entirely too caught up in their callous fun to take note of a most clever minstrel.

Cormac was staring, his lips tightened and his hand very tightly clutching his mug. The two took no note of him either, rapt and enwrapt in a diversion pleasant only to themselves. Cormac glanced at the inner doorway. No Cas mac Con. Good. Cormac was in no hurry to leave. He was minded to ask the minstrel if he knew a lay about a couple of hogherds and how they had such knowledge of fillies, but he held back; this was not his neighbourhood, or his city, or his country.

Scumac ordered two more mugs of the reddish ale he and his nephew were so assiduously stowing away. Lasrian, frowning, went to his kegs. The minstrel, apparently unnoticed save by Cormac, was weaving a clever system of verses in which appeared again and again the words *mesca* and *mocci:* intoxication and pigs.

Of a sudden Scumac, like an outsized cat—though with a lurch in tribute to the potency of Lasrian's brew—was out of his chair and at the girl. He caught her by shoulder and one breast and began dragging her from her seat, toward the rear; one of the rooms for pleasure, Cormac was sure, to which Cas had repaired with his "cousin."

Cormac had no other thought. He rose and rushed to the girl's aid. As neither Blai nor his uncle wore a sword or visible dagger, Cormac did not draw his steel. He placed a big hand on Scumac's arm and the man jerked, swinging away. In thus evading Cormac's grip he incidentally let the girl slip free of his. The man of forty or so faced the big youth angrily, and Scumac was red of face. Then Cormac saw the other's gaze leap past him. At the same time, just as Scumac started to grin, a hand fell heavily on Cormac's shoulder.

Cormac turned and drove a fist into Blai's relaxed and ale-filled belly, all in one movement.

With an ugly gagging sound Blai doubled half

over, then sank to his knees. His eyes bulged and his mouth gaped while he clutched his midsection with both hands. With an "urkk" and a gushy liquid sound, Blai messed Lasrian's floor.

From behind Cormac came another cheerless sound: a good hearty thud. He whirled, to see Scumac, his eyes rolling loosely, begin to bend both knees. His hands fell loosely open and from one a dagger dropped to the oil-dark floor. The man's falling to his knees jarred the floor under Cormac's feet. He stepped back then, as Scumac stretched his length.

Behind the fallen man stood the girl, glaring at Cormac. She held the stool with which she'd tested the hardness of Scumac's skull. It was hard; though the man lay still, he breathed naturally and there was no blood.

A smiling Cormac mac Art said, "I give ye thanks," and awaited similar words from her.

"Hmp! I struck him before I thought, when I saw the knife," she said, and tossed the stool so that Cormac had to jerk a leg from its path. "No child am I to have need of a long-nosed *protector*— certainly not a buffoon with a backwoods haircut and wrists like the slabs of pork ye doubtless raise and slaughter!" With her eyes she directed the bemazed youth's attention to the unconscious Scumac. "It's perfectly able I am of taking care of myself—see? Which is more than I can be saying for yourself, *soldier;* but for me he'd have divided your shoulderblades by another quarter-inch!"

A speechless Cormac mac Art watched her step across Scumac, nudge his nephew neatly so that he dropped from hands and knees into his own vomit, and storm from the inn in a swirl of worn off-white skirts and hair like dancing flames.

137

The minstrel rose and made as if to follow. At the door, he turned.

"Nothing harmed, Lasrian, I see; good for you a member of the Royal Army was here to restore order. Bad cess to yourself an these two don't clean up their own mess, Brughaid! The nephew's been eating his dulse half-chewed, I see." Blue eyes switched their calm gaze to Cormac, and in them he saw youth, and amusement. "Weapon—man: it's far better ye are with your arm than at the judging of womankind!"

And with a wink, the minstrel too departed.

Women, Cormac thought, feeling very warm and very confused. *Hmp! But a girl, no more than fourteen—ummm. Well...hardly so mature as I, though. Upbringing will out, as Sualtim's said so many times.*

"Ah ... soldier ... member of the Royal Army there ... would ye be helping me stretch Scumac and Blai over there by the wall? Corpse-imitating drunks lying about the floor do business no good. And might I be suggesting that it must be time for ye to be seeking your camp?

Still feeling the heat that betokened his flush, Cormac helped Lasrian move the victims. Blai had passed out and his uncle was snoring, despite the fact that he lay on his belly. The chagrined youth nerved himself to ask about the minstrel—and the girl, as if she were an afterthought. Lasrian vowed not to know either, and was sorry the minstrel had left. Cormac's impression was that minstrels were far more welcome than "backwoods buffoons" such as he'd heard himself called. He decided it was indeed time he returned to the company of weapon-men, whom he understood. Cas mac Con could take care of himself.

So can I, Cormac thought, *so long as I be staying clear of Carman's strange women!*

The unsung hero of the Blue Shamrock departed it. Directions were easily asked, and got. He made his way through a Carman dim with its closeset buildings beneath a lowering sun in an overcast sky. The while, he took note of how these city Leinstermen had their hair trimmed. Hair and its grooming were important to all of Eirrin, and those words of the girl's had hurt.

Too, he frequently held up and turned for his inspection the thick stout wrists Art and Midhir had ever spoken so highly of.

Slabs of pork? Lugh smite her backside!

Thankless blowze! The two slabs of pork lie on Lasrian's greasy floor!

With such thoughts to cheer him and aid in the regaining of his pride, the young weapon-man of Connacht returned to the camp.

During and after dinner among his fellow Blueshirts, as Leinster's soldiery were called, Cormac had opportunity to ask a number of questions. People loved to answer questions about their lands and their ways, he discovered swiftly, and were thereby made happy to ask none. Several of his queries he directed at Forgall, about the way he'd kicked that Pict on the beach. Forgall laughed and pointed out that when men were at the business of striving to do death on one another, it were manifestly stupid to be mindful of rules, and to confine oneself only to edge of blade. There was, he said rather archly, the sword's point. There was the buckler's edge, and its boss.

"And the feet," Cormac said; he knew that other.

Aye, Forgall said, and one did have to practice;

he'd seen Cormac kick that day, and lose his balance.

"Ye did! Ye said naught; methought I'd tumbled so foolishly unseen."

"Blood of the gods, man, ye were after saving my life!"

Later, Cormac eschewed the story-telling, the games of brandub and the dicing. Rather surreptitiously, he betook himself outside, and around behind the barracks where a bit of moonlight whitened the ground. There he spent many minutes alone in the gloom, swinging sword and shield and dancing about on one foot whilst kicking viciously with the other, at nothing. He fell more than once.

Then rain commenced to patter down, and left off his strange practice to join his fellows indoors. Had any asked, he'd have sworn he gave no thought to a flame-haired, fiery-tempered inn-girl. But then he'd told them other lies, too.

Chapter Eight:
The Flame-Lady

On the morning of the morrow, Forgall announced sword-training, and gave command into the hands of Bress. The captain, attired in his best, entered Carman for a conference. All knew the subject: the Cattle Tribute.

Each man in the barracks armoured and armed himself: their swords were of wood, wrapped again and again with wide strips of leather. Bress marched them to the training area. Complaints arose; the rain had fallen long and long last night, and the field was become little more than a bog. He who lost in these mock-combats would receive a mud-bath.

"So he will," Bress said. "Only the *losers,* though. It's weapon-men of Leinster we are, not children!"

"Why make mudpies then," someone grumbled.

When Bress demanded to know who had spoken, none would tell. Bress of the Long Arm chose three judges, and set to choosing teams of two. The men of each pair would fight each other. The judges announced mud-rules: ordinarily a man adjudged to have sustained a wound was required to continue his combat on his knees. In order that none might have to kneel in inch-deep mud- and worse- this day, the "wounded" would forfeit bucklers, which would certainly cripple them in ability.

Soon the field was noisy with the banging of swords of wood-and-leather on shields and helms and armour, along with the grunts and muttered curses of men and the sluck of booted feet drawing out of the mud. Too, there were splashes. Well to one side, the judges watched. Well to the other, Bress kept keen watch, that unfortunately good-looking, sorrel-haired man, a tall and haughty superb warrior all wished were not so striking—or so sour.

Cormac mac Art did not know that it was on himself Bress had fixed his gaze. The supposed Ulsterman took his opponent's slash on his buckler, turned the blade away, and struck a swift "killing blow." Thus was Donal the Slender embarrassed— though he did not fall, and was at least unmuddied.

Bress approached; then was time, he said, to *test* this great slayer of Picts from...wherever he said. "What is it your name is again, Slayer of Picts?"

Cormac was determined not to be provoked. "Partha mac Othna, Battle-leader."

"Ah. Well .. obviously this is an off-day for Donal." Bress looked about. "Eochu! Eochu Lightning-hand—hither man. Ye face, uh, Partha."

And with a little smile on his sensuous lips, Bress stepped back. Others watched, then, whilst Eochu came tramping sloshily toward Cormac, staring fixedly at him over his shield-rim. He stomped to a halt in battle-stance with his toes practically at Cormac's. "Ha!" Eochu cried, but none saw the new man twitch.

142

Cormac circled in silence, keeping his shield ever foreward and his sword ready, away from his body at the side. Eochu made attack; Cormac caught stroke and then backstroke on his shield and smote Eochu's helmet. The blow was pronounced not so hard as to have dented the steel, were the blade a real one. Nodding, Cormac slashed instantly upward at Eochu's face; Eochu's shield leapt up and in mid-stroke Cormac turned his elbow over and thrust over the shield. The blunt tip of the practice-sword struck Eochu's forehead even as Eochu's edge banged off Cormac's shield.

Eochu was adjudged dead—in truth, his brain was hardly his own for a time.

Bress called for Cethern of Dinn Rig. A groan arose from the others—and a minute later, adjudged wounded, Cethern had to forfeit his shield. Feeling naked, defenseless, he decided to attack violently in an attempt to take Cormac first. Cethern tried; Cethern "died." Bress's jaw twitched, so tightly did he clench his excellent white teeth. Men were cheering the foreign recruit. Slayer of Picts, indeed! Also "slayer" of Donal, and Eochu, and Cethern, and Bress's plans for his muddy defeat.

"A man of prowess," Bress said, through his teeth. Still the words sounded sneery, rather than complimentary. "Would ye be trying two at once, Man of Prowess?"

"NO!" That cry came from many throats.

From Cormac's: "Aye, Battle-leader. It's yourself commands, and a Blueshirt obeys!"

And so two men came, veterans slogging in mud, one in chain and the other in leather. Their fellows watched in stiff-lipped silence, tense, and accusing looks were shot at Bress mac Keth. He stood watching, eyebrows arched, chin high so that he seemed

143

to be gazing down upon the three men a dozen feet away.

Cormac met them both, and took four great loud strokes on his buckler and with his sword struck aside a fifth and took another on his shield ere he saw his opening and stabbed one of the twins so that the man were certainly dead, had the sword been of steel. Cormac did not pause to note the man's withdrawal, as no verdict of the judges was necessary; mac Art had still another foeman.

The youth was beginning to sweat. The sun brought a wriggly mist up from the water-soaked field. One blow the supposed Ulsterman took: was but a glancing one on his mailed upper arm, and all knew it would be hardly so much as a distraction to a man in combat.

"The boy swings like a farmer sowing grain, Fithil! What hinders ye, man?" This from Bress, in encouragement of Cormac's opponent.

Cormac and Fithil circled, staring each at the other over rim of shield. Fithil feinted; Cormac interposed shield and feinted in return; both men aborted their strokes and moved restlessly; staring, ever staring.

"What hinders him is Partha mac Othna!" someone called, and other voices arose in assent. One of those voices belonged to first-bested Donal, who felt not so bad now he'd seen the youth dispose of so many others.

Cormac was forced to backtrack swiftly. In the mud he nearly fell, and Fithil pressed in. His sword banged loudly on Cormac's buckler; Cormac's blade rapped as loudly on Fithil's left thigh. Adjudged crippled, Fithil would on better terrain have sunk to his knees. Amud, he discarded his shield and crouched low.

144

"Stick the boy in the stones, Fithil!"

To that encouraging cry from another partisan Bress added, "If he has any!"

"Together the two of ye might have four!" someone else bellowed at Bress.

"If the Ulsterman has three!" And great laughter arose.

Cormac grinned; Fithil grinned; Fithil risked all in a long lunge. Cormac had to leap to avoid that drive at his legs. He came down with a splash—and a ringing stroke of his sword atop Fithil's unadorned helmet. There could be no doubt of the efficacy of that blow; Fithil was "dead."

This besting of two opponents at once upset Bress, who had chosen two fine weapon-men to teach the Ulsterish boy a lesson. They had failed him. It appeared that but one man in Leinster could teach that lesson: taking Fithil's sword of leather-wrapped wood, Bress advanced on the dark young recruit. Again a silence moved over the gathering, though a few men groaned. Cormac heard some of the murmurs; Bress mac Keth was Champion of Leinster!

Aye, and in seconds Cormac knew that here was a match; Bress was beyond merely good. Too, the man had much reach on him. When Cormac was at the length of his own sword and arm, Bress was still dangerous, able to inflict the deadly wound, because of the length of his arms.

"Many men have this or that skill or gift of the gods on their side," Midhir mac Fionn had told him, more than once, for Midhir had seldom said anything meaningful only once. "Discover that. Respect that. And then seek to discover what weakness he has that works against him, for I have seen no more than five or six weapon-men in all

145

my days who had not some weakness for the exploiting."

Cormac sought, while with Bress mac Keth he fought a different sort of match; the match of two who were better than good, and knew it, and respected each the other's ability. They took their time, ever shifting, feinting, circling, testing, side-stepping, essaying strokes that were hastily blocked and as hastily aborted while the attacker covered himself. Each tried using his swift-shifting eyes to lie about where he intended to strike; neither succeeded, for the other recognized the strategem in time. The sound of leather-wrapped wood on shield boomed and rolled out across the muddy field. All about them stood staring men, their booted feet invisible in mud so that all appeared to stand on stumps. And there was much murmuring, though it was very quiet.

Cormac attacked, erred, and caught a stroke to the shoulder that was adjudged wounding. Indeed, he felt it through padded coat and mail. Unhappily, he was told he could use his buckler no longer. Cormac loosed it and sent the round shield spinning as though it weighed much less than its fifteen pounds; one man ducked, another tried to catch it, and a third succeeded. The second nursed a back-bent finger.

Shield-less, Cormac gazed into the grinning face of Bress Long-arm.

Already the youth had noted that Bress did not fight as Forgall did, for Bress was excellent, and longer of arm; he was proud to use sword alone. *Pride. And temper. Aye.* Cormac's youthful eyes narrowed to slits and his brain raced.

Now, against an unshielded opponent, Bress succumbed to over-confidence: pride in ability. He came boring in, covering himself well while he loosed a flurry of short strokes.

With his own sword Cormac batted away one, then two and then three cuts. Realization was on him that he'd not be allowed to attack; Bress would keep him busy using sword as defense only, and certainly find the opening to strike a killing blow. Accordingly Cormac bashed away a short cut with all his might, so that his arm shivered with the impact. He came back high with his own blade, drawing Bress's shield up—and whipped out a foot to kick Bress in the shin.

Bress lurched. His right foot skidded in the mud. The edge of his padded wooden blade, hard-swung, banged the side of Cormac's helm—and further unbalanced the champion. Bress Long-arm fell into the mud with a great splash that spattered Cormac as high as his chin. He did not notice; his head rang from what he knew was a killing blow.

All about Bress and the youth standing over him lofted whoops of laughter. Bress's great glower soon evaporated that noise. A judge's voice called out: Partha mac Othna was dead of a cloven head, with helmet-steel in his brain.

"Over-ruled!" Bress bawled, from the muck. "Was the flat of my blade only!"

Cormac would have seen grins and winks directed his way, but he was watching his downed opponent. *Pride and anger,* Cormac mused. *Those are Bress's weaknesses. I'll be remembering. But . . . now he wants me not "dead." He belies his own stroke, so that he may rise and tumble me into this sludge!*

He gave Bress that opportunity. Cormac made no move to attack the downed man who, in an effort to rise, slipped and splashed down anew. Cormac banged his blade against his own chest. All knew

147

he could have struck Bress then, and won, in accord with Bress's own altered rules. And Bress knew. It was enough. Backing two paces, Cormac assumed a position of readiness, though he bore no shield. He waited.

Bress began to come up, mud dripping from him. He was enraged and yet forced to take care lest he slip and fall anew. Every man stood watching as if ensorceled. Bress Big-foot would make much more of this . . .

Forgall's shout made every man jerk.

"Ho, what a fight! What a well-matched pair these be! I was telling you, Bress! Only yourself could have come to my aid a few days agone the way Partha did!"

Forgall came up grinning, holding up his dress *plaide* from the mud. His wide-open face showed only good cheer and delight. "But—it's yourself was to be teacher this day, Bress. It seems the student has been at the giving of lessons!"

Hearty laughter leaped up all about and provided the wings on which tension fled. Bress muttered a few words about having slipped in the mud.

"I saw," Forgall said smiling, looking fondly from Bress to Cormac and back.

"In truth was Bress struck the blows," Cormac said. "He both wounded me and, in my thinking, slew me."

"Och!" Forgall cried in delight. "What a pair of weapon-men!"

Bress did not acknowledge Cormac's kind words. Nor dared he fault the recruit on his foot use. Was fair, and Forgall's way of fighting, he offsetting his short-waistedness by such means; was the sensible way.

A rather startled Cormac tried mentally to

examine his sudden revelation. Why, Forgall was more ingenuous than he! Had Forgall been Bress he'd have laughed; Forgall had no intention of rubbing salt into Bress's figurative wounds with his words of teacher and student, for the captain was a good-natured weapon-man who respected those of equal and superior skill. To Forgall, it must be hardly conceivable that such as Bress and Partha did not love each the other.

Then, thinking on that, Cormac mac Art glanced up as a mucky Bress mac Keth slogged away, and the youth caught the other's darkly vengeful look.

To Forgall, was all a game; he loved fighting, even to the death that day with the Picts. To Bress: exaltation of another was not to be tolerated—nor was defeat or minor humiliation. Cormac resolved to think hard on both men, and to attempt to mould himself accordingly.

Forgall took up a comanding position and shouted his news.

"On the morrow we march northward, for the Boruma time is upon us. The victors in to-day's little combats are at their leave- to clean up and betake themselves wheresoever they will . . . you who won not must practice the more. For it's your very lives are at stake, boys. Bress . . . Battle-leader . . . would ye be remaining with them?"

The request was that, a request and ultra-politely made; obviously Bress could not refuse. He nodded.

Cormac and those others who'd won their encounters returned to the barracks. Rather more than one of his fellows let him know how they had loved seeing Bress Lamfhada mac Keth put into his place: the mire. Cormac accepted their accolades in good fellowship and kept silent his total agreement.

149

He was nervous and thoughtful while he stripped and cleansed himself for he was much bespattered. Bad enow that Bress had disliked him on sight. Now the dislike had loped into a feeling beyond animosity.

After washing, Cormac pulled on leggings of white linen. Over them he drew the blue tunic Lugaid the Fox was happy to lend him, and he drew his boots up over his tight *braecs*. Next came the vest of black leather with its shoulder-broadening guards for upper arms and shoulders, and about his waist he buckled his weapon-belt, without sword or scabbard. He took a dagger of course, sheathed at his hip, but yesterday's experience told him he'd be better off in Carman without a sword. He might draw it in anger. As for the dagger: that was after all an eating utensil.

Men were waiting for him; they wanted the suddenly-popular foreigner as part of their group.

Cormac remembered his desire to have his hair Leinsterishly trimmed, and made mention of it.

"Och, Partha! If ye'd but said that afore; it's I cut the hair of half the men here, and for a trifle. But now..."

Cormac nodded. "Perhaps this evening."

"Absolutely! But come—let us go and find a good inn and empty its larder!"

The group of full dozen weapon-men, swaggering for they'd won this leave, left the camp. They went happily and rather boisterously along the road to Leinster's gate, keeping to the grass alongside; the road was muddy and they'd had enough of that. A carter with loose red-grey hair smiled on them, and his youngish son and his daughter—who was older—turned and stared large-eyed at these fine heroes of King Ulad. Each received a wink or three; the boy

150

grinned, assuming they were for him.

Just inside the gate sat a young slender fellow, red of hair and blue of eye. He was covered in a shapeless and threadbare mantle drawn on over a once-red tunic faded to the colour of dying red clover. In his hands a lute; on his lips a song. The words included *mesca* and *mocci*.

With a smile, Cormac went to him.

"A good tune, minstrel! Have you a name?"

"Most likely. An ye go to the next cross-street and turn by your right hand—not left, right—and walk past three crossings, ye'll want to be asking someone for the Inn of the Flame Lady."

"All this I'll be wanting to do? And why?"

"A certain caustic maid we both know, and her no street-slut, has desire to see yourself again, foreigner. Whence come ye?"

"Ulster; Partha mac Othna my name." Cormac's heartbeat had speeded and the sun seemed to have grown warmer. "Ye mean—"

"I mean that though it makes me none too happy and she knows it, it's herself would have been here for all to gawp at and remark upon, did I not agree to send ye along."

"Partha!" that from one of the other waiting Blueshirts.

He half-turned waved a hand. "Go on with ye, all. I'll not be going your way; it's business this minstrel and I have."

"And him *male!*" This was followed by laughter.

"He has a sister," Cormac called, and that brought laughter and hoots, remarks and a whistle along with a stallionish whinny. Then off the others went, not without Lugaid the Fox's asking whether *she* had a sister. Cormac turned back to the minstrel. "What is she to yourself, minstrel?"

151

"One I hold in esteem," the young redhead said very seriously, and Cormac heard warning and admonition. "We are not, however, lovers."

"I hear ye. It's in your debt I am."

"Partha: you are. Begone; ye be not good enough to keep her waiting."

That grated sufficiently for Cormac to tarry: "My father commands a stronghold rath for Ulster's king, and is of clan-na Morna."

The nameless minstrel snorted. "In truth," he said, and it was neither a statement nor a question but an entirely neutral tone, unimpressed.

Cormac started away. "Ah—friend minstrel. How is she named?"

"Breotigernd," the minstrel said, and Cormac laughed; the name was the same as that of the inn: Flame-lady.

"What else!" he called and went happily the way he'd been bidden.

Soon he was aware of why the minstrel had repeated that he was not to go left; that way he'd gone yesterday. The street to the right led him into better environs. After he'd made three crossings of other streets, he asked directions to the *bruidean* called Breotigernd. The flower-pedlar pointed, and Cormac sadly told her he had naught with which to buy a blossom. Then he turned leftward and walked past an armourer's and meat-seller's. The third building was hung with a yellow sign emblazoned with a stylized red flame outlining a naked woman. Cormac entered.

He was disappointed. Of Flame Lady's nine patrons, none was the girl of the Blue Shamrock; indeed, none was female. The brughaid came to him, fast as he of the Blue Shamrock. Far from sure of himself or what he was doing, Cormac quietly asked a question. The innkeeper became visibly happier and more hospitable.

The lady awaited in a privy chamber behind the tap-room, he said, and led Cormac thither. The wary youth entered.

Cormac was astonished. Here was a board laid out with savoury viands and not ale but good mead. And here waited she, in a green gown cut closely to her slender body, and hardly so lowly as her attire of the previous day

She smiled. "Close your mouth, huge boy. Even though flies are not yet abuzz in Carman, ye might dehydrate your tongue."

"I . . . it's the same I am as on yester day, and my hair the same. What . . . what means all this?"

"It means we eat together. It means I make apology for my display of temper at that inn of *mesca* and *mocci*, and that I thank your fine strapping self for coming to my rescue as though I were a lady. And it means I bid ye be joining me."

Cormac shook his head in incomprehension. "And . . . who else?"

"None other! And would ye be shutting the door? I've no fear on me of yourself, huge boy. Look here, where we met on yester day a girl must be known to be able to take care of herself. I showed that. Now—none will join us here. I but remembered your great height and the thickness of your arms, and made sure there'd be food aplenty. What have ye been at since last I saw ye?" With a flash of white arms, she poured mead gurgling into a jack, which she extended.

"Fighting."

"I'd not be doubting it!"

Cormac laughed. He took the jack, made a tiny bow, and drank off half its contents. "This is good!"

"So I thought, when I tasted it for us. Fighting. And winning, o'course."

"Aye. But this was practice—the Royal Army's practice," he added, pridefully. "Most of the morning. Six men I was made to face, for one in command has no love for me."

"Six men *at once?*"

"Singly. Two at once. In the mud."

"Ah. Do sit down. Mightn't I be persuading ye to remove the weapon-belt and leather jack? It is most handsome—but the leather *creaks* so. New?"

"New." *Gods of my fathers, but she's so sure of herself, so full of sophistication! It's a buffoon I am indeed.* And he drained his cup.

"More?"

"Aye."

"There. My name isn't really Flame-Lady."

"It's what I'll be calling ye."

"Then ye've no need of knowing my real name!

"What is it?"

She laughed. "Aha!" she cried, and he knew he'd been successfully teased. "Aine. And do you have a name?"

He was surprised to discover he wanted to tell her his real name; he did not.

"Partha," she repeated. "A good enough name; I know it or not. Ulster and Leinster are hardly neighbors."

"Strange that names should be so different though, betwixt kingdoms, isn't it?" He laid aside his weapon belt. "Now 'aine' is in use all over Errin, surely."

She shrugged. And the jiggle that movement brought about within her bodice made his head go light while warmth came upon him. She was the

154

most attractive member of her sex he'd ever been with. Indeed, he'd been alone with none, not this way . . . none under twoscore years of age, at any rate.

"Aye, it's such a common name," she said. "It's Partha I'd rather be."

Cormac laughed. "Or Drolleen?"

Aine looked unpleasant, then smiled, then laughed; the sound, he thought, was that of a happy brook in the hills. "Do see that ye never call me that. Or filly, either!"

"Memory will be on me till the end of my days, Flame-lady; I make vow by the gods my people's people swear by. Aine. Aine. It is a pretty sound. Ye be of Carman?"

No, she told him, she was a merchant's daughter from Ailenn, come down to Carman with her father for goods. They talked of that, and of trading,, and they ate, and talked too of names, and springtime, and Carman, and other matters. She was bored with this self-conscious capital city, Aine told him; she preferred her Ailenn. When she asked about him, he mixed truth with necessary lies and made all as sketchy as possible. She filled his mug a third time and he told her that he was far ahead in the quaffing. She pointed out that he was much bigger—and then drank off hers and filled her cup and drank most of that, and filled it to the brim again. How was it no green eyes he'd seen afore had been so beautiful, so . . . green; no red hair so firelike, so beautiful?

They compared ages. She claimed to sixteen years. So did he, shy a month. Ah, he said, lifting his cup, an *older woman*! And he but a poor foreign-boy all alone in the great city. And they laughed, and drank.

"And why did Othna's son Partha leave Ulster and travel even across Meath, all the way down to Leinster?"

"Oh . . . a matter of a woman," he said, with an airy wave of his hand.

They smiled, exchanging looks; they drank. She leaned close with her eyes on his, and Cormac, staggering at the brink of those green wells, asked why she'd been in such a place as the Blue Shamrock.

Looking suddenly not happy with him, Aine straightened. "I told ye. Boredom's one me here, with my father ever busy at the dickering. I . . . wander."

"The minstrel?"

"A friend I met."

"And I?"

"A friend I met. A good friend."

"A better friend?"

"Greedy Partha! O'course. It's not the bard for whom I took room and so much food—and mead. Good, isn't it."

"It is! It . . . truth to tell . . ."

"I know! Me too: lightheaded! Well, it makes kissing easier, doesn't it?"

It did.

It did again. And even again, and a fourth time. Her mouth was like chestnuts in winter before the fire; he could not stop with but a taste.

"I was set to hurl something at you," she said softly, nestling.

"What did I do, dairlin' girl?"

"It is what you did not, oaf!"

He squeezed her slim waist, and his thumb wandered high. "Oaf, is it?"

"Ah! Oww—no no—dairlin' boy, Partha, *mo chroi* . . . mmm . . . my dairlin' boy . . ."

156

When he left later he knew that he was indeed a man, and more than mead went to Cormac's head, and he walked tall and aswagger through Carman, and proved his maleness if not his manhood with his thought: *Well, after all, it's a weapon-man of the king I am, and her but a pedlar's daughter—who wanted me.*

Chapter Nine:
On the Plain of Sorrow

The tramp of men shook the air, mingled with the lowing of kine, the creak of laden waggons, and the occasional whinny of a dray-horse. Northward marched the armed men of Leinster, toward a destination between Ailenn and Atha Cliath, up near the Meathish border. The marching men in their sleeved tunics of Leinster blue comprised a *catha*, a battle force three thousand strong. With them moved like a number of cattle, and creaking, rattling wains laden with treasure. From other areas of the kingdom other men marched, herding more lowing *boru*.

Up the Slaigne to its joining with the Bann they tramped, and followed the Bann northward to its source, and still they trekked toward the north.

Och, Leinster! Ochone! O my grief!

All knew that Meathish forces were marching southward to meet them at the border. There would they claim the tribute-under-duress, the bitter legacy of men long, long in the ground and nigh forgotten.

157

All knew too that messengers had carried strong words from the high house of Ulad of Leinster to that of Lugaid on Tara Hill, and back had come words no less strong. King Ulad had made himself plain. The High-king, he decreed, "in his weening arrogance and desire for 'tribute' the reason for which he remembers not, but demands only in greed." And Meath would not chew so great a slice of Leinster without having to bite it off.

Tradition. Neither Leinster nor Meath wanted war. There would not be war. Yet there must be these demands, the reticence, the annual negotiations, the threats—and finally the pitched battle at the border on Magh na-Broin; the Plain of Sorrow. This, annually, for Leinster's honour. And sure, was blood that fed honour, time out of mind.

Ulad's General Fergus Buadach and his two elder sons had ridden up to Ailenn already. There they awaited the troops, slowed both by their baggage and by the animals they accompanied.

The trek north was an easy one. Even the weather was kind to the troop, if the weather of wet, misty Eirrin could ever be said to be kind. To the people they passed they made a great pageant, so that the Blueshirts marched nearly every yard with an audience of russet-clad farmers.

About them the heather was rising, and the bilberry, and fields were sown with grain. Already ferns and low, woody shrubs were renewing themselves, in their annual attempt to impart a nigh-subtropical aspect to much of the Emerald Isle. Clearly visible were the spurs and corries of distant hills. The sky had left off its sullen brooding to smile on eastern Eirrin—and nowhere on all that isle could a man stand and not see hills. Cromlechs and the black of springfires crowned the hilltops, and now and again a druid of the Old Faith or a priest of the New could be seen staring, staring in silence, knowing the mission of these marching men and wishing it were not so.

Round about children stared, too, close to the shade of thatched rooves from the corners of which hung the stones that anchored them in place. Tramping men skirted the bogs and swamps that splotched green-gold Eirrin with brown, and smiled at the sweet voice of the cuckoo. On the second day they passed through grass and farm-lands, where charlocks and artichokes freely grew, and the needly junipers valued for their savoury berries and fragrant wood. Wild ducks called, and the order was passed that they were not to be molested, this early in the year.

Truag nuin! Sad evil!

Five thousand kine. Five thousand hogs. A like number of good cloaks and brazen vessels of silver. As to the silver a concession had been made; nevertheless a well-guarded wain carried two hundred pounds. The wealth of Leinster. *Ochone!*

Northward they bore it, and Cormac mac Art marched brooding as though a Leinsterman born. He thought too of Aine, his flame-lady with her hair like gold and bronze and rowan-berries, those eyes green as grass in May-time under their darkened brows; the taste of her lips, redolent of honey and herbs and her own sweet breath. Cormac brooded, and he mooned.

Truag nuin, heavy-laden Leinster! Ochone and Ochon a righ!

They reached their destination, and already they were sick of cattle and pigs.

Only a camp they had, on Magh na-Broin, where men traded with local citizens and entrepreneurs for food and drink. Within the hour kine and swine were raising a stench. All very well to go forth in armour and armed, mayhap to gain honour, mayhap with the woundy blow or death itself. But to have to nursemaid all these noisy, stinking animals as well . . . *Ochon a righ!*

Fergus the Battle-winner called in his commanders and captains for a great conference. Forgall went out from the camp, leaving Bress in command of his Fifty, with his instructions: stay in place; prepare the *Coichte* as other Fifties were being readied, to meet the enemy. Two men of each *Coichte* were to remain here, with the drovers and churls, to guard hogs and cows.

Word came then, and it was good. Leinstermen cheered and called Meathmen weak: a last-minute concession by the High-king excused his "brother-king and fellow sons of Eirrin" from the porcine portion of the tribute, and half the measure of silver, already reduced.

With scales and great care, men measured out half the thirty-two hundred ounces of good silver. Then they reloaded, and hogs and wagons moved southward. This lest Lugaid's mind be changed still again, for in truth 'twas changeable as the winds that blew the clouds overhead so willy-nilly that often the land itself seemed to move.

No man but was glad to see those stinking pigs go.

Bress made his preparations. Bress made his choices. The barber Cond he would leave to mind the camp—and Partha mac Othna. Partha who was Cormac understood what had motivated Bress to such a decision; leaving behind his best fighting man! Cormac chafed . . . and obeyed without comment, a good and loyal weapon-man of Leinster.

Anger was hot in him nevertheless, and he knew that one day he and Bress the contemner must needs settle this cloud between them. A wonder the arrogant Big-foot hadn't sent Cormac forward among the foremost men, in hopes he'd be slain.

"Be sure he considered that," Cond said, as he and Cormac commiserated. "But there is also the possibility that ye might be slaying so many Meath-men it's a hero ye'd be. That, Partha, would outweigh the other in Bress's mind."

Cormac tried not to hope for the death of Bress mac Keth.

And so the troops marched out, less than a hundred having set out back toward Carman with the pigs and silver. A hundred and forty-eight remained with the herdsmen. A hundred and forty-eight weapon-men become cowherds.

For two days Cormac was but a churl, a *buachall* or *bachlach*. He chafed with the bored men of the other companies at guarding stupid stinking beasts—against naught. All were aware that northward their fellows were doing battle with the Meathish force. Cormac hated the inactivity and despised the lowliness of his task. More than restless, he had much company in his disquiet.

The Plain of Sorrow, indeed!

And then on the second night, whilst he was at the "guarding" of silent cattle while most of the others slept, he twitched into alertness. The youth sat with his back against a tall old oak wrapped against the night-chill in its leafy hood. Cormac stared, blinked, stared again. At first he saw only the white hair and beard, silvered by the moon-light. They appeared to float, eerily riding the air several feet above the ground. Cormac's skin writhed with horripilation as he pounced to his feet,

161

spear at the ready.

Then he saw that here was no sorcery; his visitor's body had merely been invisible in the darkness, for it was swathed in a dark green robe. A woods-green robe; a druid's robe.

Out of the darkness came Sualtim Fodla. A new prickling assailed Cormac, though not in fear; he assumed he was witness to another vision, another druidic Sending.

Surely Sualtim could not be here, a Connachtish druid of considerable age in Leinster just below Meath's border. Far and far from Connacht—and far, Cormac thought with some embarrassment, from Airgialla, where he and his old tutor had agreed he'd go.

And then he heard the faint snap of a twig from the great oak that shadowed them both even from moonlight. That told Cormac that the druid was indeed come here, in the flesh.

Cormac was more than surprised. His old *fithithir* had found him, come to him as if directly, though he was afield in the night. And after Cormac had deliberately deceived him—or so the youth had thought—lest even Sualtim too be traitor!

"You did well, my boy." The druid spoke very quietly. "You sought to deceive even me."

Cormac gnawed his lower lip. He could not meet those knowing eyes. He remembered having warned Sualtim against calling him "boy"—and he said nothing.

"I understand," Sualtim told him, just as quietly; he was but a stride away, now, and there he halted. "So. North you rode, and then swung east . . . lost all to bandits in the forests . . . saved a Leinsterish war-leader and have joined his force . . . and you're after couching your first woman . . . or are after

162

being bedded by her! So now it's a man ye be in all way . . . Partha mac Othna na Ulaid!"

Astonishment mingled with chagrin in Cormac. Best he say nothing, he decided. He who'd thought himself so much the man but moments agone now felt much the boy, in the presence of him who'd been his tutor so long—and who seemed to know all things, impossible or no.

"Look up, son of your father. Give listen. I have been busy; I have knowledge to share. Think you I came so far only to tell you what you already know?"

Cormac looked up then, sheepishly. Sualtim looked naught but friendly, rather like a proudly doting parent. Then a cloud came onto his face:

"Aengus mac Domnail . . . was in fact Eoin mac Gulbain, my b—Partha. Aye: son of that same Lord Gulban your father replaced as *toisech* in Rath Glondarth. Reasoning and reasonable or no, Eoin held my lord Art responsible for the fall of his father and the ruin of his family."

"Aengus . . . Eoin . . . Gulban's son . . . "

"It's little time I have, Cormac. Eoin sought revenge then, and was inhumanly patient in his waiting for the taking of his dark vengeance. Fault him not in this, C—Partha." Sualtim glanced around; there was only the darkness, shot with snores. "He felt he was right, and justified; he died feeling that he had done vengeance for his father."

Cormac's lips were tightly compressed. Not fault the man who'd slain his father?

I wish Aengus were alive, that I might slay him! Cormac was not so calmly reasoning an animal as Sualtim; Cormac had not the benefit of time in this life.

"Yet methinks another was behind Eoin, Cormac.

163

A priest of the New Faith! A man there is named Milchu—he professes the peaceful mouthings of Iosa Chriost but serves *demains*; mayhap the Christians' 'Devil' himself! Aye . . . and now I'm after learning that Milchu has the ear of the High-king himself."

"The . . . *ard-Righ*!"

Sualtim nodded. "Milchu is surely his agent and his spy."

"Mentor . . . ye—ye be thinking was the High-king's own hand in my father's murder?"

"Cormac . . . I am. It is not unknown that Lugaid mac Laegair our own High-king held no love for Art, on account of his popularity . . . and on account of the honoured name your father put on yourself." Sualtim lifted a staying hand against Cormac's speaking. "Yet no surety is on me, Cormac. It's the answer to that question I now seek. It's north I go. Milchu is said to be on a mission to the northern kingdoms. There will I seek out that priest, *cairnech* of the New Faith or no, and learn what we must needs know."

In silence, Cormac mac Art stared at nothing while he pondered the implications of this revelation. A priest of the New Faith! The High-king! So swiftly did his mind plunge into the ugly tangle that the sound of the old man's voice caused him to jerk.

"Cormac . . . if this surmising of mine gain the seal of truth, it were best that you put from your head any thought of blood-feud, lad."

Eyes grim as a wolf's stared at the druid from the dark, lined face. Grey as sword steel, those eyes were learning to be just as implacably hard.

Sualtim made a gesture that was nigh to pleading. *"Think!"* Far better ye go and present your case to

the Kings Assembled at Feis-mor come fall ...
would be a greater shame and dishonour on
Lugaid!"

The grey eyes stared. The face remained grim,
impassive—and thoughtful. Only the mouth moved:
"Aye—"

"I will find out," Sualtim said. "And now I must
leave. Ere there can be any thought of accusation,
it's firm evidence we must have."

"The High-king," Cormac mumbled, and then
seemed to emerge from a trance. "Oh—no, mentor,
remain ye here and rest. At least till dawn—"

Sualtim shook his head. "It's no rest there'll be
here, Cormac. Leinster fares not well against
Meath. Soon will come the men of the High-king,
to claim the Boruma, and no one to be the better of
it to the end of life and time."

While Cormac stared, stunned by shock upon
shock, the druid turned and started into the night.
At the edge of the tree's shadow, he turned back.

"My b—Cormac. Remember well all those things
I was so at pains to teach you. For it's knowledge
will serve ye, and consideration. A sharp mind will
often win out where a sword-arm would fail, or but
complicate matters and bring peril. Remember
ever that the opinion of none is so important as
your own, where it concerns yourself. Just . . . just
ever seek the use of the brain, son of Art, before
you go reaching for the blade."

Surprisingly, Sualtim smiled. "And now put worry
from you, *weapon-man*. When it comes your turn
to sleep, do, even if it requires *glasreng-blaith*."

Cormac watched the white hair above the green
robe until he saw only the hair, and then his long-
time mentor was swallowed up by the night.
Thinking *brain and blade, brain then blade—
brain rather than blade?* Cormac was left alone

165

with too many thoughts. He stepped back against the tree, hearing the sound of a little breeze humming mournfully over the Plain of Sorrow. Was a lonely wind, moaning about the lone Connachtman in Leinster.

He stared into the darkness and saw nothing. *Aye,* he *mused, alone and lonely. It's Cormac* n-Aenfher *I am; Cormac the Lonely*!

Chapter Ten:
The Cattle-Raid of Leinster

The grass was still bejeweled with dew when Forgall returned with what remained of his force. Every eye among them was dulled by the cold of defeat and dismay. The battle had been a shield-splitter and Magh Broin was a plain the ravens would long be croaking over.

A full score of Forgall's men had been slain, and but eleven of the total remained unscathed. On them all was the sour taste of defeat—and weariness, to the bone. They came in like so many hounds who had tracked the quarry long and long, and had lost it. For Leinstermen in the matter of Boruma, victory and honour were elusive quarry indeed.

Shocked at how few returned, shocked at those who did not return, Cormac and Cond heard the order that went out to all the other Fifties, to all the army. The tribute was to be delivered.

Those who had fought remained in camp while those who had been herdsmen continued, now moving the cattle and the wains containing the other portions of the tribute up northward. The Leinsterish force was most heavy of heart and hardly swift in the performing of that unwelcome task. Without spirit in eyes or gait, Cormac and the others herded the livestock across a plain become a lake of blood.

A great greyed Ogham stone marked Meath's southern frontier. There, sore longing to draw steel and be men though it meant their deaths, the men of Leinster watched while the jubilant Meathmen took possession of cows fatted on Leinster's good grass.

Cormac stared deep in thought on the ways of men. He stared at two, for there side by side stood General Fergus of Leinster and Lord Conor, the High-king's cousin and commander of his force.

Would be a great shame on me, Cormac thought, *not to stand well apart from that man who commanded the slayers of my comrades The ways of nations of men are more strange than those of any man, and the ways of generals and kings are stranger still!*

By this little battle, he mused, all was settled. All? What? The battle was hardly war though to mothers and wives and sweehearts of dead men it was hardly so minor an encounter. How was anything settled by such? What could a limited war prove? Why then war at all, with boundaries around it, with rules and less than a total commitement?

And the youth of Connacht thought, for the first but not the last time: *Kings are fools, and nations of men greater fools, to do the bidding of such men and be commanded by their pettiness—and to die for their whims.*

And then the Boruma was in Meathish hands.

Meathmen went to their camp with the noisy

enthusiasm born of the joy of battle-winning. Leinstermen turned and tramped silently back to their encampment. Such a vast herd of cattle was not easily driven, and the sun was nigh to the horizon when they reached camp once more.

Spirits around the campfires that night could not have been lower. Though it was not cold, men wrapped their bodies in their cloaks and their minds in cloaks of dark thoughts. Among them, near Forgall, Cormac sat and pondered. Only partway he heard the Captain of Fifty—which was fifty no longer—swear by the blood of the gods, and bemoan the fact that once more had Meath set the bloody crown of defeat on proud Leinster.

"My grief! Once— oh but once in my life would I fain see Leinster prevail!" And Forgall kicked out at a burning log, so that sparks leaped up in spots of bright yellow and ruddy gold. And Cormac sat and pondered.

"As fresh malt is ground in the mill, so shall Meath one day be ground by the steel of Leinster!" So spoke Bress of the Long Arm, for he bore but a scratch on his sword-arm, and that not deep.

No, Cormac thought, *not with steel. It's never with the sword that Leinster will best Meath!*

"Och," groaned Cas mac Con, wearing an ugly wound that would scar his face and likely draw the left corner of his mouth, "weariness is on me like a—a cloak of wet woollen . . . but how can a man sleep on such a night?"

"How can *any* of us sleep?" This from Cond the Hair-trimmer, who had not fought.

And Cormac sat and pondered, and thought of battle, and honour, and kings, and generals and of sleep, and he looked round about him with dull eyes. He gazed, hardly seeing, on the squat plants that the cows had refused to eat. And he blinked. He stiffened, and blinked again, and there was a light in his eyes.

Into his mind came the final words of Sualtim Fodla, spoken less than twenty-four hours agone. Why aye, Cormac recognized that plant Sualtim had called *bläsreng-blath*: boar-blossom. Of old had Sualtim told him of it. Those furry leaves, when chewed or crushed for their mucousy juice, were used by the druids and the better leeches—to induce sleep! A man could undergo surgery and not . . .

An idea circled about at the perimeter of Cormac's mind, and nipped teasingly in the manner of a dog.

The brain; use the brain when the sword fails . . .

The nipping dog could not breach the defenses. What seemed an idea could not pierce into his mind. Surrounded by forlorn men who stared drearily into their fires, Cormac wrestled with his own brain.

"Ale!" Forgall called, without enthusiasm. "Ale, that I may drink to forgetfulness of disgrace and sorrow for comrades done to death."

"Aye—ale!"

Ale!

In the darkness a wounded man groaned. Then did Cormac gasp, for he knew that man could be helped a bit or eased at least, by chewing leaves of boar-blossom . . . or drinking ale into which their juice had been pressed . . .

Cormac mac Art's eyes snapped wide. With a lurch, he was up and at Forgall's side. The youth bent. He murmured to his captain. Few men so much as glanced that way, to see the face of their leader show puzzlement . . . and then seem to take

169

on a glow of happiness. Of a sudden he struck grinning at Cormac's leg, clutched a leathered ankle.

"It's no proper or decent notion ye've had, Partha, nor yet a one for the consideration of sane men. But this is no sane day, and what we've done be not the deeds of sane or proper men. And sure your idea's one that warms a heart heavy within me ... and soothes the aches of wounds put on us by Meathish swords and taunts!"

He looked into Cormac's face, and their eyes flashed.

As though well rested, Forgall sprang up.

"Ale! ALE!" he bellowed. "Casks and casks of ale, lads, and hie—put bounce in your step!"

Darkness lay on the Plain of Sorrow, and through it rattled a cart behind two plodding horses with drooping heads. The cart creaked under burden: a full score stout casks that sloshed with liquid sounds. Atop the cart, hunched, sat two peasants roughly clad in their russet and dirty leathers and mist-hoods.

The rising of a drepanoid moon saw them approaching a broad cluster of campfires, just north of Leinster's northern border. Not the main encampment of the Meathish army this, but that special space apart from it where the stenchy tribute was under guard. Well away from the sprawling encampment of the High-king's troops it was, that the nostrils of triumphant soldiery might be spared animal odours and night-noises.

A sentry came abruptly alive. He challenged; the carters halted their dray-breasts. The sentry half turned to call to his superior. That man came, stared, frowned, set his fists against his hips, and stared on.

"What means this? Who be ye? What *is* this load?"

"We be but two good honest men, Captain your worthiness," one of the carters said, adding swiftly, "and us unarmed! 'Tis the cart of our master. We would but pass, Captain. It's good honest men we be, but honest peasants, and—"

"Yes, yes, and unarmed, as if we'd be fearing ye two if ye bore axes and swords both. And why would ye be passing along here at this hour, two good honest men?"

"We . . . we're to be paid well by an honourable innkeeper but a halfscore or so miles hence, good Captain, up beyond yourself. Mightn't we be passing, Captain? We be no army, to be rousing noble well-armed weapon-men such as yourself."

"Ah-huh. An innkeeper, eh?" The captain's eyes seemed to gleam, though the moonlight scarce touched them. "And what is it ye be fetching to a moneygrubbing brughaid but a halfscore or so miles hence, eh, eh? Brion . . . go ye and rap on one or two of those interesting kegs."

"Oh, oh captain," one of the peasants nervously began, while the soldier was pacing forward, to the side of the cart.

Thump, went his spear-haft against a wooden cask, and the sound that returned was not from hollowness. Catching his spear-butt at the edge of that keg, he rocked it.

Slosh.

"Ale!" The Meathish captain's voice was as of one in awe in the presence of the very gods. "Ale, by Lugh's cup!"

"Well," the cart's driver said, "ah . . ."

"Ale!"

"Ah . . . well . . . aye, Captain." And hurriedly, "Mightn't we be passing now, Captain sir your worthiness?"

"Ha! Not without paying the toll! It's war we've had this day, man, and your innkeeper untouched by it—why had we failed in our steadfast duty, his inn might have been invaded by barbarians and who knows what damage done? Brion—*tap that keg!*"

And Brion did. And the dark liquid came spilling forth, gurgling happily like a mountain brook. And the captain, his eyes fair emitting sparks now, used his helmet to catch some, so that it frothed up golden foam in the steel pot. And the captain drank.

"How . . . how tastes it?" This from Brion the sentry, with hope.

"Like sweat," muttered one of the carters, and his companion introduced an elbow to his ribs.

"Ha! *Good!* Good, by Crom's beard. It's ale— Good ale! Not our pale stuff," the delighted captain cried out. "It's *Leinster's* good ale this be!"

"Wh—why yes, Captain, aye your worthiness, the innkeeper our lord's always wont to say there's no comparing Meathish ale to this. He imports this for Meath, Captain, ye see, your worship. Might we be going on along our honest way now ye've quenched your thirst, good Captain?"

The sentry muttered to his superior. The captain nodded, with exuberance. His teeth flashed in a grin.

"So your innkeeper says that, does he? Why, that's treason! And he's trafficking with the knavish people we've after fighting this very day. Och! For shame! I do fear me this load of ale is hereby declared contraband, my man, and confiscated—in the High-King's name!"

"The *High-king!*" The carter almost whispered, in his awe.

"Aye. Hoho! And why should not we be celebrating with the rest of the army, we those others are after turning into smelly-booted nursemaids to an army of cattle? Did not these swords spill Leinsterish blood as well and as redly as theirs?"

One of the two carters tensed and his knuckles went white on the fist gripping his horse's reins. His companion of the sword-grey eyes squeezed his arm.

"But—but Captain, fine honoured Captain, surely ye can't be meaning to . . ."

The younger carter, he of the darkish skin and the grey eyes, broke off. The captain had drawn steel, and it shone like silver in the moon's cold light. The captain's eyes were as cold.

"It's . . . to the count of twenty I'll be giving ye, boys, to hush your voices and become scarce hereabouts. Else—"

The carters stared. The captain said, "One." The sword lifted, gleamed. The carters exchanged a look. "Two . . . three . . . fo—"

Reins dropped. The carters scrambled from atop their sloshy load. Hitching up their smocks' long skirts of reddish-brown homespun, they made haste into the night, heading for shadows back in the direction whence they'd come.

Behind them, the captain and his sentry laughed.

"Spoils of war!" the captain cried, and his eyes gleamed bright as the sword he now swiftly sheathed. The slap of peasantish boots faded into the night. "Into the camp with it, Brion—it's I and yourself are about to become the most popular men in all

Meath this night!"

Brion saw the two peasants disappear from his view behind a hairy, sprawly clump of furze that reared up in the darkness. Grinning he took up the reins of their horses. He did not see the two men slow to a jog; did not see the smiles spreading across their faces. They proceeded into the deep shadows of a growth of rowan bound about with last year's woodbine and this year's new green runners.

Around them men rose up in the darkness, and Forgall and Cormac were handed their proper clothes. Soon whispering, hopefully smiling men were helping them into their chaincoats. The clump of rowan was alive with men of Forgall— and nine others, handed into his command. The nine were all that remained of their own Fifty, with their captain and his seconds all slain on the Plain of Sorrow.

Amid the trees, crouching behind the haw that partway ringed the grove like a low defense-wall, they waited.

Weary weapon-men practically held their breaths in silence. Excitement and the hope given them by the plan of their comrade Partha had restored them as though they'd slept many hours. Soon it came: plainly they heard the sounds of revelry from the Meathish cattle-camp.

"The sons of sows are snorting up that ale as if the High-king had decreed it out of existence on the morrow!"

"Hush. We hear them."

"Hump! They hear nothing."

"Mayhap it's they who'll be out of existence soon, happily and insensibly guzzling . . ."

"Pray they do indeed guzzle just so: to insensibility!" 174

"Be silent." Forgall's voice slashed among his men's, low and angry. "An . . . one of those yonder steps away to relieve himself, and wanders this way . . ."

There was no need for him to say more; there was silence. They waited, six-and-thirty men of Leinster, armoured, armed, waiting, hoping, hearts pounding, helmets doffed against a betraying flash of steel in the moonlight. Not a man but held his breath in order to hear the better—and against being heard by the joyous, ale-guzzling men of Meath.

Measured against the branches and tops of trees, the moon visibly moved in the cloud-drifted sky. A little breeze came, and tarried for a time, and retired for the night. Squatting men moved, stifling grunts, for toes and calves had begun to ache. They waited. The noises from the Meathish camp commenced to diminish. They diminished. Now but three or four continued to sing, to shout, to laugh. Then there were definitely but two voices. And then one.

That man sang a couple of lines, shouted again, bellowed curses on his weakling fellows. He essayed another line of song, an obscenity. There came a crash; wood splintered. Another great string of curses. And then silence.

And silence. Not even a cow lowed.

The men of Leinster waited. Their heads they cocked, with one ear turned toward the cattle-camp, holding their breaths and straining to hear.

There was naught to hear. Not even the wind soughed.

Forgall made them wait longer than any other man would have done. All chafed. Cormac chafed—and mentally congratulated his leader. *Patience,* he thought, and perhaps he matured a mite more.

Then, with a little rustle, Forgall mac Aed rose. All about him, with rustles and clinks and little grunts as circulation rushed back into limbs in which its flow had long been disrupted by their squatting, the others rose.

Six-and-thirty men moved from the rowan grove and paced toward the Meathish camp. Helmets capped their heads now, and shields bobbed high at their sides, and swords and axes were naked and sinister in their fists.

They discovered no need for their weapons. Drugged with quart upon quart of ale and the sleep-inducing oil of boar-blossom with which the Leinstermen had steeped it, the cattle-guards lay deep in slumber. Each sprawled where he'd sagged or toppled. The camp's only sounds were snores.

Grim-faced Blueshirts stood over sleeping Meathmen. Sword- and ax-hands twitched. Their owners looked to their captain. Forgall too gazed upon the slumbrous men, and regarded the blade bared in his fist; he reflected on slain Leinstermen.

A hand touched Forgall's arm; it was a big hand, unlined, and Gael-dusky.

"Best we leave them asleep and alive," Cormac mac Art dared counsel his leader. "Will be greater insult and shame on them and High-king Lugaid, that the entirety of the 'tribute' was retaken without the spilling of one drop of blood!"

A smile spread over Forgall's features. "Aye," he muttered low, and he lifted his blade on high so that all his men saw. Then he sheathed it.

Silent men of Leinster began to move among sleeping cattle and used spear-hafts as goading staves. Then came forward darling Bress mac Keth. Before him walked a Meathman, at sword's point.

"Thisun drank not deeply enough, Forgall. Or vomited it up, more like."

"One sound," Forgall muttered, "and you die."

"So I told him," Bress muttered, and the prisoner started, feeling swordpoint at spine.

Forgall drew steel. "Bind him. Gag him. You, my glaze-eyed friend of Meath, will be after telling your fellows precisely what took place here." Forgall smiled tightly. His sword held the Meathish weapon-man now, whilst Bress bound the fellow— with unnecessary tightness, of course.

"If these drunken sots ever awaken," Forgall said, "do ye be telling them—and His Arrogance the High-king—that was Forgall mac Aed of Athmore and Carman who did this . . . along with his sword-companion Partha mac Othna. And it's the king of Leinster we both serve, little fellow."

Bound hand and foot and gagged with cloth and cord, the single wakeful Meathman was dumped to ground—his fall cushioned by two cow-piles of excellent size—and left. His comrades slept on. Weapons and shields not worn were piled on the ale-cart with surprising lack of noise. Smiling men ringed the vast herd of cattle, knowing the thousands would follow the hundreds once they were set moving. They started the beasts amove, southward. The Leinstermen even repossessed their ale-cart, piled now with spears and shields, axes and swords, and a few helmets.

The ale had not been sufficient to keep these men of the High-king asleep throughout the raid, however silent; was Cormac's suggestion of the druid-learned soporific that accomplished the snorey slumber, and all his comrades knew it.

Several cages of fowls the Leinsterman left, and Forgall stood over the dung-besmirched man

177

they had gagged and trussed.

"The birds we leave. Tame fowls. It's feathers you fine warriors will be eating, without beef or milk, when Lugaid on Tara-hill learns of what happened here this night!"

Laughing, the Leinstermen tramped south behind their cart. Brain, Cormac mused had prevailed over blade.

Chapter Eleven:
Samaire

News of the deed reached Craman before the doors themselves.

General Fergus's men arrived to cheers, and to the discovery that a celebration had been arranged in their honour. The feast was being laid on by King Ulad Ceannselaigh himself. It would be held in the Assembly-house, to accommodate the remainder of Forgall's Fifty—and its nine new members. For craft and guile had ever been highly respected and loved in Eirrin.

However excited and anticipatory, Forgall's men and the rest of the army took almost at once to their beds. There most spent the greater part of the next twenty hours.

Then it was up to bathe and see to their hair, with Cond much in demand, and clean their boots; in high jocularity they referred to their preparations as prettying themselves for society. The while, the men of Forgall laughed and shouted jests and threats and called one another *flatha:* warrior-nobles. And then they trooped into Carman, and were cheered through the streets.

In clean unwrinkled shirt or long-sleeved tunic each man walked, with leggings of his choice over tight breeches of white linen tucked into newly-gleaming boots. Ceremoniously they carried their polished helms, and each wore his best cloak and brooch and bunne-do-ats.

The Feis-tech was Leinster's greatest hall. Present for the celebration of a Leinsterish victory over Tara were nobles from Carman and elsewhere in the realm, and the poets and historians, minstrels and mages. Finely coiffed and bejewelled ladies, too, had come to do honour on the men who had outfoxed the High-king's men—and returned five thousand cattle. The hall was scintillantly ablaze with richly-dyed robes, with buckles and ornaments of silver and gold, with pearls and gemstones, with coloured bits of glass and brilliant enamel-work, all flashing in the light of more candles and torches than any had seen before in one place.

Musicians played. Nobles babbled to each other and to common soldiers no longer so common. Servants scurried so that ale flowed like a mountain stream, foaming and bubbling.

Drisheen or black pudding there was, a rich mixture of entrails and blood; pork too in plenty, along with fresh-butchered beef (and jokes about its being the best-travelled beef in the history of Eirrin). The boards groaned beneath more side-dishes than most of Forgall's men had known could exist. Among the red trout and cakes made of oaten meal, there was an abundance of the famed honey of Carman itself, and sloak and dulse from the nearby sea, as well as its game: millicks, or periwinkles still in their shells, scallops and the meaty black sole. To wash all down the hall fair swam in good brown ale, and beer made from wheat and honey, and that different drink also made from honey and called mead.

Ladies and their daughters wore crimson dyes on their nails, the black or deep blue of berries on their eyebrows, and other vegetable dyes here and there to enhance their faces—or so at least they thought, those noble women of Leinster. Golden rings or hollow balls of gold bound hair braided and curled to hang in dangling spirals; others wore their thick manes up, held by pins and pearls of gold. Soldiers—eye, and others who fancied themselves more sophisticated—goggled at the wife of one king's cousin: she had dyed and bleached her hair so that it was an impossible silver-white. Some of these women of metropolitan Carman, Cormac noticed, even *wore* their beautiful combs of bone or horn. All the people of his isle were fond of their hair and its care, and their combs, but this style of making combs into ornaments was a new one to the youth from Connacht.

With winter-tide gone from the earth and summer not yet here, the well-born and high-placed of Leinster wore silks and satins and furs, along with light linens and heavier woolens. A filay or poet from Athaircthech over near Osraige affected clothing of peasantish russet—and displayed himself well, as he stood out among the sumptuously attired throngers.

Many wore the *peallaid*—originally a sheepskin and now a long strip of cloth adorned with stripes that crossed to form a design called *plaide*.

Fresh rushes crackled and hissed underfoot and the candles flickered so that the marvelous figures that decorated the wall-hangings seemed to roam and gambol on those huge panels of white linen.

Much in evidence all about was the superb work of the needles of Eirrin's women and the delicate, brilliant work of jewel- and metal-smiths. Clothes and ornaments were broidered and purfled and picked out in spindle-whorls and fretwork, spirals and enamel inlays. Beside Cormac, Cas remarked the fact he'd looked at seven noble necks ere he saw a *plain* torc, and Cormac advised the farmer's son that these people possessed more than one of those neck-ringing badges of Celtdom. Most he saw were indeed ornate, worn only for dress occasions, and among them were those that wore gold lunulae or bore pendent sun-disks.

Cormac saw too more than one man, and woman, and girl and boy, who wore the necklace of good fortune: garnets and jet beads strung on gold or silver wire. And despite winter's being surely beyond the point of a surprise return, he saw two who were still wary of colds, for each wore the foot of a hare around his neck.

Rich clothing and precious metals and jewels blazed, in the Feis-tech.

Cormac was hardly the only blue-shirted guest who could not control the constant swiveling of his neck and his eyes that were bright in their sockets. He saw that the women much noted one another, too. It was just, he realized, that they were more circumspect about it, as if afraid of being seen appraising or envying one another.

Twisted bands of bronze or silver-gilt or even gold flashed from womanly arms, and he was hard put not to gawk at one young woman—married; she wore the rolled linen hood. The bust of her rowanberry-hued gown was decorated with miniature shield-bosses! Of silver they were, the inward-whirling design of each centering in a wrought

181

rowanberry of red enamel. A carnelian dangled and flashed from each of her ears, and her eyelids fairly dripped some pale violet dye.

King Ulad himself, in white and yellow and gold and wearing a lunula big as his head, bespoke the heroics, the genius, and the courage of the guests of honour. Then his own filay, chief poet of Leinster, had ready a narrative for the occasion. Proud was Leinster; proud the poet; exaggerated was his droning account—and long. Ale or mead wetted his lips—and the listeners quaffed each time he did.

The eye of mac Art was drawn quite naturally to a passing pretty young lady of worth. Seated at the high table she was, and nigh-orange of pearl-strewn hair, with beside her a flame-topped lordling. Both wore *plaides* of Leinster blue criss-crossed with yellow stripes. They to the king's left; on his other side sat his elder sons. Cormac's mouth went dry and he trembled. Stunned, he promptly poured a draught of ale down the wrong tube and embarrassed himself with a long coughing fit.

Wiping away the choke-tears, he demanded of a solicitous servant the identities of the two youths to the king's left.

"Why, my lord Tara-baiter: those are Ceann Mong Ruadh and Samaire, younger son and only daughter of our king!"

And Cormac stared on them, for last time he'd seen those two they had been but a rag-tag minstrel and a merchant's daughter named Aine.

He continued to stare, helplessly, the while his full belly sank and strove to convince him it was empty. He'd thought he had lost his love, his first love, and her gone home to Ailenn. Och and ochone, but no! He had lost her the more! For it was *Samaire ingin Ulaid-Ri* she was: Daybreak, daughter of King Ulad!

It's the blood of old nobility warms my veins, but . . . it's no suitor for the king's own daughter *my father's after raising in me! Behl preserve and Crom protect, she and I have . . . we have . . .*

And gone from mac Art was the celebratory fever—though hardly from his comrades-at-arms. And he ached and felt hollow and chill within, as though some part of him were missing and his heart pumped not hot blood but cool.

At last the poem ended. Cormac hardly noticed. Up rose the king, and called out the name of Aed's son Forgall, who rose amid cheers and was asked to speak. Ablush with embarrassment and much ale, Forgall falteringly said he would not, could not take much credit. Then—once renewed cheering and board-drumming had risen and sunk—he pointed out and called loudly the name of their successful plot's master mind.

That same Partha mac Othna had to be nudged into attention, and nigh shoved to his feet, for he'd been elsewise distracted. Another great cheer rose: for this young warrior from afar who'd be receiving a golden torc from the king's own artisan. Another poet seized the opportunity to begin to put together words about Othna's crafty son, and soon Partha's canniness was being compared with that of the heroes of Eirrish legend. Cormac's blood warmed again; his face, at least, seemed to burn.

And sure all were most impressed and thrice-happy . . . saving only Bress Long-arm. His hate-filled glower Cormac saw, though he was too doubly flustered to take note. As for the young woman beside Bress—hmp. Never had Cormac

183

seen so much bosom displayed, on a clothed woman.

Somehow he managed to express his love for his "adopted land" and its "noble king" and his happiness for having aided in "easing its Burden," and the throng thundered acclaim, and Cormac sank swiftly down into his seat. There followed more drinking, and eating, and more drinking still. Only the most private of conversations could now be attended, for the members of each pair or trio of speakers sought to make himself heard above all others in the hall.

Cormac could not wrest his gaze from the high table. Thus he noted disagreement betwixt the younger royal siblings. He caught too the darkish look Prince Ceann shot him, and was amazed. Even then Princess Samaire, orange-gold ringlets of hair dangling, dancing before either ear, was calling a wand-slim servant to herself. The two girlish heads bent close, and for an instant the gaze of Aine/Samaire locked with that of Partha/Cormac. His stomach promptly executed a curvet like an unbroken stallion, and he swallowed hard.

"What think ye of our pretty princess?" he was asked, by Cethern of Dinn Rig, who sat to his left.

"Ah—she—oh. The king's daughter? It's on that girl she just spoke to I've had these eyes, Ceth—ye be looking at the *king's daughter,* man?"

"Och—I but look! And that servant of hers has less meat on her than my spear!"

Then Cethern had to lean away—for the servant in question was there! Cethern made a ridiculous face at Cormac over her back, as she bent between them. She whispered in Cormac's ear, whilst he sat bolt-still and his colour rose.

"Put your hand around me and pat my backside,

184

Partha mac Othna, so these louts think we're at the flirting, and attend me: Drink lightly, I am commanded to tell ye, for one called *Aine* would have converse with yourself later this eve. Come, man, act flirtatious—there. Not so hard!"

And she straightened, and went away, and Cethern laughed and kissed his palm; Cormac had not touched the girl at all.

Elated, he did as she'd bidden, and suffered Cethern's jesting—and Cas's too-powerful nudge in his right side—when she passed again later, behind him, and trailed her hand caressingly across the span of his shoulders. Nervous but forcing himself not to drink, he soon became very alone in that hall. At the king's leave, some nobles departed. Cormac was not even aware that he received a sheep's-eye or two from this or that noble lady. All others meanwhile, aye, including the women of Eirrin who were not chattel to their men, descended with great gusto and passing swiftness into stuffed, barbaric drunkenness. That gave way by degrees to stunned drunkenness, so that most of the assemblage were passed out across crumb- and bone-strewn boards, or amid the rushes on the floor.

Cormac smelled both vomit and fresh urine and bethought him that feasts began better than they ended.

Then the king himself rose to depart—aye, and lurching a bit, as befit the ruler of triumphant sons of Eirrin. In passing he paused to do words on "Partha mac Othna our most valuable import." Cormac flushed. King Ulad passed on, and out of the hall with his family. Instantly Cormac was up, stumbling over Cethern and then hurrying past and over and around other fallen comrades. Those whom the Meathmen had not scathed now lay downed by the sharp edge and point of fermented grains and honey.

The door led not directly outside but to an inner gallery of passing dimness. There waited the so-slender servant of the princess herself. She led him—by the damp hand, like lovers—into even darker realms and to a closed door of richly carven oak. She tapped, released his hand, patted his backside, and departed on swift feet.

He entered a most private chamber, and paused; all within was darkness.

"Do close the door, and bar it, and I shall light this candle."

He did; sparks were struck; again; a candle came alive in a yellow point that drew the eyes.

"Ah, Partha! I admit to some dizziness—I hope you drank but little!"

"Ye did dissemblage on me—why?"

"Ah. You use 'ye' to me then, do you?" Aine/ Samaire sighed. "Ah, Partha! My father does do his best to keep me most sheltered indeed—and watched! His only daughter—valuable trade-goods, you see. So . . . my brother Ceann and I make our own plots. It's good friends we are, though siblings. We disguise ourselves and slip out from that prison called the King's-house whenever we can, to wander Carman as people—*real* people!" She held high the candle; now she shrugged, and watched his eyes drop their gaze from her face. She smiled. "Hence the 'Aine the merchant's daughter role. How was I to know I'd be . . . be taking a—a liking to your huge self?—and brainy self too, isn't it, Hero of Boruma!" She gave her head a swift shake and little curls flew, dark gold in the candle's light. "Never have I heard poets compare a living man with a Cuchulain afore, Partha mac Cuchulain!"

And why not, he mused in his confusion, *for I was he, once . . .*

He but smiled. He'd say naught. Now he knew her name, and accepted that she'd dissembled for no reason to do with him. As for himself . . . he must maintain the lie of his name, even to her darling self. Feeling guilt and that strong urge to tell his real name, he tugged his lower lip in under his teeth and studied the floor.

"There . . . there is another lie ye've had of me, Partha. I have no sixteen years on me; it's Ceann who's sixteen, and he older than I."

At that he looked up, suddenly smiling happily. "Ah—and will you be keeping *my* secret—" he paused over the name—"Samaire?"

"Aha!"

"Will you now?"

Her bantering expression vanished. "For ever, Partha."

"My age is not sixteen, either. It's big I am for my years—"

"Oh."

He grinned. "—and I feared I'd not gain weaponish employment or respect, an I spoke true of being but fourteen."

She clapped her hands and her smile was like her name, for "samair" was the word for "break of day." "Ah! As if ye needed worry about respect . . . but . . . why it's little more than a darling young boy ye be . . ."

His dark brows lowered and his eyes went serious and not happy; that he accepted not well, she saw, and she spoke swiftly while she moved to him.

"And I little more than a girl . . ."

"A dairlin young girl, aye . . ."

"Your dairlin girl, Partha, drettel . . ."

187

Their arms went around each other, and he had to bend well down to join his lips to hers, and then they were holding each other more tightly, and their mouths moved, pressing, and their hands . . .

. . . and he woke hours later beside her, and smiled, and touched her beside him, asleep, and he smiled the wider. Then he saw, even through the heavy drape at the window, that the sky was going light. He knew it was close onto cock's crow.

Lugh's arms and blood of the gods, he thought (for he was training himself to warlike oaths) *to be caught here thus would be sorest trouble for her and death for me, sure!*

Very slowly, sneakily like unto a thief, he eased himself from the bed. He dressed without waking her, and was able to make his way through the deserted assembly-house. Then through the just-waking city he strode, humming as he went, and smiling upon those who stared or scolded, and he realized: *I love her!*

Aye, and he did.

And she loved him.

And the days passed, in Leinster, and the weeks. The hero of the Plain of Sorrow was offered a post as second in command in another Fifty, and he asked to remain with Forgall though Forgall had a second, who was Bress. And so he stayed with those men, without rank in a Fifty whose members now called it Tara-Baiter.

Six days Partha spent on special duty, at the palace. Each evening the winsome, spear-slim Devorgill came to him on behalf of her youthful mistress Samaire, and each evening the Hero of Sorrow's Plain said no and was adamant, for duty was duty and honour was honour, and he'd not creep like a thief for love in the House of the King. On the seventh day, as on that day before the first of the six, he met a girl named Aine in a wood at the west end of the pasture of one Bresal An-gair, and they endeavoured to make up for those missed times together. The more fool he for not coming to her in her room, she told him; the more man he, he thought.

The Blueshirts were not idle, but only at training. Now there were stories of Pictish incursions from the far side Lock Derg over to the west. The *Cruithne* seemed more and more bold in raiding into the north tip of Munster, that strip of Munsterish land separated Leinster from the western land south of Connacht. There Picts were settled still, and entrenched the way that Munster's king left them alone. Along that western border of Leinster, snuggled to Munster's "chimney," lay little Osraige or Osry, in a thin line forming a tiny realm. Were its king to cry for aid, Ulad's men would march. Already a few companies had been sent there, to crowd the border outposts lest the Picts come in force.

And so the Blueshirts waited, and talked of Cruithne, and kept limber with their daily training.

And the days passed, in Leinster, and the nights. On some of those nights Cormac and Samaire trysted, and, even more seldom and with greater care, during some days.

Even Cormac's new stature and the golden torc conferred on him by King Ulad did not dissuade Bress from his weening dislike. He called his chosen enemy "Partha n'Allmurach": the Foreigner. Nor was Bress deterred from his strong pressing of the youth. The Long-arm seemed bent on goading Cormac into drawing steel on a superior, thus to be disgraced—and perhaps slain into the bargain. Clinging to his sense of honour with difficulty, Cormac would not be so provoked. He was the better for it, in the minds fo his fellows. The supposed Ulsterman was well-liked, and respected as well; Bress's fixation cost him much respect and, as it later fell out, considerably more.

The malevolent, watchful eye of Bress mac Keth made the meetings of Cormac and Samaire more and more difficult, and thus perilous.

Now Behltain was on Eirrin; *Cetsamhain* that those of the New Faith called after some Gallish person or legend: Walpurga's night. The eve of May Day; the season's beginning and its observance more ancient among Celtic peoples than any could know.

On that happy occasion of the beginning of growth that would culminate six months later with Samhain, the end of harvest, Partha mac Othna shared words, and kisses, and much more with Aine ingin Fol, merchant of Ailenn, and they snuggled and murmured their love.

A forbidden love, they both knew. A hopeless love, he was sure. That she would not admit; Samaire held ever hope that the morrow would see to the morrow, as the old women of Eirrin were wont to say. Even her brother Ceann was more sympathetic to the clandestine lovers now, though he disapproved. Third in line or no, Ceann mac Ulaid was aware of being royalty and of the impossibility of anything good's coming of the liaisons of his sister and the foreign weapon-man. Ceann and Devorgill—with whom indeed Ceann was known to have disported himself, but he was after all male and even in Eirrin that was different. Different—he and Devorgill were the only two who knew about the adolescent lovers. So all hoped, at any rate.

Samaire owned that Ceann kept silent because she knew about his dalliances with the very, very young wife of the old, old Condla, once called *Airechta,* or King's Champion—and now called Condla Taeb-trom: Big-belly. Cormac disagreed with her, feeling that Ceann was manly, and loved his sister, and was imbued with sympathy and empathy. And Samaire told him he was both naif and over trusting.

Better had we never met, mac Art thought too often during that idyll. But it was impossible to be so dismal in her company, and her body white as the privet's dainty blossom. Nor, in youth and in love, could he exert strength sufficient to part from her for good and all.

"A pity it is to give love to a man, and he to take no heed of it," she said, reaching for a cup of mead that should have held hazel-nuts that night before May dawned. "It is better to be turned away, if one is not loved as one loves."

"You are loved as you love, and more, dairlin girl."

"Impossible that it be more, *mo chroi* . . . but don't be tellin' me: show me!"

And he did.

And later she told him, tracing Oghamish on his bare chest with her finger, "The colour of the glossiest raven is on his hair, and his skin like the finest new copper or a fawn's coat, his cheek like the blood of the speckled red calf, and his swiftness and his leap are like the salmon of the stream it fights and conquers, or the fleet deer of the grey mountain . . . and, sure the head and shoulders of Partha Othna's son are above all the other men of Leinster."

"Not all of Eirrin?"

"Be not greedy, my love."

"Hmp. And have you no pretty words for me, dairlin boy?"

"None," he told her, but he showed her instead, so that she had need of few words.

Chapter Twelve:
Picts!

Cormac returned to a garrison in uproar. Torches blazed on high and bobbed about in the upraised hands of his fellows. Voices rose in a cross-ranging cacophany of commands and queries and replies. Harness jingled, and mail; swords and knives in their oiled sheaths were being buckled on over armour of leather and linked chain. Horses whickered or neighed shrilly in apprehension or plain displeasure as they were hauled forth and harnessed. Men hurried in a dozen directions on a score of errands, their paths crossing and criss-crossing. Cormac heard the wheels of waggons and carts. Men grunted while they loaded on supplies.

"Eochu! What—"

But the Lightning-hand ran on, on someone's orders, buckling on his sword the while.

"Here you, get your—Partha! Malingering?"

Cormac stared into a pair of icy grey-green eyes above a long nose. "The opposite, Bress. I have night's leave; it's early I've returned. What is all this?"

"Picts!" a man shouted, rushing by all ajingle. Two spear-butts dragged behind him.

Cormac echoed the word, gazing about at a semi-organized bedlam of preparations. "Picts! *Here?*"

"Idiot!" Bress snarled. "Duck's anus! Of course not here. Into battle gear with ye—we march at once." And after a glower, the Long-arm executed a self-conscious heel-and-toe and stalked off.

Cormac hadn't time to seethe. He learned the situation while he made himself ready for battle-march. The *Cruithne* had raged across that tip of Munster that surged up betwixt their land and Osraige. They were in Osraige; across that tiny realm's northern strip leaving a wake of blod; the Picts were in western Leinster!

A fort of Osraige was overrun and its garrison slain to the last man; a fort of Leinster, too, had been attacked and burned out. Of its garrison, as well as the two hundred Blueshirts so recently sent to firm up defenses . . . who knew how many lived, if any? Farmhouses were ablaze in Leinster. Women and children lay dead, having been raped and mutilated; men were dead and a whole little settlement destroyed. Priests had been deprived of those bodily parts for which they claimed no use; druids lay headless.

Munstermen marched northward; Leinsterish forces hurried down from the garrisons along the Meathish border; now the forces of Forgall and others were to hurry westward "with all despatch and more," in hopes of stopping the incursion, and surrounding the Pictish invaders, and destroying them.

Hurriedly Cormac gathered up armour, weapons, and field-kit. Within an hour, Forgall's *Coichte* and several other such Fifties were amarch through the night. Supply-wains creaked and rattled along under cursing drivers. Mayhap it was midnight, Cormac mused; mayhap before. It was either the eve of Behltain or the day itself; one of the Celts' two great annual celebrations.

What a day for the onslaught of those Pictish demons, with great fires being readied for the spring rites!

Chapter Thirteen:
In the Glen of Danger

Mist rode the post-dawn air so that the sun was but a pallid glow somewhere beyond a sky the colour of dirty pearls, hanging low over the fog-cloaked glen. Through this chill gloom moved · weary Blueshirts, seeking the Picts who'd eluded them for a full week.

Oh, they'd found evidence enow. Bodies they had found, mutilated corpses caked with blood and eerily alive with flies. Burned homesteads. Slain dogs, butchered horses. But of Picts . . .

Twice had these men come on Pictish war-parties, but only that: small groups of the nearly naked, black-eyed devils, all too many of whom wore Celtic trinkets and carried Celtic weapons taken from corpses. Twice had the searching Gaels crushed the burly dark men in blood-letting combat. Leinsterish losses were few. But these had ben rencontres with two little raid-parties, hardly anything approaching a main Pictish body.

And that was all there had been in a full seven days of marching, tramping, sweating, searching.

A week of tension. A full week of searching, and of constant disappointment mingled with their tension. A week: plenty of time for men to grow disgruntled and apprehensive and tense and, naturally enough for soldiers forced to walk and walk in full battle array, spears ready but without the release of battle, to complain.

Contrary to their expectations, there was no such entity as a Pictish *army*.

Oh, the invasion was a major one, right enough. It consisted, though, of the warriors of several separate tribes of Pictdom. Each was intent on its own purposes, and booty, and glory. All pillaged and murdered in several directions at once. Without unified purpose, without semblance of unified command or a single strong leader. There were tales of one, and of a powerful shaman, too. But no soldiers had seen them.

The men of Forgall mac Aed's *Coichte*, part of Commander Conan Conda's *Notri da Ceadach*—Three-hundred—wanted and needed action, the adrenalin release of tension, the clamor of battle and the joy of *doing something*. Even men who had little stomach for blade-reddening were more anticipatory than aprehensive, now.

Partha mac Othna who was Cormac mac Art had taken a cut from a flint ax on his cheek and another across his right forearm, from a captured Celtic sword. The sword was re-captured. The wounders were dead. And while his wounds were but minor cuts, Cormac knew they'd be scars on him, all his days.

He was *tired*. All the Blueshirts of Conan Conda's command were tired; as much downcast they were, as weary. And ever, ever wary, despite their growing conviction that the Picts were as unseasonable
195

frost giving way to the sun of a clear morn; the devils had always *been* there afore them, but seemed to have melted away. This doubly damned slog-work enforced quiet and care, the skin prickling; this constant tramping about in tension without the relief and release of combat was maddening. It made men feel far more tired than they were.

And now—now, this morning, it was worse.

Visibility was such that one's shield, held out from the body by a strong arm, was but a dark blurring blob without detail or even its proper round shape. Someone to Cormac's left muttered quite succinctly, "Excrement."

Cormac agreed in silence. *Cess.* This cess-pool of a soupy fog, cold through leather leggings; this whole maddeningly frustrating quest: cess. It was Glean na-Guais they tramped, Danger Glen; it should have been called Glen Cess or Cess-pool!

He waded through it. Tall grass *wheeped* against his boots.

All around him others waded through it. Occasionally there was a little splurch or splash followed by a muffled curse, as a man stepped into a pool of water based in mud. Elsewise there was only the whisper of cloth, the occasional jingle of mental fittings, the creaky rustle of armour of boiled leather, and the strange, metallic susurrus of mail-coats.

Fog and mist. And the sun up. Cormac frowned, considering, glancing about—at pale greyness.

The picts had their druids or priests: shamans; sorcery was hardly unknown to them. Here, now Cormac was most wary of the position of his little company, on quest apart from the main army of three hundred. He was most aware and wary of the environment. It was unnatural, mist-haunted, tained with the reek of dark sorceries. For three days now they had been at the seeking out of a band of a hundred or so particularly vicious and successful foes. This band of savages was apparently led by a madman—that leader who might well become chief of a united Pictish force, for it was known he had begun with but twenty.

Too, according to words accompanied by blood from the lips of an old woman dying of obscene wounds, this band of fivescore was accompanied by a shaman she swore had sent a writhing foggy darkness on the tiny settlement of Baile Ablaich. *Ablach!* No more; all its apple trees were tattered, chopped, seared and singed and some still smoking with their smoldering.

There was no more Appletown; there could hardly be said to be apple trees, for soldiers could not pause to attempt to quench flames so hot they ate at living trees.

Now, in this silence-heavy, fog-enshrouded glen of Osraige, Cormac felt the pale white mist all about and it seemed he felt the silence as well. The fog was palpable; the silence seemed so. Surely it was unnatural. When he tilted up his helmed head he did not even have to squint at the sky. Was late in the morning—for those who rose with the sun or before, it was. The Eye of Behl should have burned off this damned creeping fog that was ever the bane of wet Eirrin with its high coasts and low damp inlands.

And surely there should be *some* sounds, he thought; this was as though their hearing had been stoppered against the world, as if the fog were chill, wet woollen pressed over their ears.

Knowing that Forgall was but three paces to his left, Cormac turned that way, to say so.

And the fog seemed to be lifted, straight up as though by a great invisible hand, from knee-to chest-level. It flowed in the manner of a swift mountain stream, in the manner of wind-chased clouds shredding into pale streaming tatters. At that instant the awful shriek arose, from only a few paces directly ahead. A short, burly, dark figure erupted from the fog-hugged earth as if ejected by the springy grass. It was a human form, if Picts were indeed human. And it sprang to attack.

That swiftly the squat dusky men of Pictdom were all about and rushing to kill.

Attack cries sliced the air and ululated like wolf-howls. The enemy had been lying await, sprawled flat and cloaked by the tall grass and misty fog—or foggy shaman-sent mist.

The first to spring up screaming was soon silent; he leaped directly at Cormac and was allowed to impale himself with ghastly neatness on a spearhead that was swung to meet him on pure defensive reflex. The spear went all the way through the leaping demon; with a grunt, Cormac released it and drew his sword.

And then that murky glen was plunged into howling battle of volcanic ferocity. The fog lifted to shoulder-level, so that *Cruithne* could see and Leinstermen had to bend or squat to bring their eyes under the cloying greyness. No Gael doubted sorcery now; the fog had lingered long enough for them to be well into the meadow and surrounded —and then risen to give vision to the waylayers when they had need to see.

The world became very loud and time rushed as it does only for lovers and those encompassed by battle.

Bracing their feet on marshy earth with grass

nearly to their knees, men who had thought themselves tired hewed and fended, slashed and stabbed. Mindlessly malevolent, Picts came at them with spear and stone-headed ax—and swords and axes too of good Celtic steel and manufacture. Baneful blows they struck in that attack of appalling suddenness and ferocity. Mail and flesh were rent open in woundy gaps. Donn, Lord of the Dead, rose up happily and spread his arms to welcome the souls sent rushing from ruined bodies.

A man staggered backward past Cormac with a spear-haft seeming to grow from his chest like a ghastly stalk, and Cormac did not recognize Fithil the Strong, nor did he recognize Bress Lamfhada who with a scythe-like swipe slew the slayer. Feet stomped grassy loam now sprinkled with blood, whilst blades of flinty stone and of steel slashed in sparkling blurs and whirls of silver and showers of crimson.

A spearhead struck to clash ringingly on the rim of Cormac's shield so that bright sparks flew and danced and he lashed back with a slash that clove the attacker's buckler and tore it from a brown arm in which a bone snapped. Past him leaped a Pict like a maddened wolf, a primal, totally savage blood-lust blazing in his terrible eyes. The aboriginal cried out hideously when the sword of Forgall Aed's son sank hilt-deep in his neck. Down he sank, whiles Cormac tore into red ruin a dusky face behind a sundered shield.

The constant clash and grate of steel was a din that smote the ears and gave threat to eardrums. Amid that awful clamor of steel and flint, wood and iron rose the battle-shrieks of Picts, and curses, and the wretched cries, moans, and blood-wet gurgles of the wounded and dying.

The dark warriors ravened into the foe they hated. They were heedless of steel, heedless of death. They were also far more vulnerable with the Gaels' carapaces of rippling steel links or coats of shining, hardened leather, and the warriors of Pictdom died in their mania. Steel-hacked corpses strewed the sod, and blood created muddy patches.

Still the attackers came, as if from the very ground itself. In their numbers and their ferocity, they took scarlet toll.

Lugaid the Fox, who had one day lent Cormac a tunic of Leinster-blue, smote a Pict like a thunderbolt, the way that he sundered chest and heart within, and a spear smote him the way that he was staggered but was saved by his mail, and he slashed maniacally to deal out death to that stocky attacker, and wounded still a third after a duel of minutes, and then even while the wood of a Pictish spear-haft splintered on his buckler and his feet skidded on on a carpet of blood-slick grass, a furiously driven spear sliced through his leather cuirass as though it had been linen, and on through the padded jack beneath, and tore into his belly an inch below the sternum. A reeking puke of scarlet gushed from Lugaid's mouth and he fell to lie twitching. He'd have been a long time dying and in agony, but was surely not mercy that prompted his slayer to wrench forth the spear and drive it into the face of Lugaid the Fox. And Lugaid was still.

From behind, Cas mac Con took off that dark warrior's head in a mighty stroke that began as a blurred arc of silver and ended in one of crimson.

While Cormac parried and feinted with the teeth-gritting savage before him, another stuck his shield with such force that its edge cut Cormac's chin, and he'd have died of the first Pict sure had not another's sword taken off the savage's arm just below the shoulder; the Connachtish youth never knew who thus saved his life. Already he had saved one, by the unwarlike expedient of kicking a Pict directly in his buttocks; the melee had deepened and thickened now so that single combats were the exception rather than the rule.

Chin dripping red, Cormac staggered back—

And slipped and fell, his boot skidding off a bloody severed hand. He looked up at the leggings of a man who stepped across him to drive his sword deep into a dusky body, and Cormac was saved twice that day. He came up lunging, to drive his own blade so violently into the side of a grinning foe that he had to fight it free of clutching ribs.

"Blood of the gods," Forgall spat out, "ye've saved my life again!"

"It's twice my own's been saved," Cormac panted, "and I've no idea by whom—uh!"

He turned the ax-blow on his shield, twisted, turned the back swing, and girded steel into that Pict's flank. "How many of these devils—uh!—are there?" That grunt was elicited by his having to twist-yank to free his blade.

"Too—damned—many!" someone muttered angrily from his left, and Cormac almost grinned.

He turned in time to see the speaker die, and the slayer was away then and Cormac had no notion who slew that Pict, or indeed whether instead he escaped. It was then the blood-mist came before Cormac's eyes, and hung there, and he saw only enemies, targets for his ravening sword. He had experienced the berserker battle-lust just once afore, and did not know that it was on him.

There were less Pictish screams. Armour turned blows. Dusky skin did not.

It was horrible, and the fog drifting, rocking like waves asea, with the sun of late morning striving to burn it away to reveal a plain of red-splattered grass littered with corpses. Was Cas raced after a fleeing Pict, and in doing so was well separated from the others. He came upon a Pictish shaman who stood rigid, eyes closed, lips amove, both hands extended. In passing, Cas took off one of those hands—at the shoulder. Like a deer, Cas sped on for all his weariness, and overtook his prey. He hacked the Pict a red line from shoulders to buttocks, a wound two inches deep. The man sprawled forward. Cas took but two more running steps, and struck, and turned from a headless corpse.

He turned to see fighting men—mostly his companions. The fog was dissipating rapidly now, writhing like a great grey serpent with its death-wound on it. Rather thoughtfully, Cas returned to the shaman, who was also down and writhing, and Cas mac Con created another headless body. And the fog vanished so that the sun blazed on grass that rose green—and scarlet.

It was over by the time Cas reached the surprisingly close-crowded scene of the final battle.

Sixty Picts lay dead or twitching and writhing; those were soon made still. Ten sons of Eirrin lay dead, and another would surely die. Six more were sore wounded and a score bore some wounds beyond scratches. Every man was messy with blood and gore, not his, but thrown by slashing swords and axes.

Panting, sweating men stared about, and saw no Picts save the fallen. Weary or no, the victors' hearts raced still. That was good; they could not yet rest. Still panting men must needs tend the wounds of others, and collect their dead ere they could make their "march" back to the balance of Conan the Wolfish's force. They did, straggling on quivery legs, and soon they must move again, to the main army that was composed of the men of both Leinster and Osraige, the tiny kingdom that might have been gathered up and dropped into great Loch Corrib over in Connacht.

Weary men collapsed and slept where they sank. When they awoke it was to the chastisement of veterans, for now it would be harder to do that which they had not done afore: they must see to dented helms, and to the scraping away of blood, that splashed mail might not rust. Too they worked at nicks in their swords—and used feet and muscle to straighten bent blades. Some shields were sundered, or so hacked that they must be replaced. Thus the dead, who had no need of marless bucklers or better spears and axes, aided the living.

A battle was fought. A war remained.

Perhaps the leader of the large band extirpated by Forgall's force had been that very important one. In that event Cuar mac Con, who had slain him, was a great though dead hero. So was Cas, son of another Con, who lived. And perhaps that leader and that shaman had been all-important. Or perhaps Pictish scouts and leaders had got together and realized that they had taken ghastly lossess on all fronts.

Whatever the reason, scouts soon reported to the Gaelic leaders that the *Cruithne* were in retreat. The northern and southern forces of Leinster, with men of Osraige, would follow them right across northernmost Munster, to join with the men of that southern kingdom; all shared a hope now of wiping out the flower and more of young Pictish manhood.

They must march on the morrow. Meanwhile they stoked themselves with meat and ale. Soon they sprawled, to gain all the sleep they could. A battle was won. A war remained.

Chapter Fourteen:
On the Mountain of Death

The broad Shannon was born in Connacht, up past Cruachan. It rushed southward, broadening into a mile-wide Loch Ree, emerged from its southern end to form the boundary between Connacht and Meath. On down through northern Munster River Shannon sliced the land, to gain its freedom at last in the Western Sea.

The Picts had crossed the Shannon at lower Loch Derg, where the lake began to narrow back into the river; the lack of current there eased their crossing. Munstermen had made the crossing from Luimneach—Limerick—just over thirty miles from their capital of Cashel. From thence they had marched but a few miles northward along the Shannon's boggy western bank, grown up with cotton grass and bog bean, alive with ravens and jays and moorfowl calling among towering birches and spear-straight rushes.

Within a day the Munstermen came upon the Pictish rear-guard.

The battle was fought there on the flood plain,

in a flashing glitter of bright steel and flint that splintered armour and bone. *Cruithne* died and died; some fled toward Shannon and were hunted down amid the hummocks and rushy quagmires of that swampy western shore.

The Gaels owned the Pictish line of retreat; Luimneach controlled the Shannon below. The victorious Munstermen gazed across the river, and their commander announced that they would cross.

Three days later the Pictish rear guard on the eastern shore was annihilated by the same Munsterish force; the Gaels owned both shores. Now too they had the fleet of skinboats with which the invaders had crossed, here at the lower mouth of Loch Derg, where mighty Shannon purled along as slowly as poured honey.

Already Meathish patrols had been trebled along their southern border, just above Loch Derg. Munsterish couriers were dispatched to apprise the Meath's garrison there of the newest development; their fellows loosed the boats and sent them floating down to be snared by the men of Luimneach.

All men respected and fearfully hated the savage less-than-men; soon Meathmen were ranked deep along every inch of their southern border. Where the border became that dividing Meath and Leinster two garrisons stood like stone sentinels only two hundred yards apart. From one fluttered the pennons of Tara and the High-king; the other displayed Leinster blue. Now those watchful men forgot their never-ending enmity and recent encounter over Boruma. Keeping a far closer watch for the mutual enemy, they exchanged gestures of good-will and humor.

The forces of Leinster and Osraige were driving the Pictish remnant before them, westward across northernmost Munster. Surely the savages would come hurrying to lower Loch Derg, for their boats.

There waited Munster; the Shannon was closed to the retreating invaders and their boats gone; troops from Luimneach and Cashel had marched up to prevent their turning southward. North waited the Meathmen and others from Leinster. The Picts were being driven into a trap. There was no escape, save through ranks of men armed and armoured and armed, too, with terrible determination.

Posting sentries thick as primroses in summer, General Ferdiad an-Airt of Munster settled in to wait. He knew the Picts were coming, and he knew from what direction, and that a Leinsterish army drove the savages like a herd of wild beasts. Hopefully they would be in panicky disarray, and would never know what hit them. If not—they would die anyhow.

Ferdiad the Bear had but to wait. Here would battle be joined. Here would the invaders, surrounded, be slain to a man—if such they might be called. (Indeed, as Ferdiad the Bear had slain none but *Cruithne* in the fifteen-year career he had begun at age seventeen, it was said of him that he was a general who'd never done death on a man. His sword had drunk only Pictish blood; animal blood.)

Here would be broken the back of Pictdom.

Unfortunately, Pictish scouts, ghosting like phantoms, discovered the absence of their boats and the waiting enemy. Those scouts raced back to apprise their leaders, who were fighting as they gave ground, not retreating pell-mell.

Then did dark, squatly powerful aborigines confer, and turn their black eyes on the blue-shimmering rise of the range just inland from Shannon's bank: Slieve Argait, the Mountain of Silver, so called for its bulging with rich veins of that moon sacred metal.

And the Picts took to the hills. And Ferdiad of Munster cursed for hours.

The men of Forgall lay weary and panting, sore of muscle and from blows and wounds. To their backs lay their own land. Ahead, Loch Derg narrowed into the Shannon just before that river widened again to join the sea, below Luimneach. Between the Leinstermen and the river reared jagged Slieve Argait.

All of yesterday they had fought, without succeeding in the attempt to prevent the enemy from betaking themselves up that great hill. From the position they at last reached atop a high-flung mesa, the Picts had an excellent view of the slope by which approach must be made. At sunset the Gaels had wearily retreated.

On this day, each of two charges against that excellent Pictish location had resulted in a mass wounding and considerable slaughter of the men of three Gaelic realms. The leaders of the forces of Leinster and Munster and diminutive Osraige licked their wounds while cursing Picts and Meathmen alike: the latter were cannily waiting, up along their border.

The Picts' position high atop the brooding pile of earth and stone was a marvelously defensible aerie. The mesa's far side formed a cliff that plunged down into the Shannon. A deeply sliced crevasse protected them on their left or northern flank. To the south and east, attackers must openly reveal themselves to scale the mountain slope—which was barely scalable, from the south.

The Picts, meanwhile, were comfortable on the broad mesa.

Keep them besieged and let the dark bastards starve, some counselled.

They'd not starve, others said; when they've eaten every egg and every bird and creeping creature, and stripped every scrubby tree and bush of bark and leaves, and still hungry—then will they come down from their aerie.

Fine, the counsellors of siege replied. Then we will fight them at our advantage.

But it was not the way of Eirrin, and some men pondered . . .

Was then one Partha mac Othna, an Ulsterman serving Leinster's king, went quietly to his Fifty-leader. That man—Forgall mac Aed—Partha drew aside. He muttered a plan whereby Leinstermen might win the victory, and great glory—here on Munster's soil.

Forgall gave listen. "Insane," he said.

"Aye."

Forgall turned to stare at the rugged slope men were calling the Mountain of Death. He remembered another insane plan of the youth's: that of regaining the enforced tribute from Meath . . .

"Take a small group," the captain murmured, reviewing Cormac's suggestion. "March south a ways, gain the bank of the Shannon, and return northward to the base of the cliff beneath the Picts . . . the shore there must be no wider than a spear's length, Partha. And . . . *scale* it? Insane. Surely . . . insane . . . to climb up there and fall on the Picts from behind—"

"Like Picts," Cormac said.

"—like Picts. Such a force *must* be tiny. It would

stand no chance of winning against the hundreds of Picts up there on Silvertip."

"No. It would but· turn them, distract their attention from this slope to their perch . . . whilst all others here, Leinster and Munster alike, charge up yon slope." He gestured at the Mountain of Death.

"In hopes that the savages would be too busy with the scalers to sling and hurl rocks and spears on those charging up this slope . . ."

"Too distracted, Forgall. And consider. They have shown us what comes of a charge. They did not even sling all those stones that killed and wounded and concussed so many; it's *hurled* down many were, Forgall! The advantage is all the Picts'. Suppose we planned, and prepared, and made a general charge, all at once. Shields and helms and armour. Suppose it's a thousand men charging up that slope all at once. How many would be falling ere they reached the top?"

Forgall's face was grim. "Hundreds."

"And if the Picts were passing busy with a group of twoscore or so maniacs who had climbed up behind them?"

"Those twoscore would surely die. But few of those who charge the slope would . . ."

"Is this not the way generals think?"

"Aye, and kings. It's 'units' men are, Partha. 'We shall lose three hundred *units* an we do such-and-so; we shall lose but two hundred *units* an we do so-and-such . . . whiles if we be asking for twoscore volunteers for death almost certain, we shall cut our losses to less than a hundred *units* . . .'" Forgall shuddered under a rush of horripilation. "Aye. It is the way generals think, and kings, Partha. It is why I can be neither."

"Suppose we take a bow, and—"

"We?"

"—and tinder, and an arrow or two wrapped in linen—soaked in oil. As soon as the summit is gained and we be in readiness, we'd be loosing flaming arrows, to arc high. That would signal the entire force here to charge up the slope, while we attack from the other direction. All the scalers need not die, Forgall."

"It's too late the chargers would be," Forgall said very quietly—with thought on him, not fear. "Those who scale the riverside cliff would surely die. We could not whirl and jump to escape axes and spears; in mail and from that height, we'd drown."

"We?" The two men looked at each other. Forgall said naught. Cormac said, "Some would survive. I cannot imagine dying, though some would go down, aye. But it's volunteers ye'd be asking for, Forgall, from all—"

"*Volunteers!*" Forgall whipped his head about to stare at the youth he respected as much for his mind as for his prowess. "No volunteers! It's *our* men will do it, or none, by Lugh's beard! Tarabaiter *Coichte* becomes Pict-slayer!"

"Munster-slayer," Cormac said quietly.

And so Partha mac Othna and his captain Forgall mac Aed met with not one, but three generals. Those wise and brave men agreed that the plan was insane, and . . .

"And worthy of those descendants of Mil, who came here to settle in a land not their own, de Dannann or no—our ancestors!"

Ferdiad the Bear looked at the youth who spoke with such heated fervor. "It's a wild wolf ye be, son of Othna of Ulster!"

"With the guile of a fox," Conan Conda said.

"A lunatic," the little general from little Osraige said. "No sane man would attempt such a feat; no sane general would sanction it."

Four men stared at him. And so it was decided, because one sneered.

Guided through the Munsterish squads by General Ferdiad's own aide wearing the general's own ring, two-and-fifty men stared upward at the pile of rock that bulked against the sky. The backside of Silver Mountain—Death mountain. The cliff was sheer. Trees and vegetation mitigated that fact by rising up it rather thickly for a score and more feet. After that a scrubby tree or scraggly bush thrust out only sparsely. And beyond that—

"And above that," Forgall muttered, "the hard part."

"Best we wait a while, until the moon comes to shine on this . . . wall," Bress said, and he was right. They waited.

After a time the moon, riding high in a sky nigh cloudless, was but minutes from bathing the cliff-face in its cold light. Forgall nodded, and the fifty men moved forward, and up through the crooked trees and tenacious bushes. Three went on from there, trailing the rope that bound them together—and that was in turn secured to thicker ropes. Cormac was not among them; these men were experienced climbers. The others huddled and waited.

They made their pact, and the vow. It had been repeated fifty-two times: an a man should fall, he would not cry out. Whether to New God or Old, each prayed that he might have strength to keep such a vow, and thus not betray his companions. But each knew that he would not fall from that tower of nature bulking so darkly against the stars.

The climbers reached the top. The heavier ropes were drawn up, slithering up past the others like serpents. Then they were still. And then they were tugged up, and released: the scalers had made fast the climbing ropes for their fellows.

With shields on backs, nine-and-forty men ascended the cliff. None fell. Each was pulled over onto the mesa and sidewise to where a clump of great stones rose up from the mainly flat surface. They lay gasping as silently as they could. Now began the longer wait. They had brought no bow, no arrows. The dark Picts had advantage at night; the attackers would wait until dawn. That light would signal those at the foot of the other side of this narrow mesa, too, and they'd rush upward in silence.

They waited, two-and-fifty men lying flat, in the darkness. They could hear the Picts. Time dragged by on feet set in muck and honey. Never had a night been so long. Two *Cruithne* approached, muttering; mailed men prepared, their helmets off against a flash in the moonlight. The two Picts relieved themselves, not the length of a man's body from Forgall mac Aed.

The Picts returned to their fellows. Naturally they'd be keeping a close watch on the eastern slope, against a night attack. The Leinstermen waited, in the moon's ghostly radiance. Time shuffled past with the gait of a tortoise heavy with eggs. The Leinstermen waited.

The blackness of the sky was mitigated. The stars dimmed. Slowly, so horribly slowly, black became indigo. It faded to a deep grey. Some stars disappeared against a sky less dark. The Leinstermen waited, and their stomachs writhed as the time drew nearer. Death seemed to grin down at them from the paling face of the moon. The sky's grey grew less deep, as though an artist mixed more and more white with his black—gradually, oh so gradually.

Hands clutched helmets. Bare heads turned to stare at the pearly hue lighting the eastern horizon. Doubts rose; the mesa's expanse cut off their view of the eastern world's edge; would the others begin their charge too soon? Should they leap up and move now? The sky went pearly. The horizon grew pink. And then gold fingers rayed upward from below the edge of the world. Every man knew, then: had they possessed a cock, it would have crowed. Brilliant yellow-gold washed up from the far horizon. The sky overhead went pinkly nacreous, like a shell lined with palest pink.

Forgall slid his helmet to him, ducked his head to the ground, helmed himself. He gestured. The gesture was passed. Helmets were pressed on. Two-and-fifty arms slid through shield-straps. Fists closed on the grips within those bucklers.

Forgall rose up to his knees and reached across his armoured midsection to lay hand on hilt.

"Now."

"*Now.*"

"NOW!"

The word burst as a shout from half a hundred throats. It was drawn out to form a battle-cry as two-and-fifty men bounded up and drew their swords, all in one motion. Before them the enemy, too, came alive.

The mesa, broad enough to accommodate perhaps seven hundred men, was occupied by three hundred Picts, and now they found themselves

213

not alone. The attackers appeared by surprise, and charged; they must not be too close to the cliff's edge. In that first attack, the latest of centuries upon centuries of yelling Celtic onslaught, thirty Picts went down in blood. After that, the battle began.

The dark men defended themselves and struck back, spreading out so as to flank and encompass the force that was armoured as they were not—but was only a sixth their number.

Yelling, hacking Leinstermen could but hope their fellows were ascending the long eastward slope of the mountain, as swiftly as they could pull and hurl themselves up among the rocks and rocky irregularities. The Leinstermen had no place to go. They could but hack and slash, fend and parry. They could but endeavor to remain a curved wall, for the enemy was so sizable as to be able to surround every man. They could but fight and fight, either to be aided by hundreds of others who'd come onto the mesa behind the *Cruithne*—or to die heroes of Eirrin. For fifty could neither best three hundred, nor retreat.

And then they were forty.

And then thirty, and Cormac knew that beside him Forgall had gone down, but Cormac could not even think about it, for Forgall's fall left him surrounded the way that he must slash his way out to have allies on either side of him again. He did, and still the Picts pressed, and no Gaels had come onto the mesa behind them. Even so, with his fellows Cormac had no time for despairing thoughts. Every man would rather have turned and fled over the cliff's edge; every man knew that way was no succor, no escape, but only a death more ignominious; here was death with honour.

Cormac struck so violently that he crippled two attackers at a blow. In that powerful half-whirl he saw Bress go down, and Cormac was not glad. His captain; the second—and Champion of Leinster! And how many stood yet? As many as a score?

No time to think; Cormac was engaged by two Picts who worked well together. He beat them away, destroyed a shield, back-stepped, let one err by advancing. Cormac showed him what Forgall had said was a Romish use of the sword: he stop-thrust the man. Even as he saw the Pict shiver, huge-eyed, the youth heard the charging Gaels of the main army falling on the Pictish rear. That brought a wave of relief, of gladness, but even so it was too late.

As he freed his sword from the muscular belly of the dying Pict, Cormac saw the man's fellow bringing down a steel ax, and knew he could neither shield nor dodge. He tried, letting himself fall, wrenching his arm for his sword was not quite free. He felt a great blow to his head, heard a terrible boom and a roaring thrumming, and saw an explosion of bright lights before his face.

He knew he was hit, knew the Pict wielded a steel ax taken from a dead Celt, knew too that it had bit through his helm and then into his very skull. And as even the bright lights vanished from before his eyes, Cormac mac Art knew that he was surely dying—dead.

Chapter Fifteen:
Scars

"Partha."

Strange word. A name? Aye, a name. I died then; it's back in a new body I am and without a glimpse of Donn or I-Breasil. *Back as someone called Partha . . .*

Partha! No, no, that's the name I'm after using these months since Connacht—why seems it years? Then . . . then . . . I am not dead?

"How is that possible?"

"Partha! Ah ye speak—what?"

"How—how is it possible I be not dead? Why is it so dark—uh!"

He opened his eyes and saw that it was not dark at all. Light seemed to sear eyeballs long covered. Something tight around his forehead seemed to press down his lids. He blinked, again and again. A face looked down at his; someone stood over him. A man. Oh, it was that minstrel. What was his—*no, no come Par—come, Cormac, Cormac, find yourself, gain control,* think!

"Partha?"

"Prince . . . Ceann."

"Aye! Ho, ye be awake! Hold ye still now; it's long and long ye've been abed, and ye'll not be wanting to disturb your bandages, Partha. At least ye know me! We feared for your life . . . then, when we at last felt ye'd live, days and days later, we feared ye'd come awake with no memory on ye. That I have seen happen, from such a slice as ye took to your skull."

"It is . . . hard."

Ceann smiled. As Cormac started to lift a hand to his head, the other youth grasped his wrist. Amazingly strong he was, for a king's minstrelly son, Cormac thought; *he holds me with ease!*

"Wh-where—"

"Carman. It's Carman this is. My father's own leech has been treating yourself, and the others, and both druid and priest have been here daily."

"The . . . others?"

"Aye. Hold still, Partha, else we must tie ye down again. Your head is swollen still, healing under a great swath of bandage. Ye've no need to be feeling of it. It's many a day ye've lain here thus, and many a change of bandage ye're after having."

Cormac relaxed his arms, repeated; "The others?"

Ceann mac Ulaid's face went very serious. "There be but eight of ye left of those who made the climb. Twoscore and four are dead, heroes in Leinster and Munster and Osraige and aye, up in Meath and Connacht once the story's spread in verse and song. But—*but,* Partha . . . only thirty others were slain! The deaths of twoscore and four, and the wounds on you and seven others . . . these saved surely hundreds of lives and limbs, Partha! As for the Picts . . . thrice a hundred and twoscore and twelve died on that mesa! And a few others; some

217

jumped over the cliff and none took trouble to search for them."

For the third time, while his sluggish brain worked to assimilate what Ceann had said, Cormac asked, "The others?"

"I . . . I cannot give ye their names, Partha."

"Forgall?"

"Dead, Partha. A hero of Leinster—of Eirrin."

Cormac closed his eyes and bit his teeth together. That exerted pressure on his cloven, tight-swathed head and pain leaped like jagged lightning. He hardly noticed. Other pain was there, too. Forgall. *First my father . . . and then Midhir and now Forgall. It continues. Those I respect, and love . . . die.*

He was not yet ready to remind himself that was stupid, but another form of in-turning, of wallowing in grief and worsening it with self-pity and -blame. That realization would come. Now, he opened his eyes to look up into the solicitous face of him who was third in line of succession to Leinster's throne.

"Cas . . . mac Con?"

Ceann shook his head. "We tried. He died in his sleep, five days agone. He never awoke, even when his leg had to be removed."

"Cas."

Then, "Five days! How long has it been, Ceann?"

"Thirteen days since—"

"*Thirteen!*"

Aye. Men have lain longer with such wounds. The leech calls it natural enough, a coma; the druid says your body needed so long to mend itself; the priest says that god and devil wrestled for your soul. It's often restless ye've been."

"Prince Ceann: it's no priest of the Dead God I'll be welcoming in here! Thirteen days!"

"Aye. A day and a night in a peasantish house, and two days in the waggon that brought ye here. Only two days agone did the leech say he'd live. On yester day ye called out *'mentor'* and a name: Sualtim. Then did ye *smile,* smile even as ye slept and release a great relaxing breath, Partha. And it's peaceful ye've been since. Sleeping, rather than unconscious from wounds."

I called. He is all left me—and did he come? Has Sualtim Fodla helped me still again?

He asked about others. He knew mixed mental reactions at news that Bress lived, whole; further, he'd been up and about for a seven-day. *The good men die,* Cormac thought with some bitterness, *and Bress lives!* Then he remembered that he too lived, and set the concept aside for consideration at another time. The while, he discovered that he had taken wounds to his chest and left leg. No longer were they hurtful, and he vowed silently that on the morrow he'd rise from this bed, lest a wounded leg stiffen into a limp. Meanwhile Ceann made sure he remained supine.

Samaire demanded twice-daily reports of him, Ceann said, and he must hurry to her now with the good news she awaited. She'd have been here day and night, but Ceann had convinced her that her father would learn of it.

"And have death done on me."

Ceann did not say him nay. "Ye know I've no liking for this . . . relationship between yourself and my sister."

Cormac stared at the wall. "Aye. And ye be right."

Ceann pursued, "You know naught can come of this, Partha mac Othna! It's the daughter of a king she is!"

Cormac had to bite back the words that wanted to flood forth; his lineage. Then a man entered the room; was Eoghan mac Foil of Forgall's Fifty. Though he and Cormac had been but acquaintances, they greeted each other now as the oldest of friends. Eoghan walked with a limp, but vowed he'd soon not. He told Cormac of the other survivors. Among them was Cond the Barber, and they chuckled—but then "Partha" frowned, for Eoghan advised him he had more need of hair restorer than clipper. A considerable swath of blood-caked black hair had been snipped from Cormac's head, and the sckull scraped in that area.

He complained of the tightness of his bandage.

"Have some ale then," Eoghan said, smiling. "A lot of it—it comes from the king's own vats, Partha! But suffer the bandage. It holds together the edge of the wound in your scalp; thus it's less scar ye'll be having, and no great patch bare of hair will show."

"Oh, *that's* important," Cormac said—only half japing—and they laughed all three, and that brought such a blinding slash of pain that he fainted.

That, the leech told him next day—and then General Conan Conda himself!—was good; "Partha" needed more rest. To that the patient replied by demanding food and ale. He received only ale and a bowl of stew with bread sopping in it. He complained—and then, when he tried to chew, thought his head was coming off with pain. After a time of rest, he finished a bowl of hot stew, and drank considerable ale, and next day he stood despite the leech's protests and Ceann's. But for Ceann he'd have fallen. He made the prince support him in walking twenty steps, and then it was more stew, with much soaked bread. He swallowed it whole rather than chew, for all his bravery and determination. And he drank more ale, which dulled the throbbing pain. The prince was not all that strong, mac Art realized; it was that he was weakened from lying so long abed.

Others, less wounded and more recovered, came. Samaire came, for the princess could come to a hero's bedside as well as could a prince. That was painful; they durst not touch each other and had to be only soldier and royal heiress. The general came again. And Ceann's older brother—the eldest, King Ulad's firstborn—Prince Liadh. And the royal poet. And another poet. And a bard, who asked questions for his lay of the Mountain of Death, where the fifty had saved all Eirrin. Hardly so, Cormac told him, but the man paid no mind; facts hardly troubled most historians, and certainly must not disrupt the creative process of bards and poets.

Bress Lamfhada did not come.

Cormac rose every day, and walked.

Nevertheless he was an impatient patient, and by the time he was allowed to leave the Royal Hospital, a bad patient. By then May was twenty days old.

On the next day he submitted to an hour of aid in bathing, and shaving, and hair-clipping and -combing (below the bandage)—it hurt—and even to help in dressing. He and the others who were all that remained of Forgall's Fifty went to fulfill a royal request: to see the king himself. Their fellows were astonished at Bress's words; he allowed that it was too bad so many good men lay in the ground, while the gods suffered their world still to be cluttered by this Ulsterish boy.

Cormac stopped short, just within the Kinghouse. He stared; Bress met the stare, and tense men stood about, watching them both.

"Say it, Ulsterish boy! And among my Fifty it's fiftieth ye'll be—and worse."

"Know this, Bress," Cormac said very quietly, and even Bress blinked; was the first time his insults and sallies had had answer of the youth. "Neither of us is boy, and neither of us is coward, or foreigner. And no matter what may result, it's in no Fifty of yours I'll be serving—or squad of ten, or five."

Bress drew in a breath. Beside him, Eoghan said, "Nor I."

"Nor I," Cond agreed, and then Laeg who was now Laeg One-arm, and then Donal of Maghna-madra and then—a new voice came, and quiet it was, and all wheeled to stare.

"Nor would I," General Conan the Wolfish said, stepping from behind an enormous oaken pillar all bound with brass. "Nor will any of ye be serving anyone at all, an ye keep waiting our king himself!"

And like egg-sucking dogs, the chastised heroes went in to see the king.

They emerged much praised, and rewarded, and Cormac's genius praised for having made a great decision and plan that cost so few lives when so many might have been lost. They emerged from that audience dizzy, and joyously happy all but one, who was infuriated but silent, for these eight were to be the nucleus around which a new *Coichte* was to be built, and its captain was named by General Conan and approved most heartily by the king, and his name was Partha mac Othna.

Chapter Sixteen:
The Trouble with Honour

That summer was for Cormac mac Art one of unequalled and almost uninterrupted happiness and serenity. Totally invisible were the terrible black clouds gathering over his head. Storm seemed to have left his life.

New Fifty-chief Partha mac Othna was allowed to pick one man from each of ten other Fifties to form his own *Coichte* around himself and the new veterans who had served under Forgall mac Aed. Ten more veterans were transferred to his command. These were chosen by General Conan Conda, who was more knowledgeable and more the soldier than Fergus Buadach, the "palace general." The recruits who completed the number of men under the supposed Ulsterish youth were in need of training.

Cormac held counsel with himself, for his command brought problems with it. Then he conferred with other leaders. All commented that he had chosen good men from their ranks, though never the very best. That, he told them, had been deliberate, and all believed their younger peer. All were pleased to listen to his problem, and to offer advice.

Having heard of those meetings, a Commander of Three Thousand called for Partha. He offered his counsel. And then Partha/Cormac went to General Conan Conda, whom he respected. Conan the Wolfish, too, was pleased to offer advice.

Next Partha announced that his *Coichte* would be called neither Partha's Fifty nor Tara-baiter, but after Forgall. Men there were who wept at that, and respect for the honourable Partha mac Othna broadened.

An enemy remained, one who carefully, necessarily gave the appearance of respect, but was nevertheless disdainful and ever a trifle surly—just enough so that Cormac could not mistake it. This was his problem, and he'd had much advice on the matter, and given it much thought. That problem was surprised when the captain of *Coichte Forgaill* quietly requested a most private conference.

The two of them rode out of camp together, ostensibly to test a new team of chariot horses. Soon, on the back pasture of the farm of Bresal Angair, the chariots stood idle while the horses happily cropped grass. It stood high and rich with the brilliant green of June.

"It's Champion of Leinster ye be, Bress Lamfhada," Cormac said, to a man hardly at his ease, "and the rank of Battle-leader. Men are honoured to be trained by your expert self. Up on Magh Broin in the Boruma matter, and at Slieve Argait against the Picts, ye did distinction on yourself yet again, and in valour and in passing ability."

Bress sat staring, forgetting in his surprise to look supercilious or even disdainful, and yet sorely

224

afflicted with wonder. What would follow this preamble of praise? Cormac spoke on.

"No certainty has ever been on me as to the reason for your instant dislike of me. Mayhap we cannot be friends, Battle-leader. That is not fortunate for we be two of the very best, and each of us knows it."

Bress continued to stare; Bress continued silent.

"Now the king and our general have made matters more difficult for us both. It's I have the post I neither expected nor requested. It's you were Forgall's second, and expected command. It gives us a problem, and thus Leinster a problem."

"Leinster?"

"Aye. For the very reason that we are among her very best. So will Forgall's Fifty be. If none of those new men can come up to what we expect, I'll be trying to have them transferred to duties that should never require them to fight."

"Is that—do ye threaten me?"

"Bress, Bress! I do not. I speak of others: recruits. What man wants other than the best beside him, in the shield-splitting? Mayhap *Coichte Forgaill* will never have to fight. It's best we'll be, anyhow. No, Bress. We are here because we have great need to talk, to come to agreement—even if it is to disagree. It's Champion of Leinster ye be. No other would I rather have training men in my command. No other, Battle-leader. Yet if it's enemies we must be, then all will know. They will feel it, however we dissemble. In that event all would be the better were yourself to be honouring the command of another captain."

Cormac raised a staying hand then as Bress opened his mouth to speak, with the look of hostility on him. "A moment, Battle-leader. Tell me

225

now, or by morning an ye wish. Will ye remain with us, with both of us trying to get along as fellow weapon-men of excellence—with a great responsibility, Bress, to these score and more of inexperienced new lads—or would ye prefer that we make a heroic announcement?"

"I—what d'ye mean, Captain?" For Bress called Cormac naught else, with care. "A heroic announcement?"

"Aye. We both know we be good. Others know. We could be going to the general, tell him we think it best for Leinster were we in separate Fifties, that they may be the two best."

"It's a high opinion ye bear of yourself."

"Bress: I do. If the general agrees, we request that he make such an announcement. Will be good for the army of Leinster, and thus Leinster, for our abilities to be put to use training a hundred men, rather than fifty. And—" Cormac smiled, "naturally our Fifties will be rivals. That could only benefit Leinster."

Bress remained squatting for a long while in silence. He rose. When he paced a few steps to lean against a tree, Cormac also straightened; both warriors knew what was good for the legs.

"Ye could go yourself to Conan Conda, or Fergus Buadach himself most likely, and merely ask that I be transferred."

"I could have done, Battle-leader," Cormac said.

"Ye're already after talking with several captains—and with General Conan."

Cormac said nothing. He'd known for a long while that Bress spied upon him. At last Bress saw that the captain would not break the lengthening silence.

226

"Yet . . . ye give me the choice."

"Bress: I do."

"Nor have ye aught of reason to like me or honour me. Why, then?"

"I do have reason to do honour on Bress Lamfhada. He has done it on himself, in training, in the Games at fair-time, and in the shield-splitting combat. How can one not respect Bress of the Long Arm?"

Bress thought about that. "It's no need I have of your respect, Partha mac Othna! I need no honouring from yourself! I will fight ye now. Or any time. I do not like ye, Captain."

Because I saved Forgall, Cormac mused, *when on his death ye'd surely have become his successor? Or for some other reason? Because I claim to be of Ulster and ye hold some grudge, bigot? Because I seemed—was!—the bumpkin, or just gained too much attention all on a sudden?*

"I know, Bress. I willnot fight ye, though. Not in words or with arms, and I know ye've striven to goad me to it." Abruptly Cormac almost smiled— almost, but not quite. "Unless it be next year at Carman's Fair, for Leinster's championship!"

"And be welcome! And why not this year?"

"This year is the Great Fair at Tara. Only once every three years is it held—and the Games. Ye deserve the chance to compete for the Championship of all Eirrin, Bress. Besides—already ye've done defeat on me, that first day I was here."

Bress gazed upon the other man in the long-sleeved tunic of Leinster blue. He shook his head, with a stirring in the air of his helm's blue plume. "I have no belief in any man's being so honourable, Captain. I cannot accept such consideration. I look for other reasons."

227

Cormac heaved a sigh. "From your mind comes that, Battle-leader, not mine."

For a long while they were silent, gazing one upon the other, and both were most aware of their helms, and armour, and of the blades by their sides.

"Captain," Bress said, "I will speak to ye, on the morrow."

Cormac nodded. He'd given Bress till then to decide. He knew both anticipation and apprehension as they rode back . . . not that Bress might decide to transfer to another's command, but that he might wish to remain. For Cormac would love to get on with this man who was so very good a warrior. Yet he did not relish daily proximity. Had it not been for his plaguing sense of honour, he'd have done what Bress had said: He'd have asked that the man be transferred elsewhere, that mac Art might handle his men in peace and happiness.

Hours and hours later, an aide to General Conan came to Cormac. The general would have converse with him: Now. Cormac cloaked himself against the night's misty chill and hurried with the aide to the house where the general both lived and held office. Cormac was most surprised to find Bress there afore him.

"Captain," the general said from behind his finely-carved oaken desk, "I ask ye to relate to me, now, what ye talked of this afternoon with Bress mac Keth."

Surprised, Cormac looked at Bress. What showed those eyes under the superciliously arched brows . . . nervousness? Apprehension? Surely not fear! Cormac set his gaze on the general's face, and did his best to recount all his and Bress's words to each other.

"And that be all, Captain Partha?"

Cormac knew it was, but felt obliged to make a show of reflection. Then he said, "Aye, General."

The general turned to Bress Long-arm who stood to his left, and looked upon him, and said nothing, and looked . . . until Bress looked away.

At last General Conan spoke. "Bress mac Keth, ye have defended Leinster well, and the Games at last year's fair proclaim ye the best weapon-man in the realm. It is a shame on us all, then, that ye be unbearable, and a troublemaker, and with no such honour on yourself as many lesser men—and a liar as well. I will not incarcerate or discharge from the army Leinster's Champion. Nor could I trust ye even in one of our border outposts. Best I know precisely where ye are, and can keep these eyes on ye. Accordingly on the morrow I will make announcement that I have want of a seasoned Battle-leader on my staff, and it's yourself will volunteer at once."

Bress spoke quietly, looking at the general's desk-top. "Aye, General."

"Go."

Bress left; Conan turned his pale blue eyes on the astounded Cormac. The general lifted a hand to push fingers through his thinning flaxen hair, and he sighed.

"I'll not ask why he dislikes ye so, Partha, and I'd not wager ye know. Nor will I tell ye what he told me. Lies. Avoid him, Partha, and do not trust him."

"General, it's—"

"Assembly an hour after breakfast, Captain. An announcement from the general. Go."

And Cormac went.

And so that problem was solved, without being solved, for Cormac had no doubt but that Bress's mind was well capable of twisting matters so that

229

the man he knew as Partha was responsible for his removal from activity. Indeed, the days passed slowly for mac Keth that summer, for he had no specific duties whatsoever but was called on now and again to carry this message or call that man for the general. Nor did Cormac mac Art ever know what Bress had told their commander, who had heard him out, and sent at once for Cormac, and had without other comment bidden Bress utter not one word whilst Cormac spoke . . . and who had believed Cormac instantly.

For mac Art the days went swiftly.

He was his own training-master, aided by the stern, hardly imaginative but superbly competent veteran he made his second. And many nights passed all too swiftly, too, in Samaire's company. And summer lengthened.

From time to time the new captain saw the new aide to the general. From time to time he thought of Sualtim, and the approach of the Great Fair at Tara, and of the Assembly of Kings later. Sualtim came not. The paths of mac Keth and mac Art crossed not. Once Cormac waited a long, long hour for Samaire to keep a tryst, and then allowed his disappointment to be alleviated by another, and her older and most willing. Upon learning that Samaire had been unable to get away from the King's House that evening and durst not send word either, Cormac felt guilt, and did not like it. Yet he liked no better the realization that he wished to remain constant to a woman with whom there could be no future.

And July came. *Coichte Forgaill* went out on maneuvers with four other Fifties, and acquitted itself superbly, new men included. Well trained they were; so said Fergus Buadach most publicly while Conan Conda smiled at his side. And July steamed on, and days came and went, and the Great Fair drew nigh.

In a room in an inn of Carman of Leinster, a pair of youths lay embracing and avowed their love. She wanted only to live out her life with him, Samaire said, and bear his sons. He wanted the same, Partha told her with sadness on him, but such could never be. He was but a weapon-man, and she the king's daughter. She sought to argue and dissuade, though was not logical or truly reasoned or reasonable.

And that evening, lying abed staring at an inn's ceiling in Carman, he told her who he was, and why he'd left Connacht, and why he lived with a name not his own. She told him that she cared not and showed him as well, and avowed that there *must* be a way for them.

He wanted that too, he told her, holding her to him and pretending not to be aware of her tears. It would be pleasant to believe, he mused, that they could surmount or smash through all obstacles, or even flee them. But the sense of honour was strong in the son of Art of Connacht in this matter as in that of Bress when he'd given the man his choice that day in June. In him too was a druid-trained pragmatism, and Cormac saw no way. She must be wed to some prince or king, thus to make alliance and bear Leinsterish sons to rule elsewhere. Such was the way of kings, and their daughters.

In truth Cormac knew in his mind that were far better he depart Leinster and hope they two could forget each other. Yet being that practical was a pain within him, and he did not say it aloud or make unbreakable resolve. He hoped still that Sualtim would bring word or send word, and that somehow all problems would be solved thus. Sure, and even that practical mind was a youth's; he entertained ridiculous and colourful thoughts of himself showing up the High-king for a plotting bit of low-life, and being forced then to defend himself from Lugaid's rushing attack, and slaying him, and being proclaimed High-king by the other monarchs assembled, so that all proffered gifts and daughters on him, and he reached forth his hand to the sunny daughter of Leinster's king.

These were dreams, he told himself, holding that sunny daughter, and unworthy.

At last it was time for her to depart the inn, and him. They would be apart for weeks: the king and his entourage left on the day after the morrow to be travelling Leinster, and visiting in Munster, with whose king they'd ride up to Tara for the Great Fair. Ulad Ceannselaigh wanted his daughter with him; his daughter would be with him, fearful of the discussion of matches for herself.

The youthful lovers promised each the other that they'd tryst in Tara, somehow.

They looked into each other's eyes, and each saw the sparkle of tears. Neither made mention. She rose and dresed. Coming first to kiss him another time, she left. Suddenly unhappy after this summer of joy, Cormac rose at once and commenced donning his clothing. It lacked but a few hours to dawn; with luck he could return to camp and gain some sleep ere dawn forced him up to be the captain who brooked no excuses, or tardiness or sloth from his men, and thus could show none himself.

After a brief interval, Cormac too left the inn.

Through dark Carman he returned to camp, and he was deep in thoughts unbidden. Thus he did not see the man who'd waited so long and long with an incredible patience born of malice, and who had seen them both leave and recognized her and knew the truth, though they left not together. And the watching Bress mac Keth smiled.

Two days later the Champion of Leinster left in the entourage of the king.

Chapter Seventeen:
A Druid and A Priest

What a throng! And I thought Carman *was a city full of people, and colourful!* Cormac mac Art, an iota of that throng of happy sons and daughters of Eirrin, shook his head. None of the noisy fairgoers around him noticed the lone so-thoughtful young man who shook his head though none spoke to him, for all were too busy going about their private pursuits—or just being joyous. He grunted when he was jostled by a hurrying purveyor of marvelously-wrought gauds of glass beads and amber and the teeth of sea-dogs. The man grunted too, and continued his single-minded hurrying through the crowd that had come to Tara from every part of Eirrin. Cormac turned to look; the fellow was gone, one among thousands.

Officially, the Great Fair began on the morrow. In truth it had commenced days ago, as pilgrims began arriving afoot, on horseback and even ox-back, in waggons and carts. Farmers and herders jostled fishermen and weapon-men and richly-attired nobles—who might well soon buy the needlework of some of those men's wives, or the produce of their farms, or the delicate jewellery made of shellfish by the wives of those who took their living from river or ocean.

Three seeming maniacs sat before a noisy inn, torturing the air and the ears of many with their yowling, howling pipes.

Bright garments fluttered and jewellery of varying degrees of worth and workmanship cast scintillant flashes with the movements of the wearers, male and female alike. Hair, cut and trimmed and washed and arranged, long combed and coiffed, glossed in the golden sunlight of July's final day. Bangles jangled and earrings tinkled. What seemed, to the youth from a Connachtish province, to be a thousand conversations were carried on all at once—some at the tops of the speakers' voices. Girls were patted and stroked and even slapped on hip or behind, and most laughed and none took umbrage. Not at Fair-time!

To this high Hill of the Kings and the renowned field sprawled about it had come peasants who'd left their russets behind; citizens of every kingdom of the Emerald Isle, bearing fruits and vegetables, embroidery and leatherwork; poets and lyrists, pipers and tympanists from the farthest northern hamlets of Ailech and DalRiadia and the farthest southern townlet of Munster; from the land round about Loch Cuan up north and Loch Conn over in Connacht and the inlet of Cobh down in the south; from Tir Connaill they came, and Antrim and Cruachain and Killarney, Dinn Rig and ancient Muirthemne; the foothills and valleys presided over by Slieve Mis and Slieve Cuilinn, from Dundalk and Dun Laoghair and aye, even the Isles of Aran, and Cait, and of the Seven Hogs.

Full twenty acres Tara Hill covered, with smaller *duns* or hills rising on it, and seven walled raths, each like unto a town itself. Long and long ago in the mists of time agone had Ollam Fodla called here the kings of all the realms of Eirrin, in solemn council. Then had been born the tradition of the great council or parliament, the kings assembled in the Great Feis. Monarchs cared not to depart their lands so often as once each year; the Assembly of Kings became a triennial occurrence.

Now fully a half-score of centuries had *Feis-mor* been held each year on Tara Hill. And before it, in late summer, the Great Fair. The great trading and selling. The relation in verse and prose of the histories of the peoples of Eirrin, spoken aloud by respected poets and historians and story-tellers who went away able only to whisper. The Games; the races and combats to determine the new Champion of Eirrin. The hearing of plaints and the redressing of wrongs. The Tales of the Finn. Public announcements of the pledging of troths. Sword-sharp satires. And absolute law.

Thus did the poet have it:

The people of the Gaedhil did celebrate
  In Tara, to be highly boasted of,
  A fair without broken law or crime,
  Without a deed of violence, without dishonour.

Whoever transgresses the law of the assembly
  (Which of old was indelibly writ)
  Cannot be spared for family connection,
  But must die for his transgression.

Aye, and still that law at Fair-time prevailed. Men wore arms but used them not. He who broke

235

the King's Peace must die. Appeal did not exist; only so could the Fair exist.

Here, amid the crowd bordering the open square where brightly bedecked tumblers cavorted, switching their back-bound hair; where hopeful satirists tried out their creations on any who'd listen; here, Samaire had sent word, would she meet Partha. And here he was, waiting and watching, ignoring even the girl tumblers. And he was sore disappointed. The sun crept measurably across the sky, steadily westering, and there came no Samaire.

She could not escape her damned gaoler of a father, Cormac thought morosely. It had happened afore. This time was a greater disappointment, for they'd been weeks apart.

And then Ceann was there, and Cormac was both glad and sad, for he knew what message the minstrel-prince brought. And he was right: Samaire had been detained by their father. Naturally she could not tell him why she was so anxious to depart his company and shirk a princess's duty. King Ulad merely needed her by him, or thought that he did. And Ceann in his Leinsterish plaide must be elsewhere too, and Cormac dolorously plowed through the throng in quest of a draught of soothing ale.

A hand fumbled at his, whilst he was locked in the crowd. Before he could draw away, in the press, he felt metal against his palm. He closed his fingers and raised the hand to look on what it contained. A moondisk. Instantly his body reacted. He knew that rune; Sualtim had scratched it there months agone.

Cormac turned his gaze on the message-bearer—a beggar.

"I want nothing of ye, young man. On Tara Hill

rises the rath of one Murcael Uais, cousin to the High-king by marriage. Directly below Lord Murcael's rath rises a grove of the oldest of trees. There, after the calling of the second watch of night, will be he who dares deface the back of a moondisk."

Cormac looked again on the symbol of the night goddess, of ancient Danu. His heartbeat was rapid and his armpits prickled. Sualtim! With information at last—and just in time! Oh; he must ask weather the beggar was to return the pendant . . .

The man was gone. The crowd, flowing like a many-hued stream, had swallowed him up, torn brown cloak and all. And in truth that human stream eddied about Cormac, split to pass him on either side as though he was a great stone in a springtime brook, and people muttered rude crudities or curses on the big youthful weapon-man who blocked them.

Clutching the pendant, he allowed himself to be carried along by the flow.

Despite his impatience Cormac had forced himself to wait until after the second night-watch had been called. Then he had taken but a few steps when he was challenged by the handsomely got-up King's Watch. At last, with mist swirling about his ankles like a wraithy grey phantom, he made his way to the yew-grove below the rath he had easily identified. And there he found Sualtim—and another.

At the feet of the druid lay another robed man, though his garb was not the green of nature's life but the black of death. A priest of the Dead God. Cormac saw the splash of colour; the scarlet on the man's forehead and left cheek, and on the ground beside that cheek. Beside him too lay a

237

good-sized stone, bigger than Cormac's fist, and on it was more of the priest's blood.

Cormac stared at Sualtim Fodla.

"A druid carries no weapons," the whitebeard said, and his voice was as though he spoke down a barrel or up from a well. "Nor is a priest supposed to do. This one did." Sualtim nodded, and Cormac looked, and saw the dagger protruding from the priest's fist; the blade was covered by his robe's skirt. "Yet the earth of our Eirrin holds weapons for one attacked. I was; the stone proved effective."

Cormac swallowed. "Sualtim—"

"Let me talk," the druid said, his voice seeming to come from a great distance though he stood but a pace away. "This man is—was—one Milchu. Him I told ye of. A priest of Iosa Chriost . . . a spy for the High-king . . . a greedy ambitious man who desired his own 'bishopric' as they call it. He was also the man who bade Aengus—that is Eoin mac Gulbain, Cormac—to do that which a more honourable priest had forbidden: slay your father."

"Sualtim—"

"Hush. Only listen. It's little time I have. I should be . . . elsewhere. Was the High-king bade Milchu to go to Eoin, and bid him do death on Art of Rath Glondarth. Our noble High-king fears one of Art's ancestry . . . and is even more fearful of a son bearing the name of that great High-king of old: Cormac mac Art. Particularly once you'd slain those first Picts, my boy, and your name and deed were becoming well-known, with comparisons to Cuchulain."

"The . . . High-king! Lugaid himself!"

"Aye, Lugaid himself. And now, Cormac . . . now does Lugaid know that the hero of Boruma—hero in Leinster, villain in Meath—is Partha mac Othna.

And he knows that Partha is also Cormac mac Art. Lugaid wanted ye dead aforetime; he does so doubly, now. The regaining of the Boru Tribute and your other successes in Leinster have but increased the *Ard-righ's* apprehension, and hatred."

"Gods of my father! Is there never to be a ceasing of—"

"Attend me! I have not done, and time is short. There is one who spied on you in Leinster. He knew of your—unwise, most unwise, Cormac—trysts with King Ulad's daughter. And he told Ulad, who told the High-king and conferred with him even this night! My boy, my boy—they two kings plot to destroy you, Cormac mac—"

Sualtim's voice had grown so weak, so seemingly distant that Cormac had bent closer, straining to hear even in the night silent but for insects. Now that voice broke off. The wise old eyes that gazed on him went vacant as though Sualtim had fled his own body. The druid made no further sound. He merely fell, crumpling like a tent bereft of its stiffening pole. As he did so, to lie face down at Cormac's feet, the youth saw that the whole back of Sualtim's robe was a mass of blood.

Ah gods—he was stabbed, and yet slew the stabber, and stood erect so as to tell me what he has told me! Cormac squatted. *Ah, Sualtim, why do you think my unhappy life could be of more import than your—*

Cormac shuddered and his nape bristled. He had put a hand to the face of his fallen mentor. What he felt was not credible, never to be believed . . . and undeniably, horrifyingly true. The old man's skin was cold.

Hurriedly, though his flesh crawled and so too his stomach within him, Cormac caught up a thin, veined, old hand.

Oh ye gods and blood of the gods!

The hand was cold. And it was stiff. Like ice it was ... no. Not like ice was Sualtim's hand. Cold as that of a dead man it was; a man from whom life had long since flown.

Shuddering so that he clamped his teeth against their clicking, Cormac rose and backed from the pair of corpses. Milchu's, too, was cold. Cormac stared down at them, and his brain spun in a maelstrom of horror, and disbelief. For he stared at the result of unhuman powers, at the incredible and unimaginable.

Sualtim had come early to meet Cormac. And so had Milchu. And Milchu had come up behind the druid, and stabbed him with his death. And then he must have gloated, sneering, flaunting his triumph over the dying druid and over the house of Art. And then, somehow, perhaps with Sualtim prostrate and dying and Milchu bending over him, the druid had smashed the stone into the priest's face.

The slain had slain the slayer. And then, because his will and his power were so great and his mission so important, and his love for Cormac ... then had Sualtim evaded Donn's dread clutch, and spoken to Cormac—from the other side of death.

Chapter Eighteen:
Fugitive

What to do?

What wonder and sore trouble on the mind of Cormac mac Art, and sadness at Sualtim's death complicated his attempts to think.

The High-king of all Eirrin plotted his death. King Ulad of Leinster knew of his daughter's affair with a common weapon-man. He plotted. And now both kings plotted together.

Am I so important then, as to occupy the time of two monarchs?

No, he thought; doubtless they'd given him but a few minutes of their valuable time, and made their plan to determine his fate, and gone right on to the other matters requiring their attention.

What to do?

He still hoped to expose the Ard-righ at the Great Assembly in the fall. *But—will I be allowed to live that long?* Or if to live ... to remain free? There was more now, so much more. Ard-righ Lugaid was ultimately responsible for the death of Art mac Cumail. And of Midhir. And of Sualtim.

241

And for Cormac's fleeing Connacht, taking on another name—a name that Lugaid now knew was an alias.

And Cormac mac Art?

He had no proof!

Bewildered, feeling once again very young and very alone, he was in need of counsel. None was available. Dead, dead, dead. Art. And Sualtim and Midhir. Dead. And even Forgall, whom though he was no great brain Cormac respected and liked—and trusted. General Conan Conda? Perhaps . . . could a general give listen to words against the highest of kings? If he did, what then when he demanded proof? No; was worse than that, Cormac realized. He could not confide in Conan the Wolfish. That would only compromise that good soldier and good man; by now Partha/Cormac was far less than popular with the general's king.

Tu, I need you!

Cormac frowned.

Tu? What word was that? A name? he knew no *tu* or *Tu*. What had been that sudden weird sensation, as of a great weight on his shoulders, a crown-like weight on his head? Were his senses taking leave of him; was his sanity staggering?

He had no idea. He was horribly alone.

Miserable, he took refuge in the company of others, and of exciting distractions. Cormac went with six others of his Fifty to watch the first of the martial games. They arrived just after Bress had fought, for he was Leinster's Champion and had won. He and the youth he knew as Partha affected not to see each other. Amid the cheering crowd, Cormac watched another pair of men circling, staring, striking at each other with leather-covered swords of wood. One combat ended, embarrassingly for the loser, in two strokes. Another went long and long, and Cormac saw how closely Bress watched. One of these men he'd later face over his shield's rim, and if he won that combat, it was another of these he'd be meeting later still, in the continuing eliminations.

"Pfah!" That from Eoghan mac Foil, on Cormac's left. "None of these puny shield-lurkers we're seeing could stand up to yourself, Captain!"

"A shame ye do not compete," another of his men said, from beyond Eoghan. "For the next Champion of all Eirrin might then be Partha mac Othna!"

"Oho!"

That from the man who stood at Cormac's right, a Meathish soldier. He went on, "So! this is the great Partha mac Othna of Ulster, hero of Leinster's king! The great herder of cows."

Most of the crowd continued to shout and wager; silence fell on Cormac's men. They stared at the Meathmen. Cormac kept his gaze on the two contenders, a young lord of Ailech and a weapon-man who represented a noble of Cruachain in Connacht.

Loud snuffing noises arose on Cormac's right. "I say this be no hero here beside me, but a coward . . . with the stench of Connachtish pigs on him!"

Eoghan gasped. Cormac tensed and his jaw clamped. He stared fixedly at the contenders.

"Aye, a base coward of the foulest kind . . . not a man at all, this cattle-thief who sells his blade to Leinster whilst claiming to be of Ulster!"

Cormac turned to look at the speaker. His was not a face Cormac knew. The fellow was not ill-favoured, and of perhaps a score of years, perhaps less. He was essaying to wear his brows as did Bress;

it did not become him either.

"Why seek ye to provoke me?"

"Provoke ye? Whyever should ye be provoked by the hearing of truth? And how could I possibly seek such—why 'tis Fair-time, weapon-boy. Even Leinsterish cattle-thieves are welcome here in *my* Meath during these days!"

"It's hardly a welcoming speech ye're after giving me, man!"

"And why should I be doing that, Partha mac Othna? It's disgrace ye and your plan put on a good captain of Meath!"

"Ah. Ye—be ye the captain of the Meathish tribute-guards?"

"Not I. He's disgraced, bereft of command and respect, for allowing himself to be tricked by some graceless fugitive who fled his own homeland rather than seek out his father's murderer."

"Partha—"

"Easy, Eoghan," Cormac put back a hand to Eoghan without looking at him; he kept his grey gaze on the Meathish weapon-man. How could the man know so much?

"It's much ye affect to know, and much noises ye allow yourself to make."

The man stared in anger. His mouth worked, drew in on itself, like a spiteful boy's. "Noise? Affect to know? *Noise?* Come away for a stroll with me, Captain Cloak-name, and it's more *noises* I'll be making for ye!"

"Rather would I see ye go for a stroll alone and let me rejoin those who watch real weapon-men." Cormac's voice remained quiet—with effort.

"*Real!* Ho—would that those two were I and yourself, swineherd turned kine-thief! Ye'd soon see what comes of facing a *real* weapon-man!"

"Words," Eoghan mac Foil said, pushing up to face the Meathman. "None others may enter the Games now, nor can Partha fight yourself, at Fair time. What would ye have him do then, man?"

"I'd have him speak for himself, Leinsterman."

"Eoghan," Cormac said quietly, desperately reminding himself of his rank and responsibility. "I do believe I'll be going along now, peradventure to taste a bit of ale."

Eoghan's face was dark and he was aquiver under the hand his captain laid on his shoulder. Without taking his eyes off the Meathman's face he said, "I do believe I'll be going with ye, Captain. The air is gone stale here."

And they moved back through the crowd, which pressed forward to fill their space. As they stepped free of the press, that same voice rose behind them; the mouthy fool had followed! "It's not staleness ye notice, Leinsterman, but the stench from that Connachtish pig-boy ye accompany."

An alarum clanged in Cormac's mind. Why was the fellow so set on trouble? How knew he so much? Why was he so—so crude and obvious? But beside Cormac Eoghan was saying *"Damn* ye!" and spinning about, hand on hilt.

The Leinsterman faced the Meathish weapon-man; the latter drew; Eoghan drew.

"Eoghan—NO!" Cormac shouted.

Eoghan paused at the cry, and thus he did not complete the movement of his blade toward the other man's, for neither of them carried buckler. The Meathish blade swerved only a little—and took Eoghan in the sword-arm. It bit deep and blood gushed.

"Eoghan!" Cormac called again, and he had a vision of a good young weapon-man no longer able to follow his trade because of a crippled sword arm, and Cormac forgot all. His blade streaked from his scabbard.

He did not hear the sudden new shouts from the crowd; a battle was being fought with real steel; blood dyed a sleeve of Leinsterish blue—and Meathish earth! Now others turned. They saw the darker man in the blue shirt strike, saw the Meathman catch the blow on his own blade with a ringing grating scream of steel on steel, and they saw Cormac's sword slide down that other blade and drive four inches of its blade into the Meathman's chest.

Onlookers were horrified; moreso Cormac mac Art, for now his full senses returned. He knew from the man's wound and his face that he'd not live to see another dawn, if indeed he survived to sunset. Cormac knew that he had slain, though he'd had no such intention.

"I broke the King's Peace at Fair-time, Samaire! I slew a man! Witnesses there were aplenty; I'm a dead man!"

She hugged him, pressing hard. "Oh Partha! Oh Crom preserve and Behl protect! Partha . . ." She was sobbing, heedlessly crushing herself against steel mail.

"I'd be dead already," he said wonderingly, for he could hardly believe it had happened yet, days later, nor was he yet able to assimilate it. "But all were as frozen in horror—myself included. What I did does not happen. The law is ancient, and clear: the punishment is death. I'd not be here," he said, looking about the inn room with eyes that scarcely saw, "but for the fact that all were bemazed, rooted. Then the King's Watch came bustling through the crowd. And I came awake—and fled. My companions *accidentally* got in the way of those Meathmen. I came upon a horse. I took it, and rode. I think I did not even slow until I realized I was entering Atha Cliath. Gods, gods! Blood of the gods; I know not even the name of the boy who bore my message to you when I learned your father's party had stopped here on the way home."

"Nor I," she said squeezing him, "but he's a circle of silver the richer—Partha! Cormac! We must flee."

"Flee? But—"

She thrust herself back to look into his face, though her hands clung to him still. "Oh dairlin, dairlin boy! Would ye remain and be slain? Think, my love. The Meathman . . . he provoked you deliberately. He had no fear on him, of the Law. How is that possible?"

"I have thought of that. He was assured of pardon, of impunity . . . and only the High-king himself could have assured him of such safety."

"Falsely?"

He looked down into her green, green eyes. "What?"

"Oh Partha . . . Cormac! Don't you see? The High-king did indeed assure him he'd be pardoned, or somehow taken care of. He *wanted* swords drawn. He had been well worked up over his captain, the one you tricked that night you gained back the Boruma. But—think! The High-king knows your prowess! My father knows your prowess. They *knew* you'd do death on their man!"

"It . . . must be. Aye . . ."

"We must flee, my love. We *must*."

No way now for me to receive any sort of hearing, fair or otherwise, before the Assembly of

247

Kings; it's a wanted, hunted fugitive I am! She's right; it's stay and die, or flee! Gods! Flee! First an exile from Connacht . . . but . . . leave Eirrin?

His voice caught when he said, "Not we, Samaire. I. It's I must flee."

"No! No-oo," she cried, moaning the word. "Not without *me!*"

Was then the knock came, on the door of that inn of Baile Atha Cliath, and when she asked fearfully who was there, a familiar voice replied. "Your brother."

They admitted Ceann—in his patched cloak and a great red mustache. He thrust a bundle at her.

"Samaire: Change clothes at once. At once! Partha: ye must decide. Stay and die, or—"

"We have just said it, Ceann. I . . . I will . . . go." The words were far from easily said; they were nigh as hideous as death itself.

"Then it must be immediately," Ceann snapped. "My father knows of this meeting; he's had you watched, Samaire. Even now he sends Bress, with a warrant for you, Partha. Resist and be slain on the spot. Neither king nor High-king cares."

"Nor Bress."

"He goes. *We* go! I will flee with him, Ceann. I love him! We—"

Her brother wheeled on her. "Think, sister! Think! An he flees successfully, evades the men seeking him, will be because the gods smile and he be no fool. But if you go with him—gods of our ancestors, Samaire! Be not foolish! Our father will search the world over for you both! All Leinster will join the search for the man who carried off the king's daughter!"

She protested, weeping, even while she changed without shame into the peasantish cloth Ceann had brought. And Ceann railed at her. The while, he too was stripping. He took up a shirt and leggings, donned them; was the sleeved blue tunic of a weapon-man. Cormac joined his efforts to make her see reason and sense, though he himself was close onto tears. *I love her! I am talking her out of going with me—never to see her again!*

Prince Ceann gathered her jewels, every smallest bauble including the pearl-encrusted comb. These he placed in the russet shirt he'd worn, and folded it with care over them, and used his cloak to make a bundle of it. His gaze met Cormac's; he pressed the valuable bundle into his hands.

"Behl smile and ever shine his light on you, Partha mac Othna. And Crom protect ye, weapon-man, for ye have enemies so powerful a prince shivers to think on't."

And Ceann whirled, and snatched his sister's hand, and practically dragged her from the room. Nor did her wailing cease as he hurried her away.

Cormac stood staring at the door, holding a ragtag disguise ... and the jewels of a princess whose father righteously—and in truth, rightfully—desired his death. And Cormac felt as if he'd swallowed a heavy stone—two, for one was lodged in his throat.

Samaire ...

Minutes passed ere he jerked, and blinked, and began again to see with staring eyes. He set his brain to work constructively. Known here, he'd betake himself elsewhere before he changed into the beggarish clothing Ceann had brought. He wrapped the little package still again in his military dress cloak of speedwell blue. He made it fast to his belt back of his left hip, behind the scabbard in which rested his accursed sword. He had no buckler; that he'd left behind in Tara. Without even glancing around at that room of sorrow, he swung to the door.

He barely avoided being bashed and swept back by it, when the door was hurled inward.

"Partha mac Othna: It's the king's own warrant we bear, for your arrest."

"Och, Bress," Cormac said so terribly quietly, "never have I seen ye in such good cheer."

Beside Bress mac Keth in the hall stood two others. Weapon-men all, in the familiar colour and leathern corselets of Leinster; swords by sides and shields on arms. The three stared at the fugitive. Then Bress reached across his midsection and drew his sword.

The Meathman was an accident, Cormac thought. *But—as well flee or be slain for a boar as for a squealing shoat! This one I'll enjoy doing to death.* And he reached for his own hilt.

The man on Bress's left started forward, stumbled—into Bress. As they scrambled, the fellow seeming all disjointed legs and arms and Bress cursing, the other weapon-man winked at Cormac. Nor did he or his companion draw steel. Indeed, in the staggering flailing entanglement with Bress, that man's shield miraculously slid off his arm.

Cormac let his sword be. He'd slain but one son of Eirrin, and he by accident; he'd redden his blade no more in this his own land. In a long stride he stepped forward and all in a rush clamped Bress's right wrist in his hand and drove his other fist into Bress's face, just at the left eye. Bress staggered; his fingers came open and his falling sword nearly impaled his own foot. With care, Cormac struck him again, in the mouth. His knuckles came away pained and as bloody as the mouth of Bress, who sagged and fell unconscious.

"Blood of the gods, but that felt good!"

Cormac spun back into the room, fist dripping, hoping he judged the two men aright. He upended the heavy oaken table; gestured. Two grinning weapon-men hurriedly lay down on the floor. Cormac paused to bid them draw their swords. They did, and he laid the upended table on them.

"In no more than minutes," one of them gasped, "the ship of Calba sails from Atha Cliath Harbour."

Cormac mac Art took up the dropped shield and Bress's sword, and fled.

From the deck of a wallowing merchant ship, bound north to Alba, a tall youth gazed on the land that slid by to port. A tattered, patched cloak covered him to the eyebrows and he held it from within against the wind that drove the merchanter past Eirrin and onto Magh Rian. Fog clung to the shoreline, and then they were past it and Eirrin fell mistily behind. He turned in order to keep his gaze fixed on that misty emerald land. Already it was becoming but a whitish outline.

Full of sorrow and bitterness, the youth stared back at his beloved land. Under his peasantish attire he wore a king's golden torc.

My voyage of exile. First from Connacht I fled, from home and hearth and those I knew. And now from Leinster . . . from all Eirrin. Long have I heard that the worst punishment for a Gael is exile from the land of the Gaels. We have roots, Sualtim said, like trees, and it's far down in the earth of Eirrin they are locked. Soon will I know. Now it is horror and pain; will it grow worse? Bereft of home and friends and woman, never to hold her in these arms again, gods, never even to see her! Will it grow worse? Can it? Will I come to wish I had stayed and died, at least to lie within the soil that holds my roots?

The tall cloakbound youth swallowed, hard; swallowed again. The sword he had carried aboard was with the ship's sailing master. He'd gain it back soon enow, were there trouble on this northward voyage, along with the fine mailcoat that had made the man's eyes go wide. Valuable accoutrements those, to be handed him by a man in a ragged cloak bearing patches, but he had said nothing, with a princess's garnet-set silver bracelet in his hand.

Now from within his cloak his last-minute passenger drew, surreptitiously, another sword. The sword that had been his father's. He clutched it, gazed upon it, felt out the familiar design of the hilt, the bear's head that topped it. He thought of how it had served his father, and then himself, of the Picts it had slain; in vengeance, in protection of Connacht, of Leinster, of Eirrin.

He raised his eyes. He saw the fog close over that land. But a single shadowy mountain peak remained visible, weirdly standing like a ghostly sentinel atop the grey-white bank of fog that was like a cloud come down to earth, to hide Eirrin from his last gaze upon it.

Then he swept his arm out in a backhand stroke, and let go the hilt. His father's sword sailed out over the Plain of the Sea, that northward sea separating the land of the Scoti from the isle his feet would never again tread. And with scarcely a splash, the sword vanished into the water.

"Holy Mary," a voice said beside him, "was that a *sword* ye hurled into the sea?"

Staring, and deep within the black cloud of his thoughts, the youth reacted with a jerk. He looked at the man who'd come up so silently. Was the ship's sailing master. He returned his sad-eyed gaze to the sea.

"Aye."

The sailor of twoscore years or so studied him with eyes set deep in the crags of a face etched by sea and sun and brine-spray, and he seemed to study the youth, to seek a view of his soul.

"I accepted your sword and that fine mailcoat when ye came aboard, along with that fine bracelet that more than pays your passage. No thought was on me of checking ye for more weapons!"

"I have none other now, only my dagger."

"Pisht: an eating utensil. But . . . by the Sacred Heart itself, man, why smuggle aboard a sword only to hurl it into the sea?"

The youth stared at the water flowing behind the ship, lapping. "In my hand it took the life of a man, a poor foolish man of Eirrin who was only the dupe of another and should not have died. Was my father's sword. He was a good man. I'll not carry it the more, lest I dishonour it again."

"Ah." The sailing master, too, gazed only at their wake. "A young man of much honour, then. And a brain as well—and prowess. Was it of Ulster your father was?"

"Na. Of Connacht."

"Ah. Connacht. Aye. Connacht . . . they talk in Connacht of a young man, vanished. Presumed slain by the slayer of his father. A great slayer of Picts the lad was, and one destined for great deeds and fame, even as Cuchulain of old."

Cuchulain? *The Grey of Macha reared . . . "Patience, my king," Tu said . . . "So you're a man of deeds, Cimmerian," Yezdigerd said, and on his head a crown . . .*

The youth jerked his head as though to clear it of fog. "Cuchulain died young."

"Aye. So I am sure did this young man of whom I

speak. A pity. A great pity. There's another young hero of Eirrin came to an early end, too. One whose deeds made me shed tears, they did. I am of Leinster; Athairctech, over near Osraige. Was this young hero brought great honour on Leinster, and her king. He outwitted the minions of Tara and took back all the Boru tribute! A great deed! A great hero. Made me shed tears, he did, of joy and pride. He restored Leinster's honour."

"Honour is not worth the pain it puts on a man, Captain."

"Methinks ye be wrong in your youth, weapon-man in your beggar's cloak. Sometimes were dishonour on an entire people, an entire land, for a man to be slain by it. And him a hero, ye see. No, were truly he a man of honour, he'd relieve Eirrin of that burden of dishonour; he'd not let our Eirrin dishonour herself by doing death on him, but sail away under a cloak of disguise. That were honour. The sort of honour that prompts a Gael to break or hurl away a weapon that had slain a countryman."

The two men stared in silence at the sea. The sailing master spoke.

"Were honour, too, for a man who felt gratitude for a deed done for his realm—and by a foreigner at that!—to assume that those two heroes I have mentioned are dead."

"They surely are," the youth beside him said, in a choked voice.

After another silent time of gazing on the quiet sea, the merchant shipmaster said, "Your sword and mailcoat are yours when we land, and I am proud to hold them for ye till then, Art's son of Connacht."

Cormac stiffened. He continued staring seaward. His jaw was very tight.

"Art's son of Connacht is dead, Captain."

"Aye. So too is Othna's son of Ulster. I never saw either of them, but have great feeling for them both. So too is Calba's son of Athaircthech dead, of a fever in the bloom of manhood. My son."

"Sadness seems to rule the world, Captain, not kings and not justice."

"Aye, philosopher. An it's a name ye'll be needing in Alba, it's mac Calba ye be welcome to call yourself."

"I . . . I will . . . remember," Cormac choked out.

And then he turned and moved the length of the ship, to turn those cold, cold eyes ahead, up toward fog-shrouded Alban Dal Riada. For there lay the future and behind him was Eirrin and the past, and the past was dead.